MASJID MORNING

A Novel

To Sharon
From Richard

Richard Morris

SQUARE DEAL BOOKS
HYATTSVILLE, MD

Printed in the United States of America

Cover design by Audrey Engdahl

ISBN-13: 9781537233277
ISBN-10: 1537233270

Library of Congress Control Number: 2016916466
CreateSpace Independent Publishing Platform
North Charleston, South Carolina

SQUARE DEAL BOOKS
HYATTSVILLE, MARYLAND

*FOR BARBARA, OUR CHILDREN
AND GRANDCHILDREN*

CHAPTER 1
THE FLAT

"Stop!" Nadira exploded, pointing through the windshield at the girl standing on the shoulder of the two-lane road by a white sedan. "That's Amy!"

"Who?" Atif asked, as he slowed the car while snatching a look into the rearview mirror to see who might rear-end him.

"Amy. She's in AP English with me. She's a senior too."

He was past her before he could stop. He glanced in the rearview mirror, expertly backed up, wove behind her car, parked, and turned on his hazard lights.

"A Lexus ES," he said. "That's about 40K. And me in my old Buick."

The girl stood with her hands in the pockets of a heavy white thigh-length coat. The sun filtered through small green leaves on trees by the road, and there was a chill in the air.

Nadira rolled down her window, leaned out, and called, "Amy!"

Amy smiled. "Nadira!"

Nadira jumped out as Atif turned off the motor, and asked, "What happened?"

"I have a flat," Amy yelled with disgust.

"Oh no. Do you have a spare?"

1

Amy shrugged. "I don't know."

"Maybe Atif can help."

"Who?"

Atif was out of the car and walking toward her. "My brother, Atif."

"Hi," Atif said in a soft, deep voice.

Amy's eyes twitched as she looked at the young man with the shock of brown hair, heavy brows across brown eyes, broad nose, light tan skin, and face tipped down with a serious, confident expression. She felt a rush.

He was about six feet tall, and his insulated gray flight jacket, with elastic waist and sleeves, gave him a muscular look.

"Hi," Amy greeted.

He avoided her eyes, and looked at the tires.

"Right rear?" he asked.

"Yes. But I already called Triple-A."

"Sometimes they take forever. Do you want me to change it? Then you can call back and cancel."

"Sure."

"Nice car. Is it your parents'?"

"No, it's mine. They gave it to me last year for my birthday."

"Nice."

"They got tired of driving me everywhere."

He nodded. It made perfect sense.

As she opened the trunk, which was empty and clean, he noticed her fingers—slender, and nails manicured with light pink polish.

He removed the temporary spare, jack, and wheel lock key, and loosened the lug nuts on the wheel. Then he unwound the jack and put it under the car.

"You really know what you're doing," Amy said.

"He's a guy, Amy," Nadira replied. "They know how to do things like change tires."

Amy called Triple-A while Atif raised the car, removed the nuts and tire, and put on the spare.

He glanced at her and saw straight hair, a darker brown than Nadira's, parted left of center, flowing down her face past her shoulders onto her chest. Her eyebrows were fine and plucked, her nose narrow and straight—unlike his sister's and mother's—cheekbones high, mouth wide, skin fair and soft.

She finished her call as Atif tightened the nuts. "You're fast."

"Oh, it's not very hard, really."

"Do you work in a garage?"

Nadira guffawed. "No."

Atif just smiled.

"He goes to the University of Maryland. He's a junior. Pre-med."

Amy blushed. "Oh, sorry."

He looked amused. "No problem."

"I'm going there next year. Do you like it?"

"Yeah, sure. It's a good school."

He cranked down the jack, put it and the flat in the trunk, and closed the lid. "There you go. But don't drive too fast on the spare, and get a new tire soon."

"Oh. OK. Can I give you something for this?"

He looked her in the eyes for the first time and spoke somewhat harshly, "I didn't do it for money. I did it to help you."

"Oh, sorry again. I'm really putting my foot in my mouth today."

"It's his Muslim good deed for the day, Amy...so he can go to heaven," Nadira said mischievously.

"It'll take a lot more than changing a tire to get me there, I think."

"Well, thanks for giving me the chance to help you get into heaven."

He laughed. "You're welcome."

They turned toward his car.

"You know, sometime I need to learn something about Muslim."

"You mean Islām?" he asked.

"Oh, yeah. I get them confused."

Nadira chuckled.

"Why are you interested?"

"I'm just curious. In Sunday school we were taught that it's a major religion, and it seems like we have more Muslims in this country now."

Nadira grinned. *Sure that's why.*

"Yes, well, I guess I could teach you something about it sometime."

"I'd like that."

He felt himself grow warm at the possibility. "I could take you through a masjid, too."

"Oh," Nadira said, almost to herself. "That would be nice."

"What's a masjid?"

"A mosque. Masjid is Arabic for mosque. It's pronounced like '**pass**-jid'."

Amy looked off into the woods beside the road. "Well, I don't know about that, Atif. Maybe." *And I could take you to a church.*

"If you want to…Anyway, it was nice to meet you, Amy."

"You too, Atif." Their eyes held their gaze for a moment. Then he broke it off and walked to the car. He let her pull out first, and then followed her onto the highway.

"So what did you think of Amy?" Nadira asked.

"She's gorgeous. Whew. A little ditzy, but she is a rich kid."

The car bounced along on its weak springs, with the windows opened an inch to let in the spring air.

"I think you like her."

He assumed a noncommittal look. "She's OK. What does she do at school?"

"Like what clubs is she in?"

"Yeah."

Nadira shrugged. "None that I know of. But I think she runs cross country and maybe plays soccer."

"What's her last name?"

"Breckenridge."

"Breckenridge! You were going to wait to tell me that until the end of time, weren't you? Her father's the farmer on the zoning board, isn't he?" She cringed. "He's the one who's been trying to block the masjid. He owns the big dairy farm, and he's on the Conservative Citizens' Council. That's like the Klan! He hates Muslims and immigrants and people of color." Nadira nodded. "He put Abu through fits!"

"But Amy's nice. You can't judge her by her family."

He scowled. "Fruit doesn't fall far from the tree."

"You don't know that."

"First they said the land was zoned agricultural, so we couldn't build a masjid there…until our lawyer showed them all the churches on this road. Then they made us have an environmental assessment and sent in biologists to snoop around looking for endangered species. Then they said that the part on the back corner that gets puddled after a big rain was a wetland, and we needed a special permit for that."

He turned off the road into the Oakton Acres subdivision where they passed one mega-mansion after another on both sides of the road, each set back on a large lot.

He shook his head in disgust. "And then they asked how many people would be praying in the masjid, and they doubled that number to give us room to grow, and then sized the restrooms and parking spaces and handicapped spaces on the inflated number. Our architect had to redesign everything."

"Does that mean the bathrooms will be big?"

"Huge."

She grinned. "Yay. Maybe we women won't have to wait in line."

"And they're requiring concrete curbs all around the parking, on the driveway leading back to it, and along the paved turning lane that they required on the entire length of the property for people to turn into the driveway and use when they come out. For safety, they said. 'We don't want any of you people to be involved in any wrecks.' 'You people,' they said. And then they're requiring sidewalks the whole length of the property, even though there are none to connect to on the farms beside us. Breckenridge! I despise that name."

"Just be nice to Amy. It's not her fault."

"She did say she wanted to learn about Islām. I mean about 'Moslem.' Ha!"

Nadira scrunched her eyes. "You're cruel."

"And I wanted to take her through a masjid!"

They pulled in the driveway of their house, a two-story structure with large windows on all sides. He drove past the three-car garage on the side and parked in the rear.

"Nadira, let's not tell Abu and Ami about Amy. I don't think they'd like us associating with Breckenridges."

"OK."

They went to the back door to the garage, punched the numbers on the lock and went in through the mudroom/laundry into the great room kitchen where their mother, Salma, was standing at the island, completing her preparation of the evening meal.

"Hi, Mother." He always used English—with no accent. He wanted no part of Punjabi. They could speak that to themselves if they wanted to, but he was an American. "Oh, that smells good. Chicken tikka masala?"

"You're late," said Salma. "I hope it's not overdone." She was removing a pan from the stove.

"Atif stopped to help a woman with a flat tire on Route 73. He changed it for her."

"Alhumdulillah," he said, his eyes focused on his mother's black hair, drawn into a bun, and her aquiline nose, like Nadira's. "Without you, oh Allāh, I would not have been able to do anything."

Nadira wasn't sure that Atif was being sincere. He was not usually so devout. Maybe he wanted to jolt Ami to avert further inquiries.

Salma watched them through her dark-rimmed glasses as they walked toward the great room and saw that Atif's hands were black. "Oh! Don't touch anything! Go back and wash in the sink in the mudroom, and don't get that dirt all over the sink and towel!"

He turned abruptly and said, "Yes, Mother. I just wanted to prove to you that I was doing honest labor for someone."

Nadira continued into the room and put her books and jacket by the stairs to the balcony. "Will Abu be here for dinner?" she asked.

"No. I thought he would, but he has surgery. He won't be home until very late—after midnight."

Now Nadira knew that she should set the table in the kitchenette where they could look out the windows into the back yard, instead of in the dining room where they ate when her father was present. Earlier, her mother had mixed lassi in the blender, and Nadira poured the sweetened yoghurt from a pitcher into glasses over ice. Soon, Salma carried over the plates of chicken, rice, and cooked spinach.

"Oh, this is good!" Atif said, knowing that his mother had spent hours mixing marinade, adding the chicken, chilling it, then grilling the chicken, making the tomato sauce, and simmering the chicken in it—a special treat for his father.

During dinner, Salma asked, "Who was this woman you helped?"

"I have no idea, Mother," he lied. "She was parked beside the road and needed assistance."

"It was his good deed for the day," Nadira added.

After dinner, while Atif glanced at the mail on a table in the hall, Nadira helped clear the table and offered to do dishes. Salma shooed her away. "Both of you. Go clean yourselves and say your

Asr prayers. Praise Allāh and thank him for our blessings. Then do your homework. And don't forget to say your Maghrib and Ishā prayers."

"Yes, Ami," Nadira said.

She walked upstairs and past her parents' suite and the other bedrooms and the guest bathroom with the Jacuzzi tub, bidet toilet, and long vanity under a large mirror, to her room, and Atif descended to his basement abode with its living area, bedroom suite, and entertainment room. They both showered and knelt on the floor in their rooms facing Mecca to say their Asr prayers. But as he studied under the artificial basement lights, Atif almost neglected to pray at dusk.

After putting away the food and filling the dishwasher, Salma climbed the stairs, washed her face, arms, and feet, and prayed, preferring her bedroom suite to the main floor den where her husband Ahmed prayed when he was home.

Amy turned into the driveway of the Breckenridges' large white colonial house. Her eyes swept across the stately two-story front portico supported by six white columns with Corinthian scroll tops. A one-story sunroom expanded the right side of the house and a carport balanced it on the left. Carlton Breckenridge, Amy's great-grandfather on her father's side, and his wife Elmira, built the house in 1920. They wanted a house in town, not just the one on the farm. At that time, Amy's grandparents moved into the farmhouse and then moved into the big house when his parents died, and Amy's parents followed them. The house was on the register of historic places despite the careful addition of new wiring, windows, appliances, central air conditioning, fire sprinklers, and a large addition on the back.

Amy loved it. Driving through the carport, she clicked open the overhead door and proceeded past the addition straight into the four-car garage at the rear. She climbed the outside stairs to the door on the side of the addition and entered with her back-pack slung over her shoulder.

Her eyes moved around what her dad had named "the trophy room," a windowless space forty feet deep and half as wide with a sloped ceiling made of timber trusses between which were six opaque skylights. Black leather sofas and chairs, resting on dark hardwood floors clad partially with oriental rugs, faced a stone fireplace with a six-foot wide TV screen above the mantle. Stuffed animal heads stared silently from the sides of the fireplace and along the walls—two eight-point bucks, a black bear, grizzly bear, cougar, moose, gray wolf, elk, fox, all spotlit like paintings. On one side, a locked oak gun cabinet housed rifles, elephant guns, telescopic sights, thermal rifle scopes, pistols, and machetes. She found her mom, Eunice, lounging on a sofa reading a magazine, while cooking smells drifted in from the kitchen.

"Where have you been?" she asked, pulling her reading glasses off her round face fringed with brown bangs and placing them on her chunky body.

"I had a flat tire, but fortunately, a nice man stopped and put my spare on. He wouldn't take anything for doing it either." She dropped her backpack on the floor near the door and slipped out of her coat.

"That's nice. Just a good Christian."

Amy tipped her chin up and pulled her long, dark brown hair behind her ears with the index fingers of each hand. "I guess, but he might have been something else. I didn't ask him. He might have been a Muslim or a Jew or an agnostic, for that matter."

"Let's not start, girl. You know the Jews killed Jesus…"

"Oh!" Amy said in exasperation. "Not that again."

"The high priests gave Jesus to the Romans to be killed because they claimed that he blasphemed. That's in the book of Matthew. You know that. And you know that these Muslims are terrorists."

"Not all of them, Mother."

"Don't forget 9/11 and Al-Qaeda, and ISIS beheading all those people."

"Yes, but not all Muslims are terrorists. There are some nice Muslim kids at school, and they're not terrorists."

"You wait. Nothing good will come out of that mosque they're building. They'll be training terrorists in there and sending them over to fight with ISIS against us, and to bomb places here, too. They'll go after the new World Trade Center next. You wait. They don't believe in Jesus Christ, and they're not saved, and we all know what that means."

"Yes, Mother." She gave up. "When's dinner?"

"As soon as your father comes home. He's meeting with Peter at the farm this afternoon."

"Good. I'm starved."

"Oh, by the way, Stewart called."

"Thanks." He had called her cell, too, but Amy hadn't answered and hadn't returned the call. Somehow, she wasn't feeling close to Stewart. She wasn't sure she wanted to marry someone like her dad who would try to keep her under his thumb her whole life. And he was so strong against Muslims and other people outside her circle that she felt like she had an extra parent. In the fall, he would be going to the University of Wisconsin to study dairy science. That might be a good time to break up, even though it would not please the adults in their families, let alone Stewart.

This older Muslim man, Atif, had arrived suddenly and excited and scared her. Agreeing to meet with him was like letting go at the top of a ski jump.

"Is Jesse home?"

"He's in his room, I think."

"You should put a baby monitor in his room." Jesse was in eleventh grade. "Then you could hear him breathing when he sleeps— which he does all the time."

She picked up her backpack and walked into the house through the kitchen past the door to the back stairs that led to the servant's room on the second floor, which Jesse had recently claimed for his own so he had more privacy and could sneak down the stairs to get food and slip out of the house unnoticed.

From the kitchen, she proceeded into the wide center hall and past the main staircase where she glanced into the reception hall at the light coming through the sunburst window over the front door and sidelights. Turning, she ascended the dark oak staircase with heavy railing and white balusters. She turned again on the landing with the nook where she loved to read and look at her laptop and gaze out the windows over the roof of the addition, at the garage, spacious yard, and the high security fence, capped with spikes, to the roofs of the houses beyond.

She passed the other door to Jesse's room, which he always kept closed and locked with a hook and eye. After climbing a few more steps into the hallway, she passed her parents' room on the front, which had a balcony that looked out under the portico and a large deck on top of the sunroom, and turned left into her room on the back of the house. She hung her jacket in the deep walk-in closet and put her backpack on the sofa bed in the room off the bedroom where her friends or cousins stayed when they visited.

Tonight they ate dinner together in the dining room because Amy's father Randall would be home and Eunice had prepared a roast. Amy liked the peach-colored walls, the dark antique furniture, and the painting of mallard ducks flying from a pond surrounded by cattails and trees.

The aroma of beef hanging rich in the air, mingled with that of rolls from the oven, made Amy ravenous. Her father sat at the end of the long table with Eunice at the other end and Amy and Jesse on the sides. Amy studied her dad as he sat down. He was tall and gaunt but strong, dressed in a white dress shirt and gray slacks, his brown hair combed straight back over his rather large head, with a pointed nose, big ears that lay against his head, high forehead, dark brows and accusatory eyes. She thought that Jesse more nearly resembled his mother: he was shorter and thicker than his dad and had a rounder face.

They bowed their heads, and Randall said grace.

Eunice began the conversation, "Amy had a flat tire today, but a man stopped and helped her."

"A good Samaritan, eh?" Randall asked as he forked in a piece of beef.

Amy blinked. She felt a threat to Atif in her father's comment. "Yes. And he wouldn't take any money."

"Makes me suspicious. I wonder what he wanted."

"He wanted to do a good deed."

"Maybe. Maybe not. Maybe he took down your plate number and will turn up later to collect his reward."

"Oh, Daddy."

He began slathering butter on a hot roll. "People are sinful, Amy. You've got to be careful."

"That's right," Eunice added. "Things are different now than when we were growing up. You can't trust people today. Even this community has changed. You never know who will be driving down the highway. We have to be careful who we associate with and watch out and protect ourselves. That's why we put the security system in."

"I'm surprised you knew where the spare was," Jesse said with a smirk.

She looked at him sweetly, but her mind's eye saw a slug crawling on a tomato in the garden. "Well, wise guy. I didn't. But the man did."

"How old was he?" Randall asked, continuing to chew and probe.

"In his twenties, I'd say."

"Did he look at you with lust?" Eunice asked.

"No, Mother, he didn't. He was very shy, really. He hardly looked at me at all. And anyway, I was wearing my white coat, which hides me quite well."

Jesse smirked. "Well, who would want to look at you anyway, ugly?"

"OK, son, that's enough," Randall said.

Atif might, Amy thought, and she lost herself dreaming of meeting with him and visiting a mosque together.

CHAPTER 2
NUMBERS

Amy's curiosity about Atif was building. For starters, where do they live? She asked Nadira the next day before class, and she replied. "In Oakton Acres, you know, the new subdivision off Father White Highway."

Amy smiled. "Oh, that's nice."

She knew their last name from listening to the teacher call on Nadira—"Miss Bhati"—so during class it was easy, with her phone hidden below her desk, to search the Internet for Bhati on Oakton Drive and get bird's eye and street views of their house. Later, she drove by for a look, and marveled at how an immigrant family could afford such a large house.

After more online searching, Amy found Ahmed Bhati, chief of surgery, White County Hospital. Clicking on medical staff, she learned that Dr. Bhati was educated at King Edward Medical University in Lahore, graduated in 1987, and finished his US residency in 1990. Atif must have been born around 1996, and Nadira, like her, in about 1999. She wondered when the parents met and married.

After getting to know them somewhat through the Internet, she couldn't believe there was such a disconnect between these people and the ones her parents hated—the anti-Christ immigrants from Pakistan—"the country that harbored Osama bin Laden and the Taliban"—the people who wanted to worship "Allāh" right in Chelmsford.

She remembered all the meetings her dad held in the trophy room, plotting strategies to stop the mosque. Her dad expected Jesse to attend the meetings, but not her. She wasn't allowed, even if she wanted to. Amy didn't think they trusted her. Maybe it was because she was a girl. But she knew what was going on. She could listen to their voices from the back of her closet.

First, they tried to block sale of the property, but they were too late. It was owned by out-of-towners who didn't care who bought it, and the financing was through an Islamic bank that was beyond their reach. This frustrated her father and made him angry.

He chaired the town zoning board, and she heard that the first time they met, they considered zoning the land agricultural so a mosque couldn't be built on it. They would protect the farmland.

"But their lawyers pointed out all the churches on the highway," Randall told some friends in the trophy room. "And then those damned developers. They were afraid that if it was zoned so you couldn't build a mosque on the land, they might not be able to build houses on it either. So they sided with the board of the Islamic association! All they care about is money."

A few days later, Atif asked Nadira a question as she was preparing to get out of the car. He dropped her off at school whenever he could to save his mother the trouble.

"Say, I wonder when you see that girl Amy, if you could ask her for her cell number."

"Ooooh," Nadira crooned. "You do like her."

"No," he said with a serious face, shaking his head in denial. "They're nonbelievers. But she said she wants to learn about Islam, and I want to see if she still does." He moved his head sideways a few more times. "That's all."

Nadira smirked. "Sure, brother, sure," she said, grabbing her backpack. "If you were as devout as you say you are, you would have me or another woman explain Islam to her."

He raised his heavy eyebrows, pleading, turned his head to one side, and asked, "Will you get her number for me, please?"

She relaxed into a normal grin, and he asked, "And not tell Abu and Ami? They don't need to know about it."

"O—kay," and she overflowed with a cascade of giggles and left the car.

He watched her go, gliding along in her white slacks, brown jacket, and backpack over her shoulder. She jogged up the stairs still smiling, and went down the hall to her locker.

She didn't see Amy until AP English. To be certain that no one overheard her, she passed her a note: "My brother wants your cell so he can call you about those lessons you wanted." Amy's desk was a few rows up, so she handed her the neatly folded paper on the way back to her desk.

During class, Nadira's mind filled with speculations: Maybe Amy wasn't interested. She was afraid her family or boyfriend would find out. A day or so earlier, Amy had asked her where she lived. But maybe she had decided that she didn't like Atif, or our family. Maybe she had decided that Atif was beneath her, and she didn't want to associate with him...

As the bell rang and the students rose to leave, Amy slipped her the note without a word while wearing a blank expression. Nadira's heart was thumping. She waited until she was outside to unfold it. And there was the number, neatly inscribed in pencil. She slipped it into a book, went to her locker, put on her jacket, loaded her backpack, and went outside where Atif said he would be waiting.

She was lucky for the days that their schedules matched, so she didn't have to catch a ride with someone else, call her mother, or take the bus. She wished that Abu and Ami would give her a car like they did for Atif, and like Amy's parents did for her, but she knew they never would unless she needed it for college. Next year, she would be going to Maryland with Atif and would be riding with him to campus, at least for a year—he would be a senior. After that, she would probably have to ride the county buses, which stopped on Father White Highway, Route 73, two blocks from their house.

Where was he? The other students were crossing the parking lot and starting to jam the driveway out to the road. She walked to the front of the school and found him there, glued to his phone.

"Did you get it?" he asked as she climbed in beside him.

"What'll you give me if I tell you?"

His eyes flared. "What'll I give you if you don't tell me, is more like it. Come on," he begged.

"Yes, yes, she gave it to me." She unzipped her backpack, pulled out the book, opened it up, and gave him the note. "I didn't want anyone to overhear a conversation, so I just gave her a note, and she gave it back."

He opened it up, typed it into his phone, quickly sent a message, "Text back if U receive. ~A," and pushed "Send."

A minute later his phone flashed, and he read, "Received, Dr. B. ~A." He laid the phone on the dashboard.

He exploded into a grin. "Ha! You told her our last name, didn't you?"

"No. Maybe she heard our teacher say it. Why?"

"Because now she's calling me 'Dr. B.' I don't know if that's because of Abu, or because I'm pre-med…"

Nadira smiled. "Or maybe so people will think you're a professor…"

His eyebrows went up. "…if they steal her phone and go snooping."

He turned out of the lot onto the Route 73, which became the tree-lined Main Street of Chelmsford town center—past the old stone bank with the high windows and the ATM out front; the red brick post office with arched windows and a cupola on the slate roof, where they mailed packages; the old restaurant that didn't serve halal meat, the tavern where Muslims didn't go; a movie theater that had long ago been converted to shops; the stone Romanesque Catholic church with a square belfry tower and a large rose window; the white United Methodist Church with tall arched windows on the side and a white steeple that pointed skyward; and rows of old Victorian homes with porches across the front, including the big one with six two-story columns that they passed every day; and on to their "suburb" in the country. The mosque, which would soon be under construction, would be a little further out.

Again the light on his phone flashed.

"That's her, Atif!" Nadira squealed.

"It has to be." He pulled onto the shoulder, stopped, and slid the message bar to the side.

"Well?" her message asked.

Nadira started waving her hand impatiently. "What does she say?"

"She says, 'Well?'"

Nadira chortled.

"A demanding woman!" he added.

"Well?" she echoed. "What are you going to do?"

He looked at her and grinned. "None of your business."

She tipped her head and smirked. "You shouldn't make a lady wait, Brother."

"OK," he said, shaking his head up and down. He thought for a moment, and then typed, "Jamaican Grill @ mall. Sat @ 2:00," and hit send. "There. Now we'll see if this fish bites."

The phone flashed, and said, "OK."

"She says OK."

Nadira grinned. "That's it?"

"Yes."

"She's on the hook, and Islām's the bait."

His expression became serious. "I'm sure she's only interested in Islām," he chided.

Nadira giggled. "If you say so, Dr. B."

"You won't tell anyone, will you?"

"Not unless you make me mad."

He arrived first, ordered a cold drink, and found a table in a corner away from the counter. The Grill was mainly a take-out place and had only a few tables and booths. Order at the counter, pick it up when it's ready, sit down and eat, or take it home. It smelled of spicy jerk chicken, curried goat, beans and rice, and other dishes, and reggae music was playing in the background.

He waited. After fifteen minutes, he began to worry. Then, in she came, wearing jeans, a white jacket, a red scarf over her hair and tucked into her jacket, and sunglasses. He stood up, waved her into the booth with her back to the door, and said hi. She removed her glasses, and her blue eyes drew him like pools in a forest.

"I can only stay an hour," she said, "and then I have to go buy something."

He blinked and then laughed. "You told them you were going shopping."

"Yes."

She slipped off her jacket, revealing a long-sleeve red floral tunic shirt with a collar and a few buttons, and sat across from him.

"Would you like something to drink?" he asked.

"Sure. A diet drink would be good."

He rose, went to the counter, and returned with her drink.

"So do you live on the farm—where that Breckenridge Farm sign is?" he asked.

"No, we live in town on the main road in a big, old house. You may've seen it. It has six white columns on front."

"Oh, yes. I know where that is. Your farm looks big too."

She nodded. "It's the biggest one in the county—almost a thousand acres."

"How long has your family had it?"

"Since the early nineteenth century."

"And your dad runs it?"

"Well, he has a manager, Peter Yoder, who handles the day-to-day operations, and they have fifteen workers. Pete and his family live in the old farmhouse. That's where we used to live before my grandparents got sick, and we moved into their house in town to take care of them. I was in middle school then. Dad had a shower put in the powder room on the first floor and Grandma and Grandpa slept in the den next to it so they wouldn't have to climb stairs.

"Then after they died, he had the trophy room built."

"What's that?"

"Just a big addition where he has all his animal mounts on the walls—you know, animals he's killed when he went hunting."

"Oh," he said. He mounts the heads of animals he's killed.

"So anyway, that's when he expanded the dairy operation—he built two big new milking barns, two freestall barns, a fresh-cow barn, and a new birthing barn, put in a new silo, and increased the herd from a hundred cows to seven hundred. Then he expanded the dairy and store, and hired more people—half of them are Hispanic—they work cheaper—to lower the cost per gallon of milk. He spent millions."

"Wow. Why did he expand it so much?"

"He said it was either that or go out of business like hundreds of thousands of other dairy farms have done. Milk prices were down and they were losing money. He said he had to get his costs down to compete with the big dairy farms. And Grandpa wouldn't do it."

"Wouldn't do what?"

"He wouldn't expand. He said it was too risky. So Dad did it after Grandpa died. He says it's still not big enough. The biggest dairy farm in the US has thirty thousand cows, and the Chinese are building one for a hundred thousand cows."

"Amazing. And your family owns that Breckenridge Dairy and store up the highway?"

"Yeah. But they're under different management."

Wow. No wonder she drives a Lexus. "And so you grew up on the farm?"

"Yes."

"What was that like?"

She looked at him. "Well—it was a lot of hard work. We all had to work and get up early. I had to feed the calves and heifers before breakfast, rain or shine, in wind and snow, before the school bus came, and then feed them again after school and do my homework at night."

He couldn't watch her face while she talked. It was distracting, so he kept glancing away and down at the tabletop. "That really kept you busy. Did you like it?"

She raised her eyebrows. "It wasn't too bad. I loved bottle feeding the little calves the best."

"Was there anything you hated about it?"

"Well, I hated it when a cow died or they had to cull one 'cause it wasn't producing enough milk."

He looked up from the table. "Cull. You mean kill …"

"Yeah. That's the business. They try to sell them to a slaughterhouse in Baltimore, but sometimes they just have to call the renderer to come and pick them up. They do the same thing with the little male calves, too—they aren't worth anything to us."

"So what does your dad do on the farm now?"

"He spends a lot of time going over the records with Pete. They keep a record of every cow—how old it is, when was the last time it calved, how much milk it produces."

He sipped through his straw. "Why do they have to keep records?"

"Well, they have to decide when to send a cow out for insemination and calving—because the only time it produces milk is after it calves—or they have to decide when to cull it."

Atif stared out the window, not knowing what to say. Then he turned back and asked, "Well. What would you like to know about Islam?"

"I really don't know anything, Atif. Why don't you start from the beginning?"

"OK. Stop me if you have any questions." He folded his hands on the table in front of him, lacing his fingers. "First of all, the Arabic word 'Islam' means 'peace, obedience, and submission to God.' Allāh is just the proper Arabic name for God."

She wrinkled her forehead. "So Allāh is not necessarily a different God from the Christian or Jewish God…"

"No. He's the creator and sustainer of the universe—all-knowing and all-powerful—and our judge at the end of life."

"Interesting."

"And there are five basic duties in Islam. We call them the pillars. First is Shahāda. In this, a Muslim declares or affirms his faith by saying, 'There is no god except Allāh, and Muhammad is the messenger of Allāh.'"

"Jesus said there is only one God, too."

"And the Old Testament prophets like Abraham also said there was only one God. The Jews believe in one eternal God, too. In Deuteronomy, Moses said, 'The Lord he *is* God; *there is* none else beside him.' And like Muslims, Jews don't believe in a trinity."

She pursed her lips. "Hmm. What else?"

"The second pillar is Salāh, the five compulsory daily prayers. The first is at dawn, before sunrise; the second, we pray sometime after midday but before late afternoon; the third, in the late afternoon before sunset; the fourth, after sunset but before daylight ends; and the fifth, at night, before dawn."

"It seems like a lot of praying, but we pray before each meal and also at bedtime—so that would be four times for me."

He looked away, shrugging. "Yes, and I'm not really a very good Muslim. I'm not devout. I usually pray once or twice a day. Most Muslims don't pray five times." He sipped on his drink and went on. "But Abu and Ami do all five prayers whenever they can."

"Who?"

"Oh. My father and mother."

Amy expressed amazement. "And he's a surgeon."

"How do you know that?"

"The Internet. I looked him up."

"There are no secrets anymore. But anyway. Yes. He has a prayer rug in his office. He just shuts the door and unrolls it on the floor when he needs to pray."

"Wow. But I guess he can't do it when he's operating."

"No. He does it later."

"What do you say when you pray?"

"We praise Allāh. We say, 'O our Sustainer! All praise is due to You alone.' And we say, 'Allāh is independent. He neither begot anyone nor was He begotten. And none is equal to Him in any way,' which is to say that we don't believe Jesus was the son of Allāh, and that divides us from Christians. We also say, 'Send blessings to our prophet Muhammad (peace be upon him).' And we ask Allāh for help and beg His forgiveness and thank him for everything. And we ask him to save us from the path of the disbelievers. We hope for his mercy and fear his rebuke. And say that undoubtedly, his torment is going to overtake infidels."

"Interesting. But let me ask you this: can you ask Allāh for specific things, like winning a football game? Will he intervene?"

"Ha!" he laughed. "No, Amy, only in a game of cricket. That's Pakistan's most popular sport."

"Yes, but this is America, Atif. So, I'm asking you—can you ask Allāh to win a football game for you? Lots of our football teams pray to God for victory."

He had a suspicious glint in his eye. "Yes, Amy. We can ask Allāh for victory in a football game."

"And what if both teams ask for victory?"

There's the hook. He tilted his head back and pronounced the answer with great solemnity: "Allāh will decide which team is more deserving and will make that team win. Or, he will let the other team win next time. Or...he will decide...not to intervene."

She smiled. "Oh. Allāh is just like God."

"Amy. Allāh and God are the same—the creator and sustainer of the universe—and our ultimate judge."

"Of course," she said, looking at him intently. "And God-Allāh is omniscient—he knows how everything ends in the future."

"Yes."

"That must be really boring. I know people like that—they always read the last chapter of a novel first to see how it ends or read movie reviews so they know how they end, even before they start watching. They don't like surprises."

"Amy. Allāh is not a mortal. He doesn't get bored. You can't ascribe human qualities to Allāh."

She looked to the side. "Yes, I know. He's omnipotent too—all powerful. He can change the outcome of any game if he wants."

"True."

She took a quick sip through her straw, then exploded, "Or any war! But he never seems to change the outcome, even if millions are killed, and even if millions of people ask him to end it."

"That's right," he said, shaking his head up and down. "He gives man free will to do whatever man wants."

"Whether it be good or evil."

"Then he punishes him for doing evil and rewards him for doing good."

"Yes."

He sighed and looked up, in thought. "All right, going on. Let's see. The third pillar. The third pillar is Zakāh, the welfare contribution. Once a year, we have to give two and a half per cent of our wealth to the poor, or to travelers in need, or to win over hearts of new converts. It's not charity or a tax. Charity's optional; Zakāh is not."

"That's kind of like Christian tithing. But tithing is ten per cent of income, not wealth."

"I'm not sure how the difference works out."

She tossed her head back and forth. "Me neither. But anyway, I don't know any Christians who tithe. People think they don't have to because they give money to the government in taxes and think that takes care of the poor, or it's supposed to."

He frowned. "But look at all the homeless on the streets."

"Yes. That's why our church has missions. We have a group in church that works at a soup kitchen and pantry in DC. I've helped them lots of times. And we have a blanket drive in the fall, and I've helped take them around to people. It's sad. There are so many people living on the street."

"And your parents support your work?"

"Yes, of course. Daddy used to drive us."

They just don't like Muslims. "Anyhow—going on. The fourth pillar is Sawm or fasting. During the month of Ramadān, all adult Muslims must fast from dawn to sunset every day—no eating, drinking, or conjugal relations."

She contained a smile. "Oh, you mean..."

He ignored her. "It is to make us experience the pangs of hunger and thirst, so we know what it feels like, so we know what suffering the poor experience, and to give ourselves self-control—to learn restraint—and to help us overcome selfishness and greed."

"I know lots of people who suffer from sexual hunger," she said with a straight face.

He scowled. "Amy. We're talking about religion."

"You brought it up, Atif, not me. But I'm glad to know you've learned to control yourself. Hmm. I can just see all you starving Muslims going at it after dark during Ramadan."

"Amy!"

She grinned. "I mean eating and drinking."

He laughed too loudly, but quickly muffled it with his arm when he saw the man at the counter looking at him.

"What do you drink," she asked, "beer, whiskey, or wine?"

"We never drink alcohol. That's against our religion."

"Really?"

"Well, we're not supposed to, but some may."

She tilted her head and looked at him sideways. "Well, we don't drink either—most people in our church."

"And we don't eat pork. And all our meat is supposed to be halal—killed and prepared according to Islamic law. But we don't really follow that in our family."

"I bet Big Macs aren't halal."

"Actually, in Muslim countries they are. The cow has to be slaughtered by a Muslim butcher and prayed over before it is killed."

"So you import your Big Macs from Saudi Arabia."

He grinned. "Yeah, sure. Now pay attention. The fifth pillar is Hajj. Once in our lifetime, if people can afford it and are physically able, Muslims must make a pilgrimage to Mecca to see the Ka'bah, the House of Allāh, built by Abraham and Ismāil for the purpose of worshipping Allāh."

"Abraham? Ismāil? Is that Ishmael? They're in your religion too?"

"Yes. They're the same. Muhammad said there are thousands of prophets who have given Allāh's guidance to mankind. Twenty-five are mentioned in the Qur'an, including the ones you call Adam, Noah, Abraham, and Ismāil, Isaac, Moses, David, Jesus…"

She blinked. "Jesus is mentioned in the Qur'an?"

"Oh, yes, we consider him to be a great prophet. But we believe that Allāh's guidance was *completed* by Muhammad…"

"Who would know?" she said, shaking her head. "But Mecca. I thought you went there because that's where Muhammad was from."

"That's true. But primarily, the Hajj reminds us that we are humble servants of our Creator."

"Have you been there?" Her eyes were wide.

"I have no money."

"Oh, poor boy," *whose father is rich.*

"My parents have been there. Two years ago. For them it was a great spiritual experience. Imagine, more than two million pilgrims go for the Hajj each year."

"Tell me about your parents."

"Well, my father grew up in Pakistan. He was poor, very poor. His father was an auto mechanic, and Abu had five brothers and two sisters. He worked sweeping stores in Lahore as a child."

"Wow. He's come a long way."

"Yes. He was the best student in his family and won scholarships to college and medical school. He graduated from King Edward Medical University in Lahore in 1987, got a visa to come to school here, and passed the medical examination and finished his US residency in 1990. Then he married my mother in Pakistan and brought her here, and he practiced in a rural area before beginning his surgical residency."

"My goodness! Did he know your mother for very long in Pakistan?" She drew a long sip through the straw, holding it with her thumb and index finger and daintily raising her little finger, while she concentrated on his words.

"Oh, many years. She is his third cousin, and they prayed at the same masjid."

"Are your grandparents still in Pakistan?"

"Abu's father has passed away, but my grandmother lives there, and Ami's parents are still living. They all live in Lahore. Abu sends them money every month."

He looked at her tentatively, unsure about whether to ask something personal. "Where did your parents meet?"

"They were showing their cows at the Maryland State Fair! Mom's family had a dairy farm in Frederick County, and Dad was older than she was—he had already been to Somalia with the Army."

"He was in the Army? In Somalia?"

"Yes."

"When?"

She shrugged. "Oh, I don't know. Twenty years ago?"

"Was he in a war?"

"Yes. In Mogadishu. He has a display of his military awards on the wall in the trophy room. He got a medal in Somalia."

"What kind?"

"Silver Star."

"Wow. That's a really high one. What did he do to get that?"

She looked at him proudly. "He crawled under fire and dismantled a mine that a Somali soldier was going to set off at some of our soldiers who were trapped—something like that. I've heard him tell that story a million times, but I don't remember the details."

"He was a real tough guy, wasn't he?"

"I guess so. He says he was 'a lean, mean fighting machine.' Ha."

"You know, maybe that war explains why he hates Muslims...."
How does he know that? she wondered.

"...The US lost that battle to Muslim soldiers, and black, at that, and had to come home. And if I remember right, Pakistani and Malaysian soldiers—Muslims—helped save the Americans who were shot down. That was in that movie, 'Black Hawk Down.' Did you see that?"

"No—I don't like war movies. But Daddy says we won that war! We killed a thousand of them, and they only killed nineteen of us. And we withdrew when the job was done."

"But how many of them that we killed were civilians?"

"He said the civilians were shooting at them. They all hated us. He has nightmares about black Somali Muslim soldiers shooting down at them from rooftops and around doorways, and firing rockets and machine guns at them from Jeeps, and crowds racing toward them with their rifles held over their heads, and dragging the naked body of a marine down a street with ropes."

Atif thought for a moment, and then said with a worried look, "Does your father have guns?"

"Sure, lots of them. He's a hunter, you know. He's been shooting since he was young—shooting rats on the farm with his twenty-two, and then going deer hunting with Grandpa, and on trips out West."

"What about your brother? Nadira said you have a brother named Jesse."

"He shoots with daddy lots of times. They have a target range on the farm. They go hunting together sometimes, too. But anyway. You were asking how mom and dad met."

"Oh, yeah."

"Well, he was going into his senior year at Maryland in agriculture. I don't think he really wanted to exhibit at the fair that much—I really think he was on the lookout for a woman and thought he might bump into someone there, someone who really liked to farm. Mom grew up on a farm and liked it, and after high school, she took a lot of Maryland Extension courses in Frederick so she knew a lot about the business. And they were both religious conservatives. They really hit it off. It took them less than a year to get hitched."

"What about your grandparents?"

"Dad's parents died within a couple of years of each other, and my mom's parents sold their farm and retired to Tucson several years ago. We don't see them very often—they don't like to come east. But I used to be real close to Dad's mom, Rebecca. She was wonderful. She worked hard on the farm and read the Bible all the time and taught me a lot. Taught me to study. She always said, 'God is love.' But she didn't get along very well with Grandpa. They argued all the time. He was a Christian, but he was a racist. He believed in segregation. And he was always ordering her around. 'I'm not one of your hired hands,' she used to tell him. 'And I'm not a cow!' Maybe she's why I like to argue with my dad. I take after her."

"Ha! Interesting."

He glanced at his watch and looked out the window. "We're out of time. I can tell you more about my family next time, if you want, and about Hajj. But you have to go shopping, and I have to study."

"OK. Great. Now, can I give you something for this, Atif, please?"

"What, money? That's what you asked when I changed your tire!" He raised his palms to her. "No, no, of course not. Nothing." He was piqued.

"All right," she said, raising her thin eyebrows.

They stood. She put on her glasses, and he watched her from behind as they walked to the door, still stunned by her beauty and wanting to know much more about her.

She turned her head to him. "Thanks, Atif."

He nodded, and they walked out in different directions.

CHAPTER 3
COYOTES

Jesse walked in the side door through the trophy room and into the kitchen, coming home from school. Eunice was making ham and cheese sandwiches and cutting carrot strips. Small bags of potato chips lay on the narrow table. It was late Tuesday afternoon. Randall was dressed in his army camouflage suit and cap, a leafy blend of tan sand, slate gray, and foliage green, and leather combat boots, heavily scuffed on the toes.

"OK, Jess-bo. Get in your combats and bring your license. We're goin' huntin'. ETD 1700 hours. It's 1633 now. We gotta get a move on."

"Gotcha. What are we huntin'?"

"Wild dogs. Peter said Jose saw three coyotes in the field on the other side of the calf barns an hour ago."

"Man. Do you think they'll go after the calves?"

"They might. We'll talk later. Go!"

Jesse bounded up the back stairs to his private lair above the kitchen, and quickly changed.

"Can you throw in some sodas, honey?" Randall asked Eunice.

"Sure. Be careful with my baby."

He strode into the trophy room, opened the gun cabinet, took out two bolt-action rifles, bipods to rest the barrels on while they aimed, riflescopes, and the predator-caller remote and speaker. He loaded them into the back seat of his pickup, and off they went.

The sun was low in the sky when they turned down the road to the calf barns. They bounced along on the unpaved road with the windows down.

"Dad, I don't understand how the coyotes would get the calves," Jesse said. "How would they get in the barns? And if they did get in, how would they get to the calves? They'd have to jump over the steel fence to get at the calves."

"Ever hear about coyotes being wily? They're sneaky and vicious. We can't take any chances, Son. They could dig a hole under the barn and get in and jump the fence and feast."

"Are they in season, like deer?"

"There's no season for coyotes. We can kill them anytime. Now if it was a black bear goin' after the calves, we couldn't kill it, unless it was bear season, and they only have that in the mountains, and you have to win a lottery to get a permit, and then you could only hunt for four days, and you couldn't kill the bear, you could only 'harvest' him—ha-ha!"

"What was the most dangerous hunt you ever did—the grizzly? The cougar? The moose?"

"Nope. It was the Mussies. They were scary."

"Mussies? What are they?"

"Moozlims. We were hunting them in Somalia when I was in the army in 1993. Over there, they were of the black variety."

Jesse grinned. "Oh yeah? What was the bag limit?"

Randall laughed. "There wasn't any. They were just like coyotes. You could shoot as many as you could find. It was open season on them—any time, any place."

"Really?"

"Well, actually, we were supposed to just kill the enemy militia fighters, but who could tell them apart? They all looked alike, and the civilians were shooting at us too."

"That's a different kind of hunting, ain't it, when the animals shoot back at you!"

"Ha! Damn straight."

They parked behind the calf barns, put the sights and bipod legs on their rifles and miner's lights around their caps, walked a hundred yards through the recently mowed alfalfa field, kneeled, and flipped down the bipod legs on their rifles.

"Focus on that wood line on the far side of the field. They'll likely come out of there. That's about two hundred yards out." Jesse nodded.

The sun was getting low in the sky and the shadows were long, but the field was still well lit. They waited silently, and then, after half an hour, two coyotes came out of the trees and began trotting from left to right along the wood line. "Hey. Here come some," Jesse said excitedly.

"I got the one on the left," Randall whispered. "You take the one on the right."

Randall set the coyote caller to bark—"whuh, whuh,"—and then changed it to the mournful howl of a pup in pain. Then he bent down and sighted across the field.

When the one on the right stopped and turned his head toward them at the sound of the pup, Jesse shot him through the forequarter on the first shot, causing him to immediately crumple to the ground. "You got him," Randall said. "Not bad shooting—for a kid."

Randall's shot missed, and his coyote began racing across the field to the right. He shot several more times, smoothly working the bolt of the rifle each time, looking through the riflescope, and squeezing the trigger, but missing, and it disappeared into the woods.

"Damn. Well, OK, Jess-bo. Let's go get yours."

"Too bad you didn't get assault rifles before the ban. Then you might have hit him."

"Oh, we gotta give these critters a chance, don't you think? Otherwise, we wouldn't have any to hunt."

They began walking in the deepening dusk, turning on the miner's lights on their caps as they went. Stooping over the carcass, they shined the lights down and examined it.

Randall laughed. "He's dead alright. OK, let's go. That's all for tonight."

"What? Don't you want to keep trying a little longer? Maybe you'll get lucky."

"Nope. It's getting dark, and I don't want to have to put on thermal lenses, and this time of year we can't hunt these critters more than half an hour after dark anyway—that's the law. Besides, this is your night to shine. We need to head on back. Tomorrow's a school day."

"But they're still out there. They still might go after the calves," Jesse said as he picked up the forty-pound furry bag of bones by the hind legs and slung it over his shoulder with the head hanging down his back, his rifle in his other hand at his thigh.

They began walking to the truck by the calf barns, and could hear mooing.

"I bet they'd be noisier if there was a coyote in there," Jesse said. "But how are we going to get the rest of them—keep hunting them? That might be tough."

"If we need to, we'll do it. But I think I'll have Clyde set some traps out here, too. He's good at that. And if that doesn't work, I'll have him put out some meat seasoned with rat poison. That'll get 'em, if the traps don't scare them away."

Jesse threw the furry bundle into the back of the truck, and then they put their rifles and the caller on the back seat and climbed in the front.

"Hungry?" Randall asked. "Want a sandwich?"

They each took one from the bag.

"I prefer warm meat," Randall said, "but I'm like a coyote—I'll eat cold carrion if there's nothing else." Jesse laughed.

Randall flipped on the headlights, revved the motor, turned around, and drove back down the farm road toward the highway.

"I think we might want to put this one on the wall in the trophy room. We don't have a coyote yet. And that way we can remember this night, and brag to everybody how you bagged it, and I can brag, too, about you. 'Yeah, I shot all those animals up there, except for that coyote over there—Jesse bagged it.'"

They pulled in the drive and parked, and Randall snickered and said, "Hey, why don't you drape that thing around your neck like one of the furry fox stoles and walk in like that. Give the women a show."

Jesse laughed and they climbed the steps to the side door and entered the trophy room. Eunice and Amy were watching the news when they burst in. Eunice looked up and said, "Don't you bring that thing in here! Get it out of here, now." Amy just gaped.

"Well, it's goin' up on the wall," Randall said. "Deadeye Jesse killed it with one shot, and we're going to keep it."

"Not like that, you're not. If you're going to mount it, that's one thing, but for now, you get that thing out of here. You'll get blood on the floor and the furniture."

"Jesse shot it?" Amy asked.

"Sure did, Sis. Want to see its teeth?" He reached his hand over the snout, lifted the head, pulled back the lips on both sides showing the fangs, growled, and jumped at her.

She cringed. "Oh! Are you sure it's dead?"

"I don't know. Maybe not." He jumped again, this time flipping its bushy tail and moving its head.

"Oh!" Amy said again, recoiling.

"It's dead all right," Randall said. "And it's one coyote that won't be coming after our calves. We just wanted you to know that we're protecting you ladies, and keeping the wolves away from the door."

Eunice smiled and said, "Well, we thank you, and now we'll thank you to get that thing out of here."

"Oh, all right. Jesse, put it in a plastic bag and put it in the freezer in the garage. We'll take it to the taxidermist tomorrow."

A few nights later, Amy was listening carefully from the back of her walk-in closet where long ago she'd discovered she could hear, quite clearly, voices coming from the trophy room. A meeting was in progress, and she strained to hear every word. What she heard, however, was a goulash of indistinguishable sounds. The meeting started at seven-thirty. *Please don't all talk at once,* she thought.

Then she heard Randall say, "And he killed it dead with one shot. Blam! And that was it."

Someone said, "Wow. Old one-shot Jesse. Yep. That's what we'll have to call him."

"One-Shot Jesse!" other voices repeated.

The voices dwindled to their normal confusion, until Randall said, "I'll call this meeting to order now." His voice was authoritative and arrogant. "Let us pray. Dear Father, we ask that you be with us tonight as we consider new ways to stop the growth of this satanic cancer in our town. With your help, we have tried and failed to stop them and their lawyers from getting their zoning and building permits, although we have managed to double their cost in the process. Yet still these moozlims and their legal curs won't be deterred and are now preparing to break ground and begin construction. Dear God in heaven, help us to find the key to halting this construction forever. In Jesus's name we pray, Amen."

The men quietly echoed, "Amen."

"Tonight I invited Tom Bender to talk with us. Say hello, Tom. Tom is a custom builder from over in Redbridge who has built a number of homes in town and knows most of the people in the building department. He shares our dislike for these moozlim immigrants and has offered to try to help us out. He doesn't know the guy who's doing the building for these camel drivers."

The builder spoke. "No, I've never met him or even heard of him. He's definitely from out of the area. They wouldn't dare try to get a local builder. I'm glad they didn't ask me for a bid. I would've told them where to get off."

"I also asked our friend in the building inspection department to come tonight. He said he better not, but that we could count on him to issue building code–violation notices and stop-work orders on every single violation he sees. He offered that we should let him know if *we* see any violations we think he should red-tag, and that he would not be hasty about re-inspecting violations that had been corrected."

"I think I'm glad I didn't get the job," the builder said, and the men chuckled.

"Oh, you'll be involved," Randall told him.

"What if we had him do inspections, too," a voice suggested. "I bet he could find violations."

Randall introduced the builder to the speaker. "Tom, this is John Dirkson—we call him 'Birdman.' He's a taxidermist— mounted all these heads up here—and he does ducks and birds, too. Beautiful work. Birdman, this is Tom. And this is Paul."

Amy slid into a more comfortable position—quietly—aware that her sounds could be carried downward.

"Like after the workers leave," another voice added.

"I could do that," Bender said, "—until I got caught."

The deep voice said, "But isn't this inspection thing just a delaying tactic? Can't we think of something to clean out kill the damn thing?"

Randall agreed. "You're right, Paul. We're just conducting a war of attrition, and increasing their costs. But it seems like they can get hold of as much money as they need. Hell, we got the codes department to double the size of that mosque and the parking and all, and those moozlims just took a little breath and went on."

"But how can we kill it?" Dirkson asked.

"Here's a thought," Paul said. "Don't you have a piece of ground on the other end of the county that we could trade them? At least that would get them out of town."

"Hmm," Randall said. "We hadn't thought of that. I'll look into it."

"I know we could sell this piece to a developer with no problem."

"I'll try it. Any other ideas?"

The meeting went on for another hour, until Dirkson and another man said they had to go, and then Randall concluded it with a prayer.

Amy had mixed feelings about him calling on Jesus to help them stop construction of the mosque. Muslims were so different from Christians; around the world, they were using violence to spread their religion, and people should be afraid of having them right in Chelmsford. Who knows what they could be plotting. But on the other hand, Atif's father was a doctor, and an important leader of the group building the mosque, and Nadira and Atif were so nice. How could these people sponsor terrorism? Still, she remembered her mother saying, "They don't believe in Jesus Christ, and they're not saved, and we all know what that means."

Atif sat in the living room studying, while Nadira set the rectangular table in the dining room. Next, she brought in a basket of roti—the flat, circular, unleavened bread that Salma had dry-baked on her tava griddle—and the pitcher of lassi with which she filled the glasses.

After taking the skewered beef kebabs off the grill and placing them on a serving dish, Salma spooned rajma—red kidney beans in a thick gravy seasoned with red chili powder, garlic, and other spices—into a bowl.

Ahmed rumbled down the stairs, drawn by the aromas, and sat at his end of the table. He was a tall man with a round face, broad nose, thick chevron mustache covering his upper lip, heavy eyebrows, a stern look, and a light tan complexion.

"How are you, Abu?" Nadira asked with a smile.

"Tired, but your mother's food will awaken me."

Atif came to the table, greeted his father, and sat on the side to his father's right. Nadira brought the rajma, and Salma carried the kebab, placed it in front of Ahmed, and sat at the other end of the table.

"It smells so good," Ahmed said to her. "We are so fortunate to have this food." Then he bowed his head and said, "*Bismillahi wa barakatillah.* (In the name of Allāh and with the blessings of Allāh do we eat.)" The others repeated his words. They passed the food, loaded their plates, pulled the meat off the skewers with their forks, and waited for him to begin. He lifted a bite of beef into his mouth and began to slowly chew. Then his eyes closed, and satisfaction spread over his face. He looked at Salma and smiled.

"How was your day, Father?" Atif asked.

"Good, thanks to Allāh. We did a quadruple bypass today. I spent four hours on my feet, cutting and sewing. The patient is doing well."

"Praise to Allāh," Atif replied. "Did you have any problems?"

"No. It was a textbook case…How are your studies going?"

"Very well, thank you," he said, hoping to end the discussion.

But Ahmed continued to probe. "Any exams coming up?"

"Yes. Biochem and advanced organic chemistry."

Ahmed leaned his head back. "Do you know the material?"

Atif looked him in the eye. "I have some studying to do, but I'm almost there."

"And you've taken good notes?"

"Yes."

"Remember that you must get As in every course to get into medical school."

"I know that," he said with some irritation in his voice.

"Do any subjects cause you difficulty?"

He decided to admit a weakness. "I have some difficulty with physics, so I have to study it harder."

"You know what you must do." Now he turned his head to his daughter. "And what about you, Nadira? Are you getting all As?"

"So far, Abu, but I've been struggling a little with algebra."

"Algebra? Invented by the Muslim mathematician Muhammad Al-Khwarizmi in Baghdad in 820. Surely you can master that."

She grinned. "Do you say that because you think I'm as smart as he was, or because I'm a Muslim?"

He opened up into a smile. "Because you're my daughter." They all laughed. "Get your brother to help you if you need to. He was good at that."

"And about you, Salma? How was your day? What did you do besides cooking delicious food?"

"I assisted with the middle school class and tutored some children."

The home line rang, and Nadira rose, answered it, and carried it into the dining room from the kitchen. "It's for you, Abu."

He rose and said, "I'll take it in the living room."

"One moment, please," she said and handed it to him. He walked into the living room.

"Yes?"

"Dr. Bhati, this is Randall Breckenridge."

"Yes? What do you want?"

"Let me start by apologizing for all the discord we've had over this mosque thing. But, you know, some of the people in town just weren't in favor of it. It's not that they're bigoted, you understand, they would just rather see you build this thing somewhere else."

"What do you want?"

"Dr. Bhati, in the service of peace, I'd just like to suggest a compromise that we all could live with."

"And what would that be?"

"Well, you see, Dr. Bhati, I own a lot of land around here, and I have a very nice piece I think you would like right down the road a few miles that I think would suit your needs very well, and it percs real well, and I think it would get these townspeople off our backs if we could swap land, and that would—"

"Stop, Mr. Breckenridge," Ahmed growled. "We are starting construction at the present site this week."

"I just thought you might want to run it by your people and—"

"No. I will not do that. We start construction this week."

"But I'm sure that…"

"Thank you for calling. Goodbye." He clicked off and returned to the dining room. His face was flushed, his mouth drawn tight, his body agitated.

"Who was that?" Salma asked.

"Randall Breckenridge," he growled. "He wants to swap our land for land 'a few miles' down the road. He says it's a 'compromise' that would get the townspeople off 'our' backs."

"What did you tell him?"

"I told him that construction starts this week. I held my tongue and thanked him for calling before I said goodbye and hung up."

"Good, Abu," Nadira said.

"The land lies properly. The masjid can be parallel to the road and our prayer room can face east. And the ground falls enough for our basement to have doors above ground. It's perfect for our purposes, and we will not change."

His scowl remained until Nadira brought dessert—coffee and fig bars. Then he relaxed, and they ended by praying, "Alhamdulillah il-lathi at'amana wasaqana waja'alana Muslimeen (Praise be to Allāh Who has fed us and given us drink, and made us Muslims)."

"I wonder what else he has up his sleeve," Atif said as they rose. Ahmed replied, "Whatever Allāh will use to test us."

CHAPTER 4

STAKES AND PINS

The late-model white Ford pickup with E&D Construction signs on the doors pulled onto the shoulder and stopped, followed by an older green GMC pickup. It was six-thirty in the morning, and the ankle-high grass was wet with dew. A cool morning fog reduced visibility and gave sights a dreamlike aura. Headlights appearing down the road slowly grew like ghastly eyes and changed into cars that whished by.

The door of the white truck swung open, and Dan Stanley, the builder, emerged carrying a roll of plans and a thermos and wearing a brown leather jacket. The foreman, Lonnie Craig, appeared from the other vehicle wearing a denim shirt over a sweatshirt and carrying his own bottle. Both men were in their thirties, and both were slender, though Lonnie was taller and more muscular.

They leaned against the cool sides of Dan's truck bed drinking coffee from metal thermos cups while looking toward the lot, telling stories, laughing, and trying to wake up.

"OK," Dan said. "We're not making any money drinking coffee." He screwed the cup onto the thermos, turned and picked up the laser level and measuring pole from the bed, and Lonnie grabbed a bunch of wood stakes, the sledge, and bag of lime. They walked about twenty paces to the middle of the lot, which gradually sloped away from the road, and Lonnie dumped the stakes and bag onto the ground. The dew soaked the bottom of their jeans and turned their leather boots dark brown.

"OK," Dan said. "Let's see if we can find the surveyor's pins again in this soup." He headed for the right side of the lot near the road, and Lonnie followed him with a stake and the sledge. "It's over here somewhere," Dan said, scanning the ground.

Lonnie looked as well. "I don't see it."

"Let's pull a tape from the road." Dan gave the end of his hundred-footer to Lonnie who walked to the road and stopped at the edge. Dan pulled it to twenty-five feet and swung the tape in an arc over the ground, searching.

"Any luck?" Lonnie asked.

"Nope. I can't find it. Let's try the other side of the lot."

They walked down to the other end, trying, but failing, to keep the tape taut and out of the wet grass.

"Right there," Dan said. "The grass is matted down a little here." Again he began swinging the tape in a slow arc over the grass. "I can't find it."

Dan pointed. "Wait. There's one of them. Over there."

Lonnie turned and looked. "Way over there?"

They walked to the stake and looked around.

Dan shook his head. "That's not where I remember it was. But I may be wrong."

Lonnie looked puzzled. "What do we do now?"

Dan turned and looked back. "Well, let's measure over to the other side and see if we can find the other one."

Dan pulled the tape out to the end, stopped, and Lonnie carried his end past Dan to double the length. They went farther, and Lonnie said, "Here it is."

Dan took in his surroundings, and said again, "This doesn't look right."

"So what do we do, just go ahead? It's not our fault if they're off."

Dan held his arms and pawed the grass with his boot. "But they look way off to me. We sure don't want to build this thing on someone else's property, or even cross the sideline."

"No."

"We might have to move the foundation if we get too close to the property lines. That would cost me big bucks. This whole job could end up in the courts, and then we'd be out of work. And they'll blame me for not catching it. 'Didn't it look fishy to you?' they'll say. 'You were with the surveyor when he put them in the ground.'"

Lonnie shrugged. "Why don't we just take a chance and go ahead?"

"Oh. That makes my ulcer rumble."

"So you're going to call off the excavator and Miguel? They'll love that. They were all set to come today. That'll put a bump in their schedules. And you'll be like that boy that cried wolf. Next time they'll whine, 'Are you sure you want us this time?'"

Dan shrugged. "I know."

Lonnie kicked a rock he found in the grass. "And what'll you have to do, have the surveyor come back and do the job over? He'll love that."

"I'll have to. But if he sees that the stakes have been moved, he'll be on my team then."

Lonnie still was shaking his head. "But who's going to pay to have it resurveyed? Are you going to pay him? Will you tell him that? And how long will it take to get him back? A week? He's got his schedule, too. This will set us back. And he's not going to want to come back and do a redo. Everyone hates that. And then, what if you're wrong? He'll be disgusted that you made him come back for nothing."

Dan spread his arms, imploring Lonnie to see it his way. "I know. It's a shitty choice. But these stakes just don't look right to me."

The two men looked at the ground and then looked up and gazed around the site.

Lonnie laughed. "I know what you're going to do."

"No, you don't. I'm going to call Maskeen and give him a heads up and try to get him to make the decision. Then I won't have to pay for it."

"Unless you're wrong."

"Yeah, well, then maybe I can split it with him. But I better call and reschedule those guys."

"They'll love that."

They walked to the center of the field, retrieved the stakes and level, and headed for the trucks.

Lonnie looked up at the blue sky appearing through the fog. "Shit. And we were looking at good weather all this week, too."

"What I want to know is who moved those stakes. Next time, you and I are both going to be there when the surveyor comes and we're going to get the foundation staked out and limed before any-one can mess with those stakes."

"Next time we build a mosque."

"Yeah."

When he reached his truck, Dan pulled out his cell, and called Maskeen.

"What was that?" Maskeen was from Northern India, a CPA with some construction experience who was watching over the construction for Ahmed and the others on the committee.

Dan explained again, leaning against his truck.

"Who would do such a thing?"

"I think we both know, sir."

"Yes."

"What do you think I should do?" Dan asked.

The young accountant cleared his throat and said he would call back. Dan asked him to be quick because he had to call the excavator and footer guy.

When Maskeen couldn't get through to Ahmed, he left a message and called Dan back immediately. "Stop the job. We don't want to end up in court. Call your subs. I'll call the surveyor."

"Thanks."

"We do what we have to do."

Atif and Amy met in a small coffee shop near the mall. She found him at a table in the back. He rose, they exchanged greetings, and he noticed that she was wearing a tan jacket over a white blouse and blue skirt, with the same scarf on her head, and sunglasses. And today, he observed a necklace with a gold cross.

"How have you been?" he asked.

"Fine. Are your studies going well?"

"Yes. You sound like my father. He's always asking about my studies."

She grinned. "Someone needs to."

Somehow, his words seemed strained to her today—polite, but cool.

"Any news?"

"Just that my dad and brother went hunting for coyotes in the field behind the calf barn, and Jesse killed one with one shot."

Atif started. "Wow. I didn't know we had coyotes around here."

"Yes."

"And he killed it with one shot. He must have good aim."

"Yes. Daddy said two coyotes were running across the field, and he made the coyote caller bark—"

Atif gave her a quizzical look.

"It's a gadget with a speaker on it that you put on the ground and it makes animal sounds. Hunters use them."

"Oh."

"And then he made it howl like a pup in pain, and one of the coyotes stopped and turned toward the sound, and Jesse shot it dead. They're calling him 'One-Shot Jesse' now."

Atif blinked. "They're killers!…But they don't scare me." Then he shook his head as if shaking out the vision and looked shyly into her face. "Do you—uh—want some coffee?"

"Just Diet-Coke or Pepsi."

He brought back her drink, and a paper cup of tea for himself, with two bags—their strings draped over the side—a spoon and napkins.

"Do you have any questions from last week?" he asked as he dipped the bags and stirred the brew.

"Yes. You say that Jesus is one of your prophets. Do you believe that he is the Son of God?"

"No. We believe that Allāh is the one and only god, the creator and sustainer of the universe, and that he has no children."

"So you don't believe that Jesus is the Son of God."

"No." He was wrapping the strings around the teabags and spoon and squeezing out the rich concentrate.

"Do you believe in the Holy Spirit?"

He looked up. "No, no. We believe there is only one God— Allāh." He laid the wet teabags on a napkin.

"Oh, my. Do you believe that Jesus had a virgin birth?"

"Yes, we do believe that, as the Bible says. We believe he had a miraculous birth. He was born of the Virgin Mary—without a father—by Allāh's command. Allāh created Adam and Eve without a father or a mother, and Allāh created Jesus without a father. And we do not believe that Jesus was conceived by the Holy Spirit."

"Interesting."

Taking a sip of the bitter tea and looking at her, he said, "Jesus began preaching at the age of thirty, and Allāh gave him miraculous powers."

"So do you believe in all the miracles he performed? Giving sight to blind people? Raising Lazarus from the dead?"

"Yes, and feeding the multitudes and turning water into wine and walking on water—yes, we believe all of them."

"But do you believe that God allowed the Romans to crucify Jesus to save us from our sins?"

"No. We don't believe that. We believe the Romans just wanted to do away with another Jewish zealot who might try to overthrow their rule."

"And so you don't believe he rose from the dead and sits beside God and judges people—you know, decides whether they go to heaven or hell."

"No. It is Allāh who judges us."

She looked directly at him. "Our beliefs follow the Apostles' Creed. It goes like this:

I believe in God, the Father almighty,
maker of heaven and earth
And in Jesus Christ, His only Son, our Lord,
who was conceived by the Holy Spirit,
born of the Virgin Mary,
suffered under Pontius Pilate,
was crucified, dead, and buried;
he descended into hell.
On the third day he arose from the dead;
he ascended into heaven
and sitteth at the right hand of God the Father almighty,
from whence he shall come to judge the quick and the dead.
I believe in the Holy Spirit,
the holy catholic Church,
the communion of saints,
the forgiveness of sins,
the resurrection of the body,
and the life everlasting. Amen."

"Impressive. Where did you learn that?"

"In Sunday school, when I was a child."

She took a long sip through her straw, and looked into his eyes.

"Yes, well, we believe a lot of that. But we don't believe Jesus was God or was Allāh's son, and we do believe that when they tried to kill him, Allāh took him up and saved him, and we don't believe he judges us—Allāh does that. And we don't believe in the Holy Spirit."

She shook her head and stared at her drink, thinking, *Then what of it do you believe?*

"When was this creed written?" he asked.

"I think it was in about 180 AD, in Rome."

He was surprised that she knew that.

"So it was written by men who didn't even know Jesus, more than a century after he died."

"Well, when did Muhammad live?"

"He was born in 570 CE—that's the same as AD—in Mecca in present day Saudi Arabia, and he died in 632 in Medina, also in Saudi Arabia."

"And when was the Qur'an written?"

"Allāh revealed the words of the Qur'an to Muhammad through the angel Gabriel starting in 609 and ending when Muhammad died. Muhammad couldn't read or write, so he memorized Allāh's words and recited them to others who wrote them down."

"Most books of the New Testament were written by about 90 or 100 AD, but I think Mark finished his Gospel by about 70 AD."

"But they were written by many men, not Allāh or God, and their stories of Jesus conflict! Search for 'conflicts in the gospels' on the Internet."

"But don't you have religious books that conflict with the Qur'an, like the hadiths? I saw some articles about that on the Internet, too."

"They don't conflict with the Qur'an. We reject religious books that conflict with it."

"What are the hadiths?"

"They are reports of what Muhammad said to acquaintances. They are not the words of Allāh. So yes, it gets complicated."

They sipped on their drinks.

Then she asked, "Well, do you believe that Muhammad was divine?"

"No," he said, and Amy blinked. "We believe that he was just a man, not a god. He was not a son of Allāh. His body did not rise. And Muhammad does not judge us, like you say Jesus does. However, we do believe that Muhammad is the final prophet and gave us all the guidance from Allāh that we need to get into heaven."

Amy looked down at the table, frowning in confusion.

He glanced to the side and said, "Amy, listen. I don't know whether to bring this up, but…I think your father is trying to keep us from building our masjid."

"I know," she admitted. "I've overheard some of their discussions."

He looked at her in surprise. "What? Well, did you know that he called my father and asked him to trade our land for another piece of land miles out of town?"

"I heard my father discussing that with someone."

"But now, do you know what else? They are taking criminal actions to try to stop us."

"What?"

He looked straight at her. "That's right. Someone moved the surveyor stakes on the corners of the lot, so that our builder has to get it resurveyed before he can begin, so he knows he's building on our property, and not on our neighbors'. That will set us back a week or more, depending on the weather…Yes, and there will be an added expense to have the lot resurveyed. And that added expense means that a larceny has occurred. Someone has stolen some of our money."

"I don't know anything about that."

"Well, I don't know how to say this, but they think that your father was responsible."

Amy's face turned red. "My father! That's quite an accusation. What proof do they have?"

"None."

She looked out the window. "Ha! Well, they shouldn't be letting slanderous accusations fly around without any proof." She looked back at him. "That's criminal, too, you know."

"You're right, Amy. But you didn't hear them talking about this, did you?"

"No, I did not. And I resent you trying to trap me into implicating my father!" She stood up to leave.

"Amy. Please. I'm sorry."

She stared at the tabletop, took a deep breath, stared into his eyes, blinked, turned, and said, "Bye."

CHAPTER 5
FOOTERS

Over a week had passed since Maskeen had called the surveyor. The builder in the group opposing the mosque went to the side door of the Breckenridge house and rang. He had another idea.

Randall greeted him. "Hi, Tom. Do you want to come in?"

"No. I just wanted to give you a report and tell you something."

"Yeah? What've you got?"

He spoke softly. "I guess you know that the surveyor was back today, and the builder staked out the building and limed it right away. I saw it from down the road. Then two of them set the temporary electric pole and staked it to the ground. And the loader was delivered right after that."

"I guess there was no chance to do anything."

"Nope. They graded the road beside the foundation and in front of it and stripped off the topsoil and piled it." As he spoke, he did a ballet with his strong, rough hands—pushing the dirt, picking it up, dumping it, smoothing it. "And then the trucks came and spread gravel on the roads, and the loader worked it down. Then it went to work stripping the topsoil off the foundation area and piling it up, and digging out the hole and dumping the dirt into big piles. These guys know what they're doing. Of course, it's just a simple rectangle on a basement, about twice the size of a house, with a porch on the front. It ain't the Turkish Mosque, you know, like over in Lanham, with all that underground parking and swimming pool."

"Yeah. Anything else?"

He grinned. "Yeah. The truck delivered the Porta-Potty."

Randall chuckled. "So is that all you wanted to tell me?"

"Well, no, sir, there's something else. I have an idea, but I don't want anything to do with it," the builder said, looking to the side. "In fact, I don't even want to tell you out loud."

Randall squinted at him. "Well, you don't have to. In fact, if it would get someone in trouble, I don't want to know anything about it. Just tell Clyde. You know, he does odd-jobs down on the farm?"

"Yeah, I know who he is. I met him a couple of times."

The weather was fair again the next day. Dan and Lonnie arrived at six-thirty with Dan's laser level and measuring pole, staked out the footers inside the foundation hole, and made a line between the stakes with handfuls of lime from the bag. Next they marked the center posts and the trenches for the porch on the road side at the top of the foundation.

The backhoe operator arrived in a dump truck pulling a trailer with the hoe on it at eight o'clock. He dug the trenches, only five and a half inches deep in the clay soil, while Dan sighted through the level and Lonnie held the pole in the footer. He dug holes for the basement post supports, loaded the machine onto his trailer and left by eleven.

While they were eating lunch in their trucks, the footer subcontractor arrived with two men and a load of lumber and steel reinforcing rods, or rebar, on a flatbed trailer. All were Mexican and conversed in Spanish, but the foreman, Miguel, spoke English to Dan and Lonnie. They installed two-by-six lumber forms around the top of the trenches and placed steel rebar reinforcing rods in the trenches, bending and wiring them together, and nailed smaller boards across the top of the forms every few feet to keep the forms twenty inches apart for the twelve-inch-thick concrete walls that would be built and to keep them from spreading when the concrete was placed inside the forms.

Finally, they wired L-shaped "J-bars" under the bottom of the other rods, every eighteen inches, so that they projected vertically two feet above the top of the forms. These were to tie to the basement-wall reinforcement rods inside the basement wall forms that would be installed later, to attach the walls to the footers. On top of each J-bar, they placed a white plastic safety cap to prevent injury.

"Should I call for the inspection at three?" Dan asked the sub-foreman at about one-thirty. "Maybe I can still get concrete after that." Miguel stopped, looked around at the remaining work, gave an affirmative nod, and Dan pulled out his phone and placed the call.

"Shit," Dan told Lonnie. "He can't come today. Says his schedule is full. I told him we were in a rush and wanted to pour today because it's supposed to rain. He said he was sorry, but he just couldn't come–too many inspections. They need another inspector...la-dee-da-dee-da. He said he'll have to get us tomorrow."

"When?"

"As soon as he can."

"Great," Lonnie groused. "You know it's gonna rain tomorrow. Sixty percent chance."

Miguel came up to them after they finished installing the steel.

"Nice job," Dan said.

"Gracias. So when we pour?"

"I'll have to call you tomorrow, after the inspector comes. If we're lucky, we pour tomorrow afternoon."

"OK. We got other job before that."

Dan and Lonnie watched them load up and leave.

"I wonder if that inspector is jerking our chain," Dan said to Lonnie. "I had a feeling."

The next day, the showers never stopped coming. Dirt washed down the piles at the top of the excavation and continued down the walls, some flowing into the trench—which soon became a moat filled with brown water—and then settling on the bottom. It mixed with the clay in the basement hole and covered it with thick, sticky mud. Dan and Lonnie looked down from the grass above in their hooded rain jackets and caps and stared. Then they went below and dug a ditch from the moat away from the basement floor a few feet to let the water drain out. Parts of the trench retained puddles, however.

"Did you talk to the boss?" Lonnie asked.

"Maskeen?"

"Yeah."

"About the delay?"

"Uh-huh."

"Yeah, I told him there was nothing we could do. You have to work with inspectors, and sometimes it rains. That's the way it is. He understood."

"That's good. At least he didn't blame us."

"Yeah. Say, Lonnie, you see all those places where dirt washed into the trench?"

"Yeah."

"The dirt is over the rebar in some places. The inspector will never approve that."

"We'll have to scoop the dirt out from under it so the concrete can get under it. Maybe Miguel can do it. Tell him to bring flat shovels."

Another shower came, and they watched the water cascade down the dirt wall. Abruptly, the rain stopped.

"I better call off the inspection," Dan said.

"Too late."

Code Inspector Gerald Damon stepped out of his car with his clipboard under his arm, wearing a red hooded rain parka, and strode down the gravel drive to the foundation. The two builders went up to meet him, and the three men walked through the wet grass to the top of the excavation, and looked down.

"You boys are in some trouble here," the older man noted. "You'll have to get that dirt all cleaned out from under that rebar before I can approve it to pour. Oh, and wait. Let me see those plans." Dan handed them to him, and he unrolled them to the foundation plan. "These call for a thirty-six-inch step down on the walkout portion on the end of the foundation for frost. Do you have that?"

Dan was flustered. He did not have that much. "I don't think I do."

"Well listen, boy. Don't call me until this here is done and done right, you hear? I'll be measuring next time I come. And remember, you need at least an inch and a half of concrete under the steel. Two inches is better." He turned and walked off without another word.

"Nice guy," Lonnie told Dan.

After two dry days, Miguel and his helpers, and Dan and Lonnie met on the site early in the morning. Puddles still lay on the clay, in and out of the trenches, especially in the low corner where the walkout was. They began using big sponges on the puddles in the trench and shoveling out under rebar that lay on the dirt, digging down another eight inches in the walkout portion, and re-bending rebar for the bigger step downs. Dan cut them some two-by-two sticks (an inch and a half square) and a few inches long to slide under the rebar to make sure they had proper clearance. By eleven o'clock, they were almost finished, and Dan called the town

building office for the reinspection. This time he was more fortunate. The inspector would be out in an hour.

Dan called the concrete company to give them a heads up, and
Inspector Damon arrived at noon and stood again at the top of the
hole. He wasn't about to get into that sticky mud. Miguel squatted
all around the trench and showed him how the spacer slid under
the rebar and how everything was wired strong and tight. Then he
showed him the extra depth they added on the walkout portion.

Gerald watched closely and finally gave a nod.

"Are we approved?" Dan asked.

"Yessir." He signed the form and handed it over.

Dan thanked him, Damon left, and Dan immediately called for
the concrete. They said they could be there at three.

At quarter of three, the concrete truck with the big mixer
drum and the pump truck with the folding crane and hose arrived and set up at the top of the foundation hole. The drivers
worked together, mixing the concrete and hooking up the pipes
between them. Then the mixer driver went into the hole to guide
the concrete from the hose into the trench while the pump-truck
driver controlled the pump in the truck. The crane reached all
the way over the hole, delivering the concrete down the tube and
into the trenches so that no wheelbarrows were used to place the
concrete. At the same time, one man from Miguel's crew tamped
the concrete and pulled up on the steel with a rake to make sure it
would be inside the concrete, and another shoveled concrete into
low spots and straightened the J-bars into their vertical positions.
Miguel smoothed the concrete even with the top of the forms. By
four-thirty, the job was done, and they rinsed off their tools and
left. The fresh concrete glistened between the forms as it waited to
harden, the J-bars with white safety caps sticking straight up two
feet out of the footers every eighteen inches.

"Finally," Dan said to Lonnie as they got to their trucks.

"Yeah. Finally we get a little luck. Say, want to grab a beer?"

"Naa, I better get home. The boys have a ball game."

"OK. Are they bringing the wall forms tomorrow?"

"They're supposed to be here by nine."

"Good. Maybe we'll get them set and ready to pour tomorrow. It's supposed to be another good day. If our luck holds."

They climbed into their trucks and pulled away.

About two in the morning under an overcast sky, a form appeared from the woods at the back of the property—a brawny man wearing a black hoodie, dark cargo pants, and work gloves, holding something on the inside of his right arm—and moved to the rear of the excavation. From there, he could not be seen from the road. He went to the rear wall footer, slipped on knee pads, kneeled, and went to work, attacking the J-bars with his hacksaw an inch or so above the top of the newly hardened footer, cutting them half-way through, while bending the bar slightly away from the blade. Then he seized each with his left hand, snapped it off, and tossed it aside. One after another, he removed them all from the back wall. Next he went to the other walls and removed every other bar. At four, he stood up and walked to the back of the property and into the woods.

When he got to his old green Chevy pickup, he removed his muddy boots and gloves, changed his pants, folded the soiled ones neatly, pulled on clean boots, and changed into a navy sweatshirt. He placed the pants in the bed with the boots and gloves on top, threw the knee pads into the truck tool box, which extended across the bed under the back window, climbed into the driver's seat, and lit a filter cigarette. He bumped down the back road to the highway, always staying on the hard gravel. He flicked the butt out the window and turned onto the asphalt road.

A mile down the road, he turned right down a gravel road past the main entrance to the farm. Continuing a quarter of a mile into a stand of woods, he stopped, picked up the muddy pants, boots, and gloves, and a shovel, and gave the evidence a decent burial two feet deep, carefully replacing the soil and leaves and tamping it all with his boots. Returning to the truck, he slung the hacksaw blade, end over end, far into the woods, turned the vehicle around, and returned to the highway and drove down to the farm. He parked by the closest dairy barn as first light was emblazoning the low clouds in the sky and beginning to illuminate the gravely wounded mosque. He dozed in his truck until Peter Yoder came out of the house.

"Morning, Clyde," Yoder said at his window.

"Morning, Pete."

CHAPTER 6
J-BARS AND JACKHAMMERS

Lonnie discovered the vandal's work at six-thirty, and minutes later, when Dan arrived, Lonnie shouted to him from the top of the excavation, "Someone messed with the footers!"

"What?"

"They broke off the J-bars!"

Dan walked quickly to the hole between two piles of dirt and looked down. "Damn. Looks like he sawed them half-way through and then broke them off."

"What do we do now?"

Dan gritted his teeth, and growled, "First, we call the cops."

He started pacing in circles in the damp grass, dialed the police station, and reported the crime. Then he called off the delivery of the wall forms, left a voice mail for Damon, and called Maskeen.

"Yes, sir. They broke off the J-bars that tie the footers to the basement walls."

"What will you have to do?"

Dan began gesturing with his left arm and hand to accentuate his words and make them more convincing, even though Maskeen could not see him. "I don't know. It's up to the inspector. Maybe we can drill holes in the concrete beside the pieces of the J-bar that're still in the concrete and weld the broken pieces back onto the side of it, or maybe we can drill some new holes in the concrete and pour in epoxy and glue the pieces to the concrete."

"Will that be as strong—either way?"

"I don't know. We might have to completely tear out the footers, and start over. It's up to the inspector."

"What?"

"That's right. We might have to tear out the footers and re-pour them."

"Is he coming soon?"

"I don't know. I left a message with his office. I'll call him again soon."

"I wonder why he didn't use a bolt-cutter—you know, one with long handles," Lonnie said to Dan. "That would have been easier and faster."

Dan shrugged. "I don't know. Maybe he thought it would make too much noise. He'd have both hands on the cutter handles, and the bar would fall and might jangle when it hit the concrete. By sawing and breaking it, he could keep his hand on the bar and keep it from hitting the concrete and then just throw it in the dirt. That'd be quieter."

He put in a call to Alec Smith, the architect who had drawn the blueprints. He was not paid to supervise the construction, but could consult with them. Dan knew it was really up to the inspector to decide what had to be done, not the architect, and there probably wasn't time to get into a hassle between the two. But he still thought he would get his opinion. Alec told Dan the J-bars were essential, and that welds or glue would be much weaker, so they would have to tear out the footings.

"Thanks. Oh, the police are here. I'll get back to you."

Maskeen called Ahmed on his cellphone. He was at home.

"As-salaam-alaikum (the peace be upon you)," Maskeen said.

"Wa-alaikum-salaam (and unto you peace)," Ahmed replied.

"I'm sorry to bother you so early."

"I'm still at home—I haven't left for the office yet. What is it?"

"Dan Stanley called and said that someone had vandalized the building site. They broke off the steel rods that tie the footers to the basement walls. He doesn't know what he will have to do until he talks to the building inspector, but he might have to tear out the footers and start over."

Ahmed was silent. Then rage leaped into his chest and his eyes started to burn. He pushed on them, back and forth, massaging with his thumb and middle finger. "Breckenridge!" he grunted, his cheeks twitching. "Did Dan call the police?"

"They just arrived."

"Please. Go down there and make sure the investigation is thorough. We must apprehend this criminal!"

"I'll go right now."

"And notify the others."

"I will."

"Khuda Hafiz (may God be your guardian)."

"Khuda Hafiz."

Dan went to the road to wait for the police. When the first car pulled in, he approached the officer, a heavy-faced man in his thirties with a massive chest and back and curly black hair. Dan read his brass name tag: "Rossini." Another car pulled in behind him.

"Who are you?" the officer asked.

"Dan Stanley. I'm the contractor for the mosque."

"What's the problem?"

"Someone vandalized the footers—thousands of dollars' worth of damage."

"How can you damage footers?"

"Can you take a look? Then you'll see real quick."

"OK." He got out and motioned to the car behind him. The other officer, who was slender, walked up. They went to the top of the hole with Dan and looked down while the builder explained what happened.

The big man peered into the hole. "I think I see some footprints in the mud down there. Don't go in there until our lab guys look at it. They might want to take some impressions. What say we put some tape around this place, Kurt? I think we've got a crime scene here."

They went to their cars and retrieved rolls of yellow tape and wire stakes from their trunks. Then they walked the tape around the entire hole and staked it to the ground.

Maskeen pulled up in his shiny silver late-model Ford Explorer and strode toward the foundation in his khakis, tie, and blue sweater vest as the officers were finishing pulling the tape: "CRIME SCENE DO NOT CROSS." He crossed the tape to the hole and stared down, and Dan joined him.

"Hi Maskeen. Do you see what they did?"

"Yes. They broke off those vertical bars."

"Yes. And I don't know how to fix it. And the more time goes by, the harder the concrete gets, and it has all that steel in it."

"You can't go in there," the big officer said to them, pointing to the tape.

"We're coming right out," Maskeen told him.

They walked with the policemen to the road, and Maskeen put on a stern face. "I am Maskeen. I represent the owners of this mosque, and I want to know what you are going to do about this crime. This will cost us thousands of dollars to repair."

The policemen were taken aback. "We just got here, sir. We taped it off, and now I have to call in the detectives."

"Thank you. Please do. And tell them to hurry. The concrete keeps getting harder."

Meanwhile, Dan called the building inspector again, but once more heard his voicemail message. Dan told Maskeen, and the lanky accountant jumped into his SUV, did a U-turn in front of the police, and barreled toward town, returning in half an hour followed by Inspector Damon. They marched to the top of the excavation—again ignoring the yellow tape and police officers—and gazed down, with Dan and Lonnie beside them.

"My goodness," Damon said. "Looks like you all are in some real trouble now. You know I can't approve these footers without those J-bars."

"Well, what do we need to do?" Dan asked.

"I hate to say it, boys" Damon answered, "but I'm afraid you're going to have to break it all up and re-pour the footers with new J-bars."

"Wha--what if we drilled beside the broken-off bars and welded pieces to them?"

"I couldn't approve that, Mr. Stanley, unless you could demonstrate equivalency with what is currently required in the code—the J-bars wired to the continuous bars on the bottom. Do you have any structural engineers on the payroll?"

"No. What if we drilled holes down to the bottom and glued new bars down in the holes, you know, with epoxy. That stuff is really strong."

"I'll say the same thing—you have to demonstrate equivalency. If you can get a structural engineer to sign off on that, I might consider it. Otherwise, I think you better start breaking up this concrete while it's still green, or you're going to have a hell of a mess. It'll be a hundred times harder to get the concrete out after it's reached its full strength. If you break it up right now, you may be able to use the steel again. But I'll have to approve that before you do. Or, you can wait a day and get a great big crane to take out the whole footer in one piece. But then I don't know what you'd do with it. Maybe you could sell it on eBay, but it would be hard to ship."

Dan's eyes grew as he imagined the crane. "I think we better get that jackhammer," Dan told Maskeen. "But I don't want to start until police investigators look at everything. They may want to take some plaster casts of footprints before we walk all over everything and dump chunks of concrete everywhere."

"I agree," Maskeen said, making a fist. "We must find out who did this!"

"We know who did it," Dan replied. "What we need is evidence."

"Yes. A trail of evidence."

"In the meantime, I better call Miguel. See if he can help. I don't know what we can do with all the concrete. Bury it in a hole out back? We can't use it for backfill. And it's no good for on top of the drain pipe."

Lonnie looked at him. "Tell Miguel to bring wheelbarrows and shovels. I'll go get the compressor and jackhammer from the rental place."

Maskeen said OK, and then turned and walked to the officers.

"When will your inspectors be here?" he asked Rossini.

"They're working a burglary in town right now. They said they'll try to be here after lunch."

Maskeen scowled. "That's not soon enough. We have to start breaking up this concrete before it gets too hard."

"You'll destroy all the evidence if you do."

"Well, maybe they can leave that other investigation for now and go back to it later. Ours is time sensitive."

"I'll ask them, but I know they won't do it."

Maskeen frowned. "Oh, is that so? Where are they? I'll ask them."

"Sir, they won't like you interfering with them."

"Maybe they won't like the publicity if we accuse them of dragging their feet, either. And maybe they won't like us suing the city."

"They won't like being threatened, sir. Maybe you better take this up with the chief. He's in his office this morning."

"I will. And maybe I'll speak to the mayor, too."

"Whatever you want."

Maskeen stalked to his SUV, climbed in, and drove away. Officer Rossini speed-dialed the chief.

By eleven, Dan was getting nervous. Lonnie had arrived with the compressor and parked it on the driveway beside the excavation, and Miguel was waiting with his two helpers in pickups on the road. They had decided where they would bury the concrete, close enough for Miguel's men to wheel it. Now, where were those inspectors?

To Dan's relief, the police inspectors arrived soon thereafter, their car followed by Maskeen. Dan had to smile, inwardly, at Maskeen's grit and persuasiveness.

"Tough dude," he said to Lonnie.

The inspectors conferred with the two officers who had arrived first, and then everyone except Miguel and his men followed the path through the grass to the excavation and peered down. Maskeen explained to them about the J-bars and the need to break up the concrete soon.

Sam, the taller of the two men, asked, "Who was the first one here today?"

Lonnie raised a hand. "I was."

"Who are you?"

"Lonnie Craig. I'm the foreman. I work for him, Dan Stanley. He's the contractor." Sam jotted it down on a form in his notebook, while the other man, Bud, took notes in his.

"OK. What time did you arrive?"

"About six-thirty. And Dan came right after that."

"Did either of you see anybody else around the foundation or in the woods over there or hear any noises?"

Both replied no.

"Did you walk inside the excavation?"

Both said, "Nope."

"So any footprints around the footer are likely to be the perpetrator's, correct?"

Dan looked at Lonnie and then at Sam. "As far as we know, sir. We left at about five yesterday, after we finished pouring. I don't know who might have walked inside after that."

Sam looked at them and Maskeen. "And did anyone walk around the outside of the foundation today?"

"Just the officers who stretched the tape. We all stayed up here."

"OK. Please, everyone go back to the road," Sam said. "Except you, Mr. Stanley. You come with us. Bud, bring that castings kit, if you will."

The three men walked down the driveway to the bottom of the hole and around inside taking photos. Dan was shaking his head, cursing. Numerous places they could make out the vandal's boot prints, and the inspectors made several plaster of Paris castings of them.

"We know what size boot he wears now," Bud said to Sam and Dan.

They put the castings in his car. "Let's see if we can track him now," Sam said, "before the dew all burns off."

Dan asked if they were finished looking at the foundation, because they needed to start breaking up the concrete. Sam said yes, so Dan told Lonnie they could start. "Try not to damage the steel. We don't want to have to replace it if we can help it."

The inspectors walked with Dan behind the hole toward the woods, following a faint path in the trampled grass. Maskeen declined to accompany them in his dress clothes, but called Ahmed at his office. The receptionist said he was with a patient, so he left a message to call him back.

Dan and the inspectors entered the woods, but soon lost the trail.

"Do you know what's behind these trees?" Sam asked Dan.

"No. I'm not from around here. Maybe we can do a map search and see." He pulled out his phone and searched. "I don't see any roads on the map." Then he switched to satellite and zoomed in. "Wait. That might be a road, or a logging road." He showed it to Sam.

"OK. Let's keep going."

They arrived at the overgrown hard-gravel road and walked both ways, until Sam said, "Here's where he turned the truck around—there are some broken branches, but no tire prints." He snapped a few pictures. "And there's where he parked and got out and in. There are a couple of clumps of mud there from his boots." He photographed them, too.

They could hear the percussions of the jackhammer through the woods.

Bud squatted, looking at the dirt on the road, trying to discern tire tracks. "We can't get any good prints here, I'm afraid. The clay is packed hard."

"How far does this road go?" Sam asked Dan.

Dan looked at his phone again.

"It looks like it goes about two miles and then connects to the highway."

"Anybody up for a hike?" Sam asked.

"I need to get back to the job," Dan said. "But if you call me, I'll come pick you up."

"OK," Sam said to the shorter man. "Let's go."

Half an hour later, they arrived at the highway without seeing any tire tracks and without noticing the butt that carried Clyde's DNA.

Word spread quickly in Chelmsford. Maskeen had contacted Ahmed, and he had told him to call the others on the masjid board and tell them to spread the word. Their leader, Imam Mufti, had called the ministers of several of the large churches in town, including the United Methodist church where the Muslim congregation rented the basement for their prayer services. Some ministers had asked what they could do to help. Imam Mufti had said that they might need some volunteers to guard the construction at night, at least for tonight, and that he would call them back with more information.

Back at the foundation, Dan watched Miguel and Lonnie breaking up the concrete with the jackhammer. Being weak and green, it broke off in big chunks, and Miguel's helpers were able to pick them up and quickly load them into the wheelbarrows, which they rolled down the boards, out of the hole and into the circle that Dan had drawn on the grass with lime. But there was so much of it. And the longer they worked, the harder the liquid rock became.

The concrete under and between the rebar was most problematic: it was sticking to the rods. Another helper had to beat it off the rods with a two-pound sledge.

After working most of the day under a hot sun, they finished. Dan inspected it, and except for a few places where dirt or concrete needed to be removed from the trenches, he decided it was ready for reinspection by Damon. He called the city, but it was "after hours" for the inspection department.

He called early the next morning, and Damon came out at eleven. Before he arrived Miguel and his crew had installed new J-bars beside the old.

"OK. I'll sign off on that," Damon told Dan. "What are you going to do to protect it now?"

"Some people are coming to guard the site at night."

"Really? Who?"

"Some of the ministers in town have offered to stand watch with us tonight, along with some of the Muslims, so this doesn't happen again."

Damon walked to his SUV, and Dan called for concrete again, and then called Maskeen.

"Maybe you could set up two-hour watches," Dan suggested, "starting about eight at night and running till six. That should cover it. They wouldn't come in daylight."

"We should consider an electronic security system with cameras," Maskeen suggested. "Then post some signs. I'll call the board members and look into it."

"Good idea." Dan's eyes watched Miguel's crew taking a break in the shade. "I hate to have to do and redo. It's hard on the men, too."

The concrete arrived at two-thirty, and the crew was out by four. The mosque was resuscitated.

Randall was livid when Damon called and told him that ministers were assisting in the security. "Those mush-headed liberals! They'll hand this country to the Islamic terrorists without a fight. Find out, if you can, which ones are in the moozlim camp. Maybe we can call some of their parishioners and let them know that their pastors are supporting terrorists. Maybe we can get some demonstrators out there to picket."

"Too bad these boys didn't wait a little longer. Then they'd've been in a fix. They would have had to hire a great big crane to pull that whole footer out of the ground all at once."

At eight, Atif arrived for his shift and brought a strong LED flashlight. Reverend Carson from Christ United Methodist church, where the Muslims met, joined him along the road. They leaned against Atif's car and talked about the mosque, medicine, school, Pakistan, Islam, Christianity, and evil.

"Who could have done this?" Reverend Carson asked.

"We have suspicions, but no proof," Atif said. "Say, Reverend Carson, I've been meaning to ask. Why are you helping us?"

"We believe in freedom of religion, Atif, for all religions. Who knows when someone will attack our religion, and then we'll need your help. And we believe in doing unto others as we would have them do unto us—the Golden Rule."

"Yes, and Muhammad said, 'Be merciful to others and you will receive mercy.'"

They talked until the next pair came at midnight—Maskeen and a priest from St. Paul's Church in Chelmsford.

In the morning the forms arrived, and Maskeen called Dan to tell him that the security company would install cameras on the temporary pole and put signs on the property that afternoon.

Ahmed called Maskeen from his office. "I want to know how much this is going to cost us! Ask Dan to prepare a bill for the extra. I want to know. And let Imam Mufti and the board know. This is going to take a big chunk out of our allowance for extras, and the job has just begun!"

"Yes, Ahmed."

"And I want to know if we can get some newspaper coverage. Call the Post and ask for a reporter. I won't put up with this. And another thing: I want to know if we can get the FBI to investigate this as a hate crime. This Breckenridge is trying to destroy our masjid."

Atif was furious with Amy's dad and suddenly distrustful of her. He was in no mood to see her soon. This latest attack was far worse than just moving surveyor stakes.

CHAPTER 7
TERRORISTS

Amy hadn't heard from Atif in days. She was worried. And Nadira seemed cool toward her at school. Amy sent a message: "Meet Sat?"

After no answer for two hours, she added, "Pls."

Atif was still boiling. But he recalled Nadira's words, "You can't judge her by her family." And he had said he would teach her about Islam. Yes, and maybe he would learn something about her evil father's plans.

"McD's, mall, 3:00."

"CU," she responded.

As he had expected, the place was nearly deserted at that hour. He bought a diet drink for her and hot tea for himself, and sat in a corner, sipping the brew with the lid off, staring at the liquid, swirling it with a plastic stirrer, inhaling the vapors. The smell of French fries and grilled beef permeated the air.

She came through the door, took off her sun glasses, saw him, and their eyes locked. *Oh!* she thought.

Again he was struck by her beauty, her dark hair creeping out from behind the red scarf, her pale skin, blue eyes, thin eyebrows and lips, and the lush figure concealed by her tan jacket.

He stood as she approached, and they greeted each other.

"I got you a drink," he said, now avoiding her gaze.

"Thanks."

As they sat, she accidentally bumped his leg with hers, and said, "Sorry."

"No problem." He looked up. "Oh, here." He pulled out some pamphlets from his notebook. "These are for you. I got them from Imam Mufti. They give a pretty good background on Islām. Then you can ask me more questions."

She took them, thanked him, and asked, "What's an imam? Is that like a minister?"

"Sort of. But he's not ordained. In Islam there's no hierarchy or ordaining body. The congregation selects the imam from their own group to lead the prayers because he's the one who knows the most about the Qur'an and can pray in Arabic. So what do you want to talk about today?"

"Well, I have some questions."

"Shoot."

"That's a violent expression," she said.

He smiled. "And very American."

"Well, my question is about violence. It seems like Islam is a violent religion, you know, with Al-Qaeda destroying the twin towers and part of the Pentagon, and ISIS beheading people, and all those terrorists, and the Sunnis and Shia always blowing each other up, and Daddy even said that ISIS and the Taliban declared a holy war—jihad—against each other. No wonder so many people are afraid of Islam. By the way, which one are you, Sunni or Shia?"

"Our family is Sunni. Most Muslims are Sunnis. But Iran is mostly Shia, and about ten or twenty percent of Pakistanis are Shia, and we live together peacefully most of the time. The founder of

Pakistan was Shia and many of our presidents have been, although I have to say that there is occasional sectarian violence by terrorist groups. But Amy, you've got to understand that we don't really consider terrorists to be Muslims. Terrorism is against our principles. And secondly, jihad doesn't mean holy war."

She looked puzzled. "My dictionary says it means 'holy war.'"

"The Arabic word jihad means a struggle, any huge struggle. It can be inside you, like a struggle against evil. Or it can be fighting a war, in self-defense. You know, the Qur'an teaches us not to kill people, just like the Ten Commandments. It says, 'Do not take any human being's life—that God willed to be sacred—other than in justice.'"

She tilted her head. "But wait a minute. Does that mean that there are some people that God doesn't will to be sacred—like non-Muslims—and you can take their lives?"

"No. It means that God made all human life to be sacred."

"Are you sure?"

"That's what I've always thought, Amy. You could consult an imam for another opinion."

He glanced out the window at the passing cars.

"OK. But what does it mean—'other than in justice?'"

His eyes turned back to her.

"Well, I think most people—at least in the United States—believe we can take lives in justice, like capital punishment for heinous crimes. And we believe in just wars, like World War II, where we fight against an enemy who has attacked us. We're only allowed to strike back in self-defense."

"Where does it say that?"

"In the Qur'an. It says we're supposed to fight in the cause of Allāh those who fight us, but if they stop fighting, we're supposed to stop, because Allāh is oft-forgiving and merciful. It's clear that ISIS is not following the Qur'an."

She still looked skeptical.

"Let me give you an example. Muhammad fought back against the pagan Meccans when they attacked the Muslims in Medina, but later he invaded Mecca peacefully, pardoned the people who converted to Islām, and had all the statues of pagan gods and goddesses destroyed. Muslims must strive for peace whenever we can."

"But didn't Islam expand by attacking countries all over the world—in Africa and Spain and Europe and India and the Far East. Didn't their soldiers ride on horses and fight with swords and bows and arrows? I read that somewhere."

"Well, yes, but Allāh says in the Qur'an, 'There is no compulsion in religion.' As long as people submitted to Islamic rule and paid taxes, they were free to practice their own religion."

"But see?" She grinned. "Islam was still spread by conquest." She loved to argue with him. It was like debating her father and mother. And she loved to win.

He pulled his head back and scowled. "See what? Didn't Christianity oppose idol worship and spread religion through conquest, too? Spanish and Portuguese conquistadors conquered the New World and China and the Philippines, and spread Christianity and colonialism, and killed or enslaved anyone who wouldn't accept Christianity and submit to their rule."

"I-I guess that's true."

"And the crusader knights in the Middle Ages fought to drive the Muslims out of the holy lands. And Queen Isabella and King Ferdinand sent Christian armies south in Spain and killed all those Muslims in the Spanish Inquisition. Before that, Jews, Christians, and Muslims had lived together in relative peace for hundreds of years under Muslim rule."

"Yes. They drove them out of Spain."

He gazed at some people ordering sandwiches while his mind spun. "And what about Catholics fighting Protestants in Germany and England, and bombing each other in Ireland, and fighting forever. Aren't they like the Sunnis and Shia? There's been a lot of violence between Christians."

"Yes. But you must know that Jesus preached forgiveness, and said, 'Do unto others as you would have others do unto you.'"

"Yes, and Muhammad (peace be upon him) said, 'Be merciful to others and you will receive mercy. Forgive others and Allāh will forgive you.'"

"That's like Jesus said, 'Blessed are the merciful: for they shall obtain mercy.'"

"And Muhammad (peace be upon him) said, 'None of you truly believe until he loves for his brother what he loves for himself.'"

Her eyes brightened. "That's the Golden Rule."

"Yes."

She searched her mind. "But one difference is that Jesus was a pacifist. He said, 'Blessed are the peacemakers,' and He said that if someone smites you on one cheek, turn and let him smite you on the other. Do not return evil for evil."

He replied, "Oh? So I guess the conquistadors and crusaders were not really Christians."

"And you say ISIS and violent Muslims are not really Muslims. That's one way to get around calling Muslims terrorists."

She watched some people enter, hoping she didn't recognize anyone, and was relieved to see that she didn't.

Atif glanced out the window. "Maybe Jesus had to be a pacifist because he didn't have any power," he suggested. "He knew that if he and his followers openly fought the Jews and Romans, they would be destroyed. Like Gandhi and Martin Luther King would have been. And Muhammed couldn't attack the pagans when he first started preaching about one God in Mecca. He was powerless, too. But in Medina, the Muslims gained strength and started to defend themselves militarily against the Meccans. That's in the Qur'an."

"And then they started trying to take over the world, like the Romans and Mongols did. I looked up 'Muslim expansion' on the Internet. It said that Muhammad was a great general, and in the century after he died, the Muslim armies conquered all the countries from Spain and North Africa to India."

"Well, the Christian empires expanded that way too—like the British and Spanish," Atif retorted.

She squinted at him. "Doesn't the Qur'an say the soldiers could keep most of the booty they took from the people they defeated as the spoils of war."

"Where did you see that?"

"I saw that on the Internet too. I've been surfing on Islam a lot."

"Well, yes. They had to give a fifth to Allāh and the Messenger, and to near relatives, orphans, the needy, and the wayfarer. But Amy—"

"So then the soldiers could keep eighty percent of the loot for themselves! No wonder the empire expanded. It wasn't just about spreading Islam, it was about plundering non-Muslims. And now it looks like ISIS is trying to expand into Africa and Afghanistan and maybe into Europe."

"But Amy. You are cherry picking and taking things out of context. The Qur'an says Muslims have a right to defend themselves. There was no such thing as a standing army at the time of the Prophet; so it was normal for all participants in battles to take a portion of the spoils of victory. This was part of the culture of the time. What was different was that a portion has to be provided to Allāh and the Prophet to be used for the benefit of the Muslim community."

"I still say that it looks like Islam was spread by the sword by armies drawn by the spoils of war."

"Look, Amy. I know Christians here are afraid that American Muslims are terrorists, too." Now he looked into her eyes, pleading. "But Amy, let's get back to reality—here, today. My father is not a terrorist. He is a doctor—a surgeon! He wants to help cure people, not kill them. And he's not alone. There are more than fifteen thousand Pakistani-American physicians in the United States treating US citizens, and thousands more Muslim doctors from other countries like India, Egypt, and those in Northwest Africa and Nigeria, and other African countries. Like Elias Zerhouni from Algeria, who was director of the National Institute of Health from 2002 to 2008, appointed by George W. Bush. Go to the website of any hospital and look at their staff of doctors and see where they received their degrees. Many received them overseas. What would you do without our doctors?"

Her eyes widened. "I had no idea."

"Of course, many Muslims receive their degrees here, too. Muslims are a part of American society and in every ethnic group. About a third of Muslim Americans are White, a quarter Black, and somewhat fewer are Asian. The rest are a mix."

She was still unconvinced. "I don't know, Atif."

"Think of all the Muslim athletes and musicians and businessmen in America—even Congressmen. They're not violent."

They were silent for a moment until Amy called it a draw. "I guess not. And I can see a lot of similarities between Muslims and Christians, too."

He blinked and said, "Yes, but now we have Christian terrorists trying to destroy our mosque, right here in Chelmsford."

"What?"

"You haven't heard? Someone vandalized the foundation, and we had to break up the concrete footers we built and pour them all over again!"

"What? Do they know who did it?"

He turned his head away and spoke softly. "I hate to say this, but once again, people suspect your father."

She snapped. "And again with no evidence, I suppose."

"The police are investigating, but there is no chain of evidence yet."

"Atif, maybe we better not see each other for a while," she said, frowning, confused.

He shrugged. "Amy, I don't blame you. But your father has tried to stop us from building in the past, and now this has happened."

She rose, pulled on her jacket, buttoned it hurriedly, tugged at the lapels, and turned toward the door.

He looked at her eyes, pleading. "Amy. I want to see you again. Please."

She turned toward him. "And I want to see you again, too. I just don't know what to do."

He rose, and Amy glanced out the window.

"Jesse! My brother! He just drove by."

"What should we do?" Atif asked.

"I'll go out this side, and you wait a few minutes and go out the other one."

"I'll go to the restroom first."

"Good. Bye."

She stuffed the pamphlets into a McDonald's bag, went out, and didn't notice that Jesse was watching her get into her car. But she skipped shopping today. She would tell her mother, and Jesse, that she didn't see anything she liked, or got tired, or whatever. She went home, wondering all the way if Jesse had seen them. More importantly, she wondered whether her father was behind the vandalism, and whether her friendship with Atif could survive this conflict.

When she arrived home, she slipped the pamphlets into a notebook and walked into the kitchen where Eunice was preparing dinner. Eunice told her, "Your father is having friends over tonight in the trophy room. Oh, and Stewart dropped by looking for you. He said that you weren't returning his calls."

"I know. I'm afraid I'm losing interest in him, Mother. I'm just not sure I want to be a farmer's wife, you know, and he's going away to the University of Wisconsin in the fall and he'll be meeting new people, and I feel like I want to be open to some new experiences and new people, too."

Eunice stood at the narrow table dipping catfish in milk and dropping it into a paper bag with cornmeal. "Oh, that's too bad. He's a good Christian boy, and your father likes him a lot. He's from a good family, and he's our kind of people, Amy."

"I know, and maybe we'll get back together sometime, but right now I'm ready for a break."

"Has he asked you to go to his prom, and have you asked him to yours?"

Amy looked away. "Not yet."

"You haven't been returning his calls."

She shrugged. "I've been busy."

Eunice put her hands on the table and looked at her. "Amy! You shouldn't keep him dangling. He'll get mad and ask someone else. Then what will you do? You need to talk to him and let him know."

"I will."

She passed Jesse on the stairs, and he looked at her suspiciously.

"Where've you been?" he demanded.

"Who wants to know?"

"Stewart," he sang. "He stopped by. He said you aren't answering his calls. Do you have something else going on, sis-ter? Where were you today?"

She casually explained, "I was shopping, as usual."

"Oh, yeah? What did you get?"

"None of your business, Jess-bo."

"That depends on what you've been up to. I saw you down at McDonald's, you know."

She frowned. "What? Are you spying on me now?"

"Never."

"And what were you doing upstairs, little brother? You didn't go in my room, did you?"

"I would never think of doing that!"

"You stay out of my room! Or else I'll start inspecting your room—for those joints you roll up there."

He tried to push her against the wall, but she slipped by him and stomped up the stairs, past the nook, around the hallway, and into her room.

Oh, she thought. *He makes me mad.* But sometimes she was glad that she always had someone to fight with. It relieved the boredom.

Then she started carefully inspecting everything that he had inspected shortly before. But he had been careful, and she found no evidence of his presence. She glanced at the pamphlets. Each one explained a different topic: Islam, Muhammad, God, Jesus, human rights, and terrorism. She slipped them back into the notebook, and put it in a desk drawer.

She had to get away and clear her mind. She pulled on her sweats, shoes, and Nationals cap, slipped her phone and change purse into her pocket, circled the hall, skittered down the stairs, yelled, "I'm going for a run," and bounded through the front door, across the porch, and down the stairs. Pausing to stretch at the bottom, she headed out of town, turned down a dirt lane, and soon was on a path through second growth timber along a stream—her favorite place to run. She drew deeply of the fresh spring air, fragrant from new leaves and rhododendron flowers, and listened to the chatter of a woodpecker. Then she "spaced out," dreaming about the shy and intelligent young pre-med student who was willing to teach her about Islam and argue with her, but who was blaming her father for vandalizing the mosque. That made her mad. But she did want to see him again—for certain.

An hour later she cruised up the front steps, through the door under the sunburst window, pounded up the stairs, shouting, "I'm back!" and jumped into the shower.

At dinner, with the four of them sitting around the dining room table eating succulent catfish, mashed potatoes, green beans, biscuits, and gravy, Randall began to interrogate her.

"Mother says you're breaking up with Stewart, and you haven't been returning his calls. What's that all about?"

"I'm just not as interested in him as I used to be, Daddy, and he's going away this fall to the University of Wisconsin, and he'll be meeting new people there, and may find someone he likes better, and I think I want to be able to meet new people here, too. And I'm not sure I want to be a farmer's wife."

Randall waved a biscuit at her. "Amy, dairy farming today is big business. You won't be milking cows and working in the garden. And you could do a lot worse than Stewart. He's smart and hard-working, and a Christian from a good family, and they have a big dairy farm and plenty of money."

She stabbed several green beans with her fork. "I know. I just think we'll both be better off if we meet some other people so when we decide on marriage, we won't be tempted by anyone else, and we'll know we're making the right decision."

"Have you met anyone else already?"

Amy looked up. "No, Daddy," she said, but she blinked and had difficulty maintaining eye contact. *And now I'm lying like Pinocchio… like Grandma used to sing…"those little white lies"…but sometimes I can't help it—they make me lie.*

"OK," he announced, giving up on his inquiry. "We have a meeting here tonight at seven. Amy, why don't you call Stewart and see if you can go out with him."

I don't need him to arrange my social life! He just wants me out of the house. She sighed. "I'm kind of tired, and I have some reading to do for AP lit."

On a Saturday night. He looked at Jesse. They'd already had a discussion in which he'd asked Jesse to see if he could "find out if she's up to anything."

"As-salaam-alaikum, Mother."

She looked up from reading on the sofa in the great room. *Why is he so polite and happy?* "Where were you?"

"At the library, studying, as usual. I have a microbiology test coming up."

"And you can't study here? You have the whole basement to yourself."

"It's easier to get in the mood in the library where others are studying."

"But what about the distractions—those girls dressed like prostitutes?"

"I'm used to them. They don't bother me. I can concentrate with them around. But you know, sometimes I just have to get out of the house and see the sky and breathe the air."

"You know what you must do. You must get straight As to get into medical school."

"Yes, Mother." *She's acting suspicious. I must be giving off signals.*

CHAPTER 8

ESCAPE AND EVASION

Amy went to her room and plopped down on her bed. *I might as well get it over with.* She dialed Stewart's number.

"Hi."

"I was beginning to wonder about you, Amy. Are we still all right?"

"Yeees," she drawled. "I've just been busy, that's all—studying and shopping and what all."

"I was hoping we could go out tonight."

"Oh, not tonight. I'm just too tired. I don't know. Maybe I'm coming down with something."

"Oh, sorry to hear that."

That stopped him. "I'll be all right."

"Well, say, Amy, I've been meaning to ask you if you can go to our prom, and I was kind of expecting you to invite me to yours. I guess I always just assumed we'd go together, and that's why I haven't asked you. But now I'm getting scared. No one else has asked you, have they?"

She leaned back against the pillow and headboard. "No, not yet. Everyone knows we're going together, and maybe that's why no one has asked, or else maybe I'm losing my attraction."

"Not to me. I still want you, baby."

"Well, I'm glad to hear that, but to answer your question—I'm thinking I'd kind of like to skip your prom."

"What?"

She scooted up to a sitting position. "You know, I don't know anyone over there," she explained, "and it just wouldn't be fun."

He stiffened. "But I thought we were going together—"

"Well, I'd still like you to go to mine."

The phone was silent. Then he asked, "So am I supposed to go to mine with someone else?"

"It's up to you, Stewart. But that wouldn't bother me."

"What? I don't understand what's going on, Amy. I really don't."

"You know, next year you'll be going off to Wisconsin, and I'll be here, and I think we should just be free to meet new people. And then if we decide to get married, we'll know we're making the right decision."

"Amy, are you breaking up with me?"

She looked out the window at a big oak tree in the yard. "Not really."

"Have you already met someone else?"

"No, Stewart, I haven't."

Her mind was seething. Was it true what Atif said? Had her father committed a criminal act to try to stop the construction? She had to know.

She wasn't sure why she wasn't invited to the meetings, but she suspected that her father didn't trust her. Maybe he and her mother didn't like the positive things Amy had said about her Muslim friend at school. And maybe they didn't know where her head was, what with her distancing herself from Stewart. Regardless, she would have to listen from her dark hole, straining to hear what was said.

Gazing out the window in the nook, she watched the guests roll in. Tonight, the meeting included the same small group as before.

Then she went into her bedroom and ensconced herself on the floor in the back of her walk-in closet where she could hear voices through the section of the house wall that was below the trophy room cathedral ceiling.

She heard her father praying about saving the town from "satanic moozlims," and asking God to halt the construction, and then reporting on the stakes and footers.

"I don't know who moved the stakes at the corners of the lot, but they had to have it resurveyed. Unfortunately, the builder noticed that they were off and didn't go ahead with the foundation. That might have gotten them in some serious difficulties if he had built on his neighbor's land."

Someone laughed. "And then someone else broke off the J-bars in the footers, and they had to re-pour them. It's just too bad the construction wasn't delayed longer, by rain or something. I would have loved to have seen some big crane come in and lift the whole footing out of the ground in one piece." The men laughed louder.

"That would have been something!" one cackled.

Oh! It was true. She was sure her father was involved in moving the stakes and vandalizing the footers, just as Atif had said. Her father was spouting Christianity from one side of his mouth but ordering crimes from the other. He did not live by the Bible: "Thou shalt not steal," and "Do unto others as you would have them do unto you."

"Do the police have any leads on who did these things?" somebody asked.

"Our friends in the police department say no—nothing but a boot print and boot size—10M—at least as far as breaking the J-bars goes."

"Do they suspect anyone?"

"Me, maybe. They asked me what size boot I wear, and I told them 12M. But I don't think they can see me breaking those bars off."

"It didn't stop them from continuing to build," someone observed.

"No, it just slowed them down and cost them some money."

"Are there any plans for something more permanent?"

"I've heard of no plans. I don't know what these people might try next. We'll just have to wait and see. But they'll have to be careful. That security camera might catch them."

Somehow Amy knew that her dad would not be divulging his plans in a meeting. Who knows who might be recording their voices. He was a careful man.

Monday morning, Miguel and his crew wired vertical and horizontal rebar to the J-bars, and erected the narrow steel wall forms on both sides of the rods. When all was finished, Damon made his inspection and failed to find deficiencies.

The following morning, the big pumper and concrete-mixer truck arrived and set up on the driveway above the hole. The mixer drum rotated and the pumper sent concrete up its high boom, down the flexible pipe, and between the forms, as a worker guided the pipe and moved it along the top of the foundation. In little more than an hour, the job was done.

The trucks left and Miguel's people pushed vertical rods into the soft concrete every four feet, allowing them to project two feet above the wall, to tie to the eight-inch-thick concrete block wall that would be laid on top of it. Next, the men stripped off the forms and the crane returned and lifted the baskets of them out of the foundation.

The crew then set about leveling dirt in the basement, the plumber came and installed sewer drains and pipes for the basement bathroom and ablution area, and the plumbing inspector came and approved the pipes. The gravel truck arrived and shot stone all over the dirt, four inches thick, and the crew covered the gravel with plastic vapor barrier to keep moisture from the ground

from entering the basement and unrolled six-by-six-inch reinforcing wire over the plastic. Screed rails—steel pipes—were installed
to set the height of the concrete floor. Inspector Damon came and
approved the slab for pouring.

The next morning, the two cement trucks returned and
pumped concrete over the ground. Miguel and his men spread
it, "screeding" it to the proper level on their knees with a long
two-by-four, and bull-floating it smooth with a board on a long
pole. When it was hard enough to walk on, Miguel smoothed the
surface with a power trowel, which rotated four blades in a circle,
while the others used hand trowels around the edges and pipes.
Finally, they sprayed curing compound on top to hold in the moisture, strengthen the concrete, and reduce cracking. The trucks
departed at eleven and the workers cleaned their trowels and left
by midafternoon.

Amy had to see Atif. She wanted to tell him about the meeting. But
now Jesse was following her! They would have to try some new tac-
tics—escape and evasion, as her father, the Somali War vet, would
say. Restaurants were too risky.

She sent a message: "Sat @ 2:00? Must see. PU behind Macy's."
"PU?"
"Pls"
What does that mean? he thought. *She wants to ride in my car?*

Amy pulled into the mall, parked in front of Penny's, hurried down
the promenade into Macy's, walked down the moving escalator,
and trotted out the back, affixing her sunglasses and scarf as she
went. She saw his car in the loading zone, with his form bent over
the wheel. She could tell he was nervous and wondering, "What
did she want?"

Quickly she walked around to the passenger side, got in, closed
the door, crouched, and said, "Go!"

"What is this all about?"

"Jesse's following me."

"Where should we go?"

"Glover Park. It's not far. I don't know anyone around there, do you?"

He shook his head and rattled his brain.

A car that looked vaguely like Jesse's appeared in the parking lot, and Amy dropped out of sight, down onto the bench seat with her head in Atif's lap.

"Oh!" he gasped, frantically moving his hands from four and eight o'clock on the bottom of the wheel to stiff-armed positions at ten and two.

"Don't get any ideas," she said as her head found a comfortable position. "Just go. We have to get away."

Breathing heavily, he drove past the stores, out of the lot, onto the connecting street, and onto the highway, every bump bouncing her soft head. And every time he moved his foot to the brake pedal, her head went up and down, until he was entering the blind realm of delirium.

"You…you can sit up now," he stuttered breathlessly.

"Do you want me to?" she teased. This was not the first time she had had her head on a boy's lap in a car.

"Yes!"

"All right," she drawled in feigned disappointment, and sat up but still slid down in her seat.

He sighed and asked why she'd said she "must see" him.

She looked out at the fields and woods and felt the warm breeze from the open window on her face and inhaled the fresh country air.

Then her voice grew serious. "I had to see you. Listen, I overheard their meeting last night, and you were right, Atif. My father is involved. He won't say anything that incriminates himself, but I just know he's involved, the way they were all laughing about the footings. He said it was too bad the construction wasn't delayed by rain or something, that he would've loved to have seen a big crane lift the whole footing out of the ground in one piece. Then everyone laughed."

"How did you hear this?"

She explained how she could hear voices in the back of her closet, which adjoined the vaulted ceiling space of the addition.

"I don't understand. He's a Christian, but is this vandalism something a Christian would do?"

"I don't know if he really is one or not, Atif. He's certainly not following the Golden Rule."

He turned into the park and followed some curves between the trees. The azaleas and dogwoods were in bloom, and the red oaks and maples were leafing. He pulled into a shaded parking space near a picnic table, and she removed her glasses and looked into his eyes.

"Wha...what do you want to know about today, uh...Miss Breckenridge?"

She smiled and thought, *I finally have you alone in a car in a semiprivate place.* She took off her scarf, shook out her hair, and unzipped her jacket. He could not help but wonder what would come next.

"You know, maybe we should go sit at that table," he said, "then we wouldn't have to turn sideways."

She was disappointed, but saw some wisdom in the suggestion. "OK."

They moved out, he watching her walk in front of him, and she, aware of his eyes. They sat across from each other—she with her back to the road, her elbows on the table, her chin in her fists, looking at him.

"So?—"

"So, Dr. Bhati. Are women under men in Islam?"

He looked her dead in the eye and said, "Do you mean 'subordinate to?'"

"Yes, yes. You know what I mean. I know that in Saudi Arabia, they can't drive or go outside without a guardian, and young girls can be sold into marriage to old men, and women are segregated from men and can't get a job where men work, and in Afghanistan the Taliban wouldn't even let women go to school or work outside the home and made them wear clothing that covers everything but their eyes."

"Yes, that is true in some countries, but women have many more rights in most Muslim countries. In fact, women have been heads of state in lots of Muslim countries, like Pakistan, Afghanistan, Bangladesh, Indonesia, Malaysia, Turkey, Jordan, Yemen, Kyrgyzstan, Kosovo, and maybe some others."

"But our country has had to wait for a female head of state," she said.

He tried to keep his gaze off in the trees and not look at her face. She was too beautiful.

"But you're right that the Qur'an calls men and women to have different roles. The Qur'an says that men are the protectors and maintainers of women, because Allāh has given them more strength and because they support women from their means. And righteous women are supposed to obey them and guard the family and home in the husband's absence."

"That's just like it used to be here, men brought home the bacon, and the women took care of the house and the kids. But our roles have changed a lot. Now most women work too."

"Yes, things have changed—everywhere. Even in Pakistan. I know that a majority of students in the medical schools are now women. I think in the United States about half of the medical students are women. But in Pakistan, all of men who graduate go into practice, but at some schools only half the women do. There's a strong pressure to get married and have children."

"That's the way it used to be here, too, I think. But now lots of women have careers and delay marriage and kids."

"Does your mother work?" he asks.

"She runs the household, and keeps Jesse and me in line, and does some things at church."

"That's what my mother does, besides helping out in the schools and tutoring children."

"And is your father in charge, and does your mother have to obey him?"

He laughs. "He thinks he's in charge, but Ami isn't always obedient. They get into some fights sometimes."

"So do my parents. She claims her right to run the household."

"Mine does too."

"But aren't women kept separate from men in the mosque?"

"Oh, yes, women stand in the rear of the prayer room or in a separate room, and we have separate places for men and women for ablutions, of course."

"Ablutions? What's that?"

"In Islam, people must be clean before they can pray, or Allāh will not accept the prayer. We must wash the right hand and then the left hand, three times. Then the inside of the mouth three times, and splash water into the nose three times, then wash the face. Next, the right arm, then the left, then the hair and wipe it down, then wash the back of the ears, then the right foot and left foot. It's called Wudu."

She smiled at him. "My goodness. That must get messy. Do you rinse after you wash, or just let the soapy water dry?"

"The washing is done without soap—just clean water."

"Well, that doesn't sound very effective. Sorry. I could never get my hair clean without shampoo."

"It's ritual washing, Amy."

"Oh. Where do you do this?"

"Mosques have ablution areas, usually between the bathrooms and the prayer area. First, people take off their shoes and put them in the shoe racks. Then they enter the bathroom, if necessary, then the ablution area, then the prayer area."

"Oh, so they can use soap in the bathroom."

"Yes. Oh, and another thing. In the bathroom, some of us Muslims don't use toilet paper."

She smiled in surprise. "What? You just…stink?"

"Amy! Of course not. We use water."

"Oh, like those French bidets."

"Not exactly. We usually pour water into our left hand and splash it on our privates. That's called Istinja. But lots of Muslims use paper before they use the water and to dry themselves off with it afterward."

"This may be more information than I need, Atif. Did I ask you to tell me about Istinja?"

He smiled condescendingly. "I don't want you to live in ignorance, Amy."

"Is all this in the Qur'an?"

"No, actually, the Qur'an just says that Allāh loves people who purify themselves. The hadiths give more specific instructions. Istinja is in the Bukhari hadith, I think. The hadiths are further clarified in Fiqhs—interpretations of the Qur'an and hadiths by Islamic jurists who issue rulings or fatwas on questions presented to them."

"It's complicated."

"Yes. Oh, another thing: because the left hand is used for hygiene, we always eat, drink, pass items, and shake hands with the right hand."

"But you doctors know how germs are spread by shaking hands, and you always wash your hands with soap."

"Yes, but our right hands are not used to clean our bottoms."

She clapped her hands over her ears, pinched her eyes shut, and begged, "Enough! I don't want to hear any more about it."

"OK. Be ignorant."

She opened them to his grinning face and said, "I'm thirsty. But I didn't bring anything to drink."

"I have my plastic bottle in the car, if you don't mind drinking after me. But it's not cold."

"As long as you didn't wash yourself with it."

Making no reply, he retrieved it and handed it to her with his right hand. She noticed, and then said with a smirk, "I'd like to see you open that bottle with your right hand. What do you do, kind of spin it around like a ratchet toy? Or hold the bottle with your right hand and bite the cap with your right side molars?"

"No, I hold the bottle with my left hand and twist the cap with my right."

"So how am I supposed to hold it when I drink? Oh, I know. With my left hand."

He watched her lean the bottle up and gulp, and followed the liquid as it slipped past her larynx. She handed it back, and he tipped his head back and swigged, being careful to leave some more for her.

She burst into laughter. "You have a very talented Adam's apple, Atif! I'm so impressed."

He feigned humiliation. "Go ahead. Make fun of me."

"You know, Atif, I've noticed that Nadira doesn't wear a hijab. Why is that?"

"Well, the Qur'an doesn't say how people should dress, except that they should dress modestly and with piety. So much of it is left to local custom and climate. In Pakistan, we don't dress like desert people, with long white robes to reflect the sun. Our women usually cover up pretty well. Some do hide their faces and eyes with burkas. Others show their eyes with niqabs, and still others wear hijabs that show the whole face. And then some just wear a long scarf over their head. And most of our clothes for men and women have colors and patterns. And much of our clothing is loose and flowing. The climate in Lahore, where my parents are from is kind of like Brownsville, Texas, only a lot hotter in the summer, so they have to dress cool."

"Was your dad ever in the military?"

"No, no. The military is voluntary in Pakistan, and he was in school. How did your dad get in the Army?"

"He was kind of wild when he was young. He told us that when he was a teenager, he and a friend used to blow up rocks with dynamite to see how high they could make them go."

"Wow."

"And he wanted to get away from the farm, so he volunteered."

"Is he still involved in the military?"

"No....Oh, he may be in some organizations, but he's not active." She looked at her watch. "Oh! I have to get back! They'll be wondering where I am. And I have to buy something, or Jesse will really be suspicious."

CHAPTER 9
STEEL JOISTS

A my went from the garage through the side door into the trophy room and on into the kitchen. Eunice was taking two pizzas from the oven, and Jesse was lounging at the built-in table in the breakfast nook with his legs stretched out and crossed at the ankles. The aroma was rich with melted cheese, spices, pepperoni, and tomato sauce.

Jesse looked up and said, "So where were you today, big sister?"

"At the mall, as usual, trying things on." She started slipping off her jacket.

"I didn't see you. I happened to be there too."

She shrugged. "Oh, and what store were you in?"

"Macy's."

She went for the kill. "And you were going through the changing rooms?"

"No."

She hung the jacket on a hook on the back of the closet door and leaned against the wall beside the refrigerator glaring at him. "You can get arrested for that."

"I wasn't going through the changing rooms."

Eunice put the pizzas on the narrow table in the center of the room, looked at Amy, and listened.

"You were just watching them—watching the ladies go in and come out."

"No, I wasn't watching them."

"But you were following me."

"No, I was just passing through."

Eunice took plates from the wall cabinet and put them on the table.

"Maybe you didn't see me because I was in Penny's."

"You never shop there."

"Except when they have sales."

"OK, children. Stop bickering." She looked at Amy. "Did you find anything you liked?"

"Not really. A couple of things, but they weren't in my size."

Jesse squinted at her. "Funny how you never seem to find things."

In the basement, the center beam was set on temporary posts from right to left until the concrete-filled steel pipe columns arrived. The rough plumbing was complete, and the floor poured, except for squares omitted around where the columns would stand. Steel decking was stacked beside the foundation, waiting for the joists to arrive. Steel ledger angles had been bolted to the top of the foundation to speed the screwing of the bar joists. And the crane truck had just pulled parallel to the front of the foundation. The driver was loosening the chains holding the open-web steel joists. Kyle Matthews, the steel-erection sub, and his men stood on rolling scaffolds at each end to bolt the joists to the foundation, while he stood on a scaffold in the center to weld the joists to the center beam. Damon had just stepped out of his truck and was striding toward Dan, Lonnie, and the truck.

"Let me see those plans," he ordered Dan. *Oh, no, here we go,* Dan thought.

"Sure. Here."

Damon unrolled them to the joist page. "Let's see. These are 16K6s, and you're putting these flimsy things four feet apart?" he asked Dan.

"That's what the engineer called for."

"And he thinks you'll get less than a one-in-three-hundred-sixty span deflection with all the live load plus the dead load of the joists, decking, and concrete?"

"Yes, sir."

"And this is supposed to support the live load of all those people crowded into that room doing their standing and kneeling and bending-down calisthenics when they pray? Why, they'll be bouncing all over the place. The vibrations'll make them think the whole building's coming down. They'll think Allah's angry."

"Your plan review department approved these plans, sir."

Damon thrust his chin out at Dan, squinted at him from his round, freckled face, and with increasing volume spat, "Well, I'm telling you, Mr. Stanley, I don't. This is an assembly occupancy, and you'd better put those joists two feet on center instead of four, or I'll shut you down, you hear?"

Dan lashed back. "What?! But that'll mean twice as many joists, and it'll take another two weeks to get them, if we're lucky!"

"I'm sorry about that, Mr. Stanley, but it's my job to protect the public and to ensure the quality of these jobs. I'm the last line of defense in this system to keep you from putting up shoddy work, and I'm going to do it."

"Shoddy!" Dan barked, his eyes flaring.

"Do what you want, Mr. Stanley." He turned and walked back to his truck and eased out onto the highway without disturbing a single piece of loose gravel.

Dan was hot.

"What are you going to do?" Lonnie asked.

"I'm calling the city. That son-of-a-bitch can't do that. Shoddy! No one ever dared call our work that."

He told the truck driver to hold on, and quickly dialed the Inspection Department. "Plan Review, please."

"One moment, please."

The call transferred to voice mail, which told him to leave a message.

He called back and asked for the chief of inspections, who was also not available at the moment. This time he left a message: "Inspector Damon is requiring twice as many bar joists as called for on the plans by his engineer and approved by the department's plan reviewer. If we don't follow his order, he says he'll shut us down." He left his number.

Next, Dan called Maskeen and briefed him. Maskeen said he would try to call Ahmed, and if he couldn't get through, he would call the mayor.

Twenty-minutes later, Dan received a call-back from the chief, who told him the decision was up to Inspector Damon: "It's his prerogative. That's his job. But if you would like a hearing to contest his decision, we can schedule you one for next month."

"Next month!"

"That's when the hearings board meets."

He called Maskeen, told him, and advised him that the driver would soon start charging the hourly rate for delaying the delivery. Maskeen had not been able to reach Ahmed and told Dan to go ahead with the closer spacing and order more joists. Dan told Lonnie, who walked to the foundation and told Kyle to lay out the joists two feet on center. Dan filled in the driver and called the manufacturer with a rush order for more joists.

"You know that'll add twenty percent to the cost," the salesperson warned.

"Twenty percent! Why?" Dan asked. "You already know what we want. You have the engineering done and everything."

"I'm sorry, sir, but we have to charge that because it disrupts our schedule. We have to delay other deliveries or pay overtime to get yours built. Even twenty percent doesn't cover the cost lots of times. So do you still want them expedited?"

"Yeah. We'll pay the extra. We have to. When can we get them?"

"I'll get back to you. Probably in ten working days."

Two weeks! Dan thought. "Oh, wait!" Dan yelled. "We can't set the joists we have now because we don't have the two-foot bridging. We just have four-foot." Silence. "I'll just have to stack these things and set them when I get the other joists."

After more silence, the factory man said, "That's right, you need bridging for two-foot spacing. And remember, when you stack the bundles of joists, you have to put them on timbers on flat ground so they don't twist. And return the four-foot bridging on the truck. We'll send the two-foot on the next load."

"OK."

"Good luck."

Dan told the driver what they had to do and asked him if he had any timbers he could lend him until the next load came. He didn't, so Dan sent Lonnie to the lumberyard to get some.

He called Kyle over and told him they had to stop.

"What?" Kyle asked. "We come all the way down from Baltimore, and you're sending us home? This is gonna cost you."

"I can't help it. We don't have the two-foot bridging. Until we get that, we're stuck. And we might as well not start up again until we have all the joists."

Kyle cursed and said, "OK. But you know I have to charge you for a whole day's work for me and the crew, plus transportation."

"I understand. Sorry about this."

"OK, pack it up," Kyle yelled to his men. "Allah doesn't want us to work today." They began rolling up the hose for the welding gun and loading Kyle's portable welding machine onto his pickup.

Dan leaned on his truck, drinking coffee with the driver for an hour, slamming the inspector, and chewing antacid pills that he kept in his glove box. He called Maskeen again and told him how they had not been able to do any work because they didn't have the right size bridging.

"Oh! How much is this going to cost?"

"I don't know. Thousands. First, we double the cost of the joists and add twenty percent for expedited delivery. Then, we add an extra trip from Philadelphia for the crane truck."

"Philadelphia!"

Dan nodded. "That's where the manufacturer is."

"Wasn't there one closer?"

"Not one that could compete with their price and quality."

"Oh."

"Then I have to pay Kyle and his crew for a whole day's work, plus transportation. Then I have to pay Lonnie and myself for this lost time. And I'll have to mark it all up for my standard profit. Otherwise I can't stay in business."

"So, we have to pay the entire expense."

"I'm sorry, sir, but that's our agreement. You pay for the extras. This was not my fault. I did everything right."

"We'll sue the city," came Ahmed's tinny voice over Maskeen's cellphone. "They're going to make us run out of money!"

"I thought of the same thing, but the inspector will just say he was doing this in our best interest. As I understand it, the floor will be stiffer with the joists two feet apart instead of four feet, which is higher quality for us."

"Ugh! We can't build this thing out of solid gold, Maskeen. This has got to stop. The next thing we know, the inspector will be increasing all the specifications just to make us exceed our construction loan. One by one, he'll increase them all. It's his plan, I know! Breckenridge is behind it. He wants us to run out of money."

"I believe you're right."

"The inspector must be in bed with him. Breckenridge is probably paying the scoundrel!"

"What can we do?"

Ahmed paused a moment in thought.

"Well. We will have to tell the city that we don't want to exceed the specifications called for by our architect and approved by their plan reviewer—not ever again."

"Yes."

"Draft a letter to the mayor and copy the chief of inspections."

"Yes."

"And Dan Stanley? Do you think he will use this to suck more money from us?"

"I think he is fair, Ahmed. But I also think he is a businessman and requires fair compensation for his work. He is correct that all this extra cost must bear on us, not him. It's in our contract with him."

Ahmed paused again.

"Call the others and let them know what happened."

And the mosque waited.

Nadira and Atif came in through the mudroom into the kitchen. They greeted their mother, who was cooking, and Atif went downstairs to his bedroom. As Nadira started upstairs with her books, Salma called to her.

"Yes, Ami?"

"Come here, please." She did, and Salma began speaking in a low voice. "Nadira, do you think your brother has been acting strange lately?"

Nadira searched her eyes. "In what way?"

"He seems distracted, like he's thinking about something."

She shrugged. "I haven't noticed."

Salma looked at her. "Nadira, do you think he has been seeing someone?"

"Like who?"

"Like a girl?"

Nadira laughed. "Oh, Ami. Atif is so shy. I do not think he is seeing a girl."

"But every Saturday afternoon, he leaves here to go to the library to study. Have you noticed that?"

"No."

"Do you know of anyone he may be seeing?"

Nadira knew it was wrong to lie, but she did not want to expose her brother. "Not really," she said. "Just one time a few months ago, I think he met someone to talk about Islam."

"A girl?"

"I think so, but I haven't heard anything about it since."

"A Muslim girl?"

"No, I don't think so."

Salma went back to preparing the meal. "Humph. Well, keep your ears open. I'd like to know what is happening with him."

Ahmed came in from the garage, and found Salma, Nadira, and Atif camped in the great room, reading. Salma went to him. "You look distressed, Ahmed," she said, her hand on his sleeve.

"I have to relax. Breckenridge is at it again." Salma helped him out of his suit coat, and hung it in the closet.

"What's he up to now, Father?" Atif asked.

"The building inspector is requiring that the joists be put closer together, to make a stronger floor, he says. But it will delay the job two weeks and raise our cost by thousands of dollars."

"But the plans were drawn by the architect," Atif protested.

Ahmed nodded. "Yes. And approved by the engineer and the city engineers. But apparently this inspector has the final authority, and he says he'll stop the work if we don't make the change. He must be in the pay of Breckenridge."

Salma groaned.

"And if they keep increasing the requirements, we'll run out of money!"

"Sue them," Atif said.

He shrugged his shoulders. "For what, increasing the quality of our building? We have no choice. We have to do it. And I must get it off my mind. It's distracting me from my work. I have patients to think about, and operations—not floor joists!"

Salma looked at him. "Come, sit down. Nadira, get him some tea. Atif, put on some music—Shaukat Ali—but not loud."

Ahmed sat in the deep chair, closed his eyes, and slowly stroked his mustache with his forefinger and thumb. He breathed deeply, and Salma crept behind him and began massaging his shoulders.

"This will end, Ahmed. You will see. Allāh wants the masjid built, and it will happen. It is not in your hands. It is in His. You are only His servant, you and the others, His agents on earth. The load is not on your shoulders. Pray to Him this evening and tonight. He will bring you peace."

The music drifted in—a flute, then the mournful voice of Shaukat.

Ahmed said, "Yes, we will go on, in Allāh's name," and he opened his eyes.

Nadira gave him his tea, and he asked her his usual question about how school was going. She responded with her usual, "Fine, Abu," and returned to the stove on the wall behind the island.

Soon the smell of onions, garlic, ginger and cinnamon permeated the air as Nadira stirred a simmering pot on the gas range, and Ahmed turned his head to one side, and asked, "Oh, what is it tonight, pindi chole?"

"Yes, with lassi. Nadira is cooking."

"I look forward to that."

"Will you be able to go to Jumu'ah tomorrow?"

"I think so, unless something comes up."

"Good." *Then I can go*, Salma thought.

CHAPTER 10
CONSPIRACY

On Friday, the Muslim congregation held their congregational prayer service—Jumu'ah—in the basement of the Methodist church. The men prayed in the recreation room, women and children down the hall in a classroom. The church had allowed the Muslim congregation to install carpet in the large room with diagonal lines to demarcate where people would stand, kneel, and bow as they prayed. The lines were at an angle to the walls of the room and faced east, where a movable stage was placed on which the imam would stand while leading the prayers and delivering his Khutbah (sermon).

They used the bathrooms for ablution, and water for Istinja was provided in a pitcher beside the toilet in the bathroom stall.

Women entered the basement through a separate door in the rear. Movable screens between the men's and women's restrooms divided the basement and ensured privacy for the women. A microphone in the recreation room broadcast the prayer service and Khutbah to the women in their room so they could participate.

Though criticized at the time for allowing the Muslims to rent the space, the Methodist congregation voted to welcome the Muslims as another faith that believed in one God and even considered Jesus to be an important prophet. The minister had participated in many ecumenical meetings with other pastors, imams, and rabbis in the area, and felt that this was an extension of their service to God. He had come to know and like Imam Mufti, who also had a law practice in a nearby town and had a good sense of humor.

Ahmed and Salma arrived at the church for the Jumu'ah at about twelve thirty and went to their separate entrances in the basement. Ahmed entered and greeted Imam Mufti and the other men, removed his shoes and put them on the rack in the hall, and strode into the bathroom to perform Wudu (ablution) in preparation for Salāh (prayer). He went to a bathroom sink, allowed water to flow into his hands, washed them without soap, and washed his mouth, nose, face, arms, and hair, and dried off with paper towels. Then he sat on a stool by a floor drain and washed his feet with water from a pitcher.

As Salma was nearing the door to the church, she met a friend and greeted her. "Hello, Nawaz. How are you and Sadiq?"

"Fine, but Sadiq works too hard at his law office."

Salma looked at her and smiled. "Is Jasmin with you today?"

"No. She isn't back from school yet."

"Do I remember that she goes to Bryn Mawr?"

"Yes. She'll be home in another week."

"She's a junior, isn't she?"

"Yes."

Nawaz began wondering what this inquisition was about, especially as Salma moved closer and spoke in a quieter voice.

"And what is she studying?"

"Middle Eastern Studies."

"Ah. Very nice."

"She even takes some art history and archaeology." Now she thought she knew. "And where is your son, now?"

"Atif is a pre-med student at Maryland and is getting very good grades. He is a junior like Jasmin."

"Yes. I remember."

"So is Jasmin engaged?"

"No. Not yet. Bryn Mawr is a women's college, and she takes many of her courses at Haverford, which is a small coed school with few Muslim men, and I don't think any Punjabi men."

Salma adopted a worried expression. "There are so many chances she might be tempted to marry outside the religion, to a non-Muslim—and outside our culture, too."

"She's thought about using the Internet, but then, too, she's been so involved in her studies that I really don't think she's been thinking about marriage yet."

Salma scowled and looked away. "Oh, the Internet. There are so many criminals on the Internet. How can anyone trust that?"

"I don't know. And I think she wants to work after college, perhaps in Washington or New York."

She looked back. "That's more temptation. Our children could slip away and break up our families. You know, maybe we should get Atif and Jasmin together sometime, just to see if anything happens between them."

In the car on the way home, Salma said to Ahmed, "Ahmed. I'm worried that Atif may be seeing a nonbeliever." Nadira was staying to meet with some young people.

"Atif!" he said in disbelief. "He is involved with his studies, Salma. When would he have time to see a woman?"

"I have noticed that every Saturday afternoon, he goes to the library to study. Nothing will stop him from going. And I've even seen him check his watch before he leaves, like he doesn't want to be late."

"He's probably on a schedule, and wants to be sure he has time enough in the library."

She looked up at him. "But I asked Nadira if she knows of anyone he may be seeing, and she said that a few months ago, she thinks he met with a girl who wanted to talk about Islam, and she wasn't a Muslim."

He leaned his head back and glanced at her. "Really?"

"Yes. It makes me worry, Ahmed. You know, we can't keep control of these children these days when they are going to school with children of the other sex who don't believe what we believe and are not of the same background. They could fall in love, and then nothing will stop them from going their own way with some nonbeliever. And they could get married and have a baby, and then he might have to drop out of school and work to support them."

His eyes narrowed. "Nothing must stop his studies!"

"I hope nothing does."

"What do you think we should do?"

She looked up at him again. "Today I spoke with Nawaz, Sadiq's wife, and asked about Jasmin."

He stopped at a light and glanced at her. "Yes, I saw him at Jumu'ah. Was the girl there?"

"No. She isn't back from school yet. You know, she goes to Bryn Mawr."

"Yes. An expensive private school. They have money. He's contributing generously to the masjid."

"She'll be home in another week. She's a junior, like Atif, and is studying Middle Eastern Studies, which even includes art history and archaeology. And she is not taken."

He smiled mysteriously. "What egg are you hatching, Salma?"

"She said Jasmin has met very few Punjabi Muslim men at school, and is thinking about using the Internet! And you know how dangerous that can be."

"So you think we might be able to do better."

"Perhaps. So I think we should invite them over when Jasmin gets back and let them get to know each other."

"We'll talk about it. I need to get some of the men from the masjid together anyway to discuss what we need to do and whether any of them can give any more money to the effort."

"Sooner is better than later."

Amy was sitting at the desk in her bedroom when her phone vibrated. She clicked. "Sat @ 10? Behind Macy's? Inspctr reqd twice as many joists, cost us thousands..."

"OK," she messaged back.

She rose and headed for the door when she heard her father's voice in the hall talking on his cellphone. She stopped and hid by the door. "Yeah...No, let's not do anything else just now. Let's see if they sue anybody or raise hell at a hearing, and then let's see what happens...Yeah...I know they have lots of money—like Bhati, that surgeon—but if we keep bleeding them, sooner or later they've got to run out....Yeah...Uh huh...Yeah, well, for now, let's just play it by ear and see what happens...Roger and out."

She cringed and kept still until she heard his feet go down the stairs.

Later, before dinner, she went into the trophy room. Randall was having his drink, sitting in a big leather recliner with his feet up, watching the news. He always had a cocktail before dinner.

ISIS had just taken credit for bombing a Shiite mosque near Bagdad, killing sixty-two people, and US jets were bombing ISIS in Syria.

"Daddy," she said. "Why do you hate Muslims, but the Methodists in Chelmsford let them use their church for a mosque?"

"Those people in that church have mush for brains, Amy. They don't know what's going on."

"What is going on? Tell me again."

He put his drink on the coffee table and his feet on the floor. "Those moozlims are slowly taking over the world, that's what. You know that. It's worse than when the Ottoman Turks were taking over, or when the moozlims went all across North and West Africa and took Spain and Mali and Timbuktu, and then went east to Pakistan and India. Now they have half of Africa and all those Russian republics and Indonesia. And their illegals are moving across the Mediterranean into France and Germany and England. And we're letting them come here, and they're building mosques everywhere and telling their young men to go fight for ISIS, which means to fight against us. And it won't be long before there are suicide bombers all over the United States. They'll destroy Christianity, you wait."

"Daddy, do you know there are fifteen thousand Pakistani-American physicians in the United States, and thousands more Muslim doctors from India and Egypt and North Africa and Nigeria? I found that on the Internet. Are they going to try to destroy us?"

"And where do you think their money goes? It goes to spreading their religious plague all over the world."

"Is that where Shaquille O'Neal's money is going, and that other basketball player, Kareem Abdul Jabar?"

"I don't know where their money goes."

"And I think you don't like Muslims because a lot of them have darker skin than we do."

"That's one reason. They'll start mixing in and making the whole country brown—them and those Hispanics and Blacks."

She looked at him angrily. "Don't say that! That's ignorant! You sound like a racist redneck."

"You show a little respect, girl, or I'll ground you right now and take away that car."

"Oh, you'd like to do that. Then you and mom can start driving me to school again."

"You can just stay home in your room."

"I can't wait till you need some surgery and the hospital has a Muslim doctor start cutting on you. Ha!"

"Go to your room!" he roared, his eyes quivering, slamming his fist onto the table. "Right now!"

Amy was quiet as they sat around the table at dinner. She didn't feel like renewing the argument with her dad.

"What are you doing tonight?" Eunice asked her.

"Looking through the newspaper ads for prom dresses. I want to buy one tomorrow."

"Do you want some help?"

She chuckled silently. "No, Mom. I don't think you really know what's in style these days. I'd rather do it myself."

"OK. Just keep it reserved, dear. Nothing too revealing. And remember, you may want to wear it for another occasion, so I wouldn't get one too frilly."

"I'll help you," Jesse said with a grin.

Amy sneered. "Oh. That's an idea…for the trash can."

"I know what looks good on a girl."

"You're only interested in what's under the dress, Jess-bo."

"Don't say I didn't offer."

Eunice broke in. "Where are you going to look?"

"Macy's, for sure. But there are a lot of other shops I want to look in, too."

"Why don't you take Stewart with you," Jesse put in.

"He knows a lot about cows, but not much about dresses, thanks."

After dinner, Randall told Jesse, "You follow her tomorrow, and this time, don't lose her. But don't let her see you, either."

Amy parked behind Nordstrom's, dashed through the mall to Macy's, trotted down the escalator and out the back, climbed into Atif's car, and plopped her head in his lap.

"Oh!" he puffed. "Don't do that." He pushed her head aside. "Put your head between your own knees."

"Go!" she ordered as she moved away. "Glover Park."

He pulled away from the store entrance out into the parking lot.

"I thought you liked that," she said.

"I do and I don't. It's like riding a rapids without a life jacket."

"Have you done that?"

"No."

On the way, he told her about the inspector and the joists, and how it would add thousands of dollars to the cost. "That's their strategy, I think—to make us go bankrupt. And we don't know what they'll do next."

"I heard my dad talking to someone on his cell yesterday, telling him to just wait and see what happens. He said he knows that you all have lots of money—'like Bhati, that surgeon'—he said, but that they would keep on bleeding you until you ran out. But they're not going to do anything else right now."

They pulled onto the highway, and she sat part-way up and looked out the windows for cars.

"They're evil, Amy."

"He thinks he's doing it to save our Christian country and to save us from getting bombed in our churches and homes. And to keep your mosques from sending fighters to ISIS to fight against us. And to save us from browning."

"Browning?"

"From getting our pure white skin, which isn't white at all, from getting turned brown by mingling with Hispanics and Africans, and Muslims!"

"He's a religious bigot and a racist!"

She looked away. "Yes, but he believes that Jesus is God."

"But he doesn't believe in the Golden Rule!"

"No, he doesn't. He's trying to save the world from Islam."

Atif glanced skyward. "Allāh, save us from her father."

They found a different table in the park, this one more concealed from the road, and she walked close beside him until their bodies bumped a few times, unintentionally. They sat across from each other again, and today Amy said, "Tell me about Muhammad."

"Well, he was just a man, not God."

"You mean not God like Jesus is."

"Yes, Muhammad was a man, a prophet, like Abraham and Jesus and many others. He was born in Mecca in 570 CE."

"That's like AD."

"Yes. His parents died when he was young, and he was raised by his grandfather who was the most powerful man in Mecca. But he died when Muhammad was eight."

Amy kept looking at him, but Atif wouldn't return her glance. He kept staring away across a field to the woods.

"He became a camel driver, and took his first business trip to Syria when he was twelve. He gained a reputation as a good and honest trader, and when he was twenty-five, he was hired by a widow, whose name was Khadija, to take her merchandise to Syria. She was fifteen years older than he was, but she proposed to him, and they were married for almost twenty-five years."

She turned her gaze to a group of blooming azalea bushes, purple and white, but kept listening.

"He was a man of thought, and would go to a cave on the Mountain of Nur, near Mecca. In that cave in 610 CE, when Muhammad was forty, the angel Gabriel brought him the first revelation from Allāh—the first verses of the Qur'an. His wife Khadija was Muhammad's first Muslim convert."

"Huh," she said, turning back and finding him looking at her. But quickly he looked away, into the trees.

"Muhammad could neither read nor write, so he memorized the revelations, and his companions wrote them down later.

"Over the next twenty-two years, Gabriel brought him the remainder of the book, the last part just before Muhammad's death in 632 CE."

She turned back, and again he looked far away.

"After the first revelations, Muhammad preached only to people he trusted. But when he started preaching publicly, he started encountering increased hostility from the people of Mecca, who worshipped idols. Muhammad and his Muslim converts were harassed and abused.

"His wife died in 620, and in 622, he led his converts to Medina to escape the persecution. Then in 624, an army of a thousand pagans from Mecca attacked Medina in the Battle of Badr, and a Muslim army of three hundred led by Muhammad defeated them. Finally, in 630, Muhammad, leading an army of ten thousand Muslims from Medina, took Mecca peacefully, declared a general amnesty, destroyed the pagan idols, and the people converted to Islam."

"So they wouldn't be beheaded?" she asked.

"No. It was voluntary. Anyway, Muhammad died in Medina in 632 after the last revelation of the Qur'an. That's the short version of his life. I can tell you much more …"

"That's enough for now."

As they walked back to the car, she slipped her hand into his and whispered, "Next time, I'll tell you about Jesus."

She strode through the double-door air lock into Macy's basement, and walked up the escalator into "women's clothes" and back into "evening wear." She was not particular about what she found. She was in a hurry. In fact, she wanted something ugly, something that Stewart would not care for or be turned on by—just something to cover her, head to toe, wrist to shoulder, in a nauseating color. She found a clerk and described her gown.

"Why would we have something like that?" the clerk asked.

She grinned. "For an old woman?"

"A prom dress for an old woman. OK. What price range?"

"It doesn't matter."

The woman was mystified, but said, "Let's see what we can find."

They went to the racks, started swishing through them, and after half an hour, there it was, in her size, a shapeless lime green gown that hung loosely from the high collar to her shoes like a dead oak leaf. It had three quarter sleeves, so almost no skin escaped the cloth. She read the label: *100% polyester.* It felt crisp to the touch, like paper (*who would want to feel it?*); it crinkled when she moved and had a slight chemical odor. The only decorations were sparkling sequins around the neck. She tried it on, glanced in the mirror, and smiled. *Yes—totally unalluring,* she thought, *hideous even. It'll do. And it's cheap. I wonder why. And it looks cheap, too. Perfect.*

"Wrap it up," she told the clerk, who gave her a bewildered smile.

At home, she tried it on for Eunice who was not impressed. "I should have gone with you."

"You don't know what's in style, Mom."

"No, I lost her again," Jesse told his dad secretively in the trophy room. "I kept looking through the stores—from a distance—I didn't want her to see me—and I never saw her until she was walking to her car with that Macy's bag."

"I think maybe you should try a new line of work, Jesse. Being a private eye doesn't seem to suit you. But I'm surprised. I thought a deadeye shooter like you would do better in the hunt."

CHAPTER 11

JOISTS AND JESUS

Ahmed perused the letter from the mayor. They were standing at the island in the kitchen.

"What does it say?" Salma asked.

"It apologizes for the problem, but says yes, it was within the authority of the inspector to require the closer spacing of joists. However, in this case, the appeals board had gone against the inspector and decided that the spacing given on the plans could be used. Blah, blah, blah. That won't help us now! The additional joists have been ordered and are due to arrive this week! It's too late to change the order. If we cancelled, we'd have to pay for them anyway. That's infuriating!"

Salma shrugged. "What can we do?"

"We might as well use them."

Atif walked into the family room aiming for the basement stairs. Salma was sitting on the sofa reading. "Oh, Atif."

"Yes, Mother?"

"We're having some friends from the congregation over Saturday afternoon for tea and would like you to come."

A red flag unfurled. "Oh?"

"Yes. We want to show off our children to them. And they will bring some of theirs also, I think."

Now he understood. "Oh, OK. Little kids?"

"Some may be older."

Maybe he didn't. "Do I know any of them?"

"I don't know. I don't think so. But you'll get to meet them."

He shrugged and looked away. "As long as it's not just a bunch of octogenarians—that could be really boring."

"I don't think you'll be bored. Dress nice."

He looked puzzled.

The crane truck had returned and pulled parallel to the front of the foundation, and the driver was loosening the chains holding the joists. Kyle Matthews's steel erection crew stood on the scaffolds at each end to bolt the joists to the foundation, while he stood by the center beam holding the welder, which had a hose leading to the portable welding machine on the bank. Dan and Lonnie waited by the truck.

"We're gonna get some work done today!" Dan shouted to the driver over the hum of the truck and roar of the welder.

The driver unfolded the crane and lifted the bundle of two-foot bridging onto the bank, and then began lifting the long, flat trusses high into the air—one at a time in a vertical position—and slowly lowering them to the foundation, being careful not to start them swinging. The crew grabbed each one and placed it on the marks. The end men bolted it to the concrete wall, and Kyle welded it to the steel beam. The end men also installed the bridging between the joists as they went. When they were done setting the joists, they broke for lunch, and the crane truck left. Then they slid the pieces of light corrugated steel decking on top of the joists and attached each with self-tapping screws, finishing the job at about four o'clock.

"The plumber and electrician come tomorrow morning to put in openings for their pipes and conduit," Dan told Lonnie as Kyle's crew left, "and Miguel comes to put in the forms and wire. Then concrete the next morning."

"The weather's supposed to hold," Lonnie said.

Dan said, "Yup," and called the concrete plant.

The next day at eight, Miguel's crew spread reinforcing wire across the steel decking and installed two-by-four forms around the outside and the stairwell to the basement. The plumber and electrician arrived later, conferred with Dan, and did their job. The plumbing and electrical inspectors approved the work, and Damon signed that the slab was ready to pour.

The next morning the cement trucks returned, and the big pumper delivered the concrete to the steel decking. Miguel and his men raked it out, screeded, floated, troweled, and sprayed it, and left by midafternoon. Now the mosque was a concrete box with a floor, walls, and flat roof, sitting in the ground.

They found their shady table in Glover Park, and Amy began. "OK. So now it's my turn. Jesus was born to the Virgin Mary in Bethlehem more than two thousand years ago."

"Yes. We believe that."

She looked directly at him. "And for his first thirty years, he was raised in Nazareth and later worked as a carpenter, and he was Jewish. And Romans ruled the land."

"An ordinary man."

Shaking her head, she said, "No, Atif, he was not an ordinary man. John said, 'For God so loved the world that he gave his only begotten Son, that whosoever believeth in him should not perish, but have everlasting life.' That's in 3:16."

Atif parried, "The Qur'an rejects the claim that Allāh begot a son. It says, 'Allāh is the One and Only. He begetteth not, nor is He begotten; and there is none like unto Him.'"

She stomped her foot on the turf under the table. "Be quiet. Luke says that when Jesus was twelve, his parents took him to the Passover

Festival in Jerusalem, and when it was over, they couldn't find him. They searched for three days, and finally found him in the temple listening to the teachers of law and asking them questions, and the teachers were amazed at his understanding and answers. And Mary and Joseph were angry with him and asked why he had done this to them, and Jesus asked, 'But why did you have to search for me? Didn't you know I would be here doing my Father's business?' That was the first time he told anyone that he was the Son of God."

"Like I said, we believe he was a man, not God."

She looked at him. "You already said that. But Paul says that in Jesus, God was manifest in the flesh, and John wrote that after Jesus made a lame man walk, he said that God was his Father, and that made he himself equal with God."

Atif looked away. "So many different people wrote the Bible, Amy—forty or more people. How can they all be right? Only God wrote the Qur'an."

"We believe that the Bible is the Word of God."

"And we believe the Qur'an is the Word of God."

"But listen. In Acts, Luke says to the jailor, 'Believe on the Lord Jesus Christ, and thou shalt be saved.' Jesus can forgive sins, Atif."

"Only Allāh can forgive sins."

Her eyes pleaded with him to believe. "But John says that in the temple in Jerusalem, Jesus told the Jews, 'I and my Father are one' and they picked up stones to stone him for blasphemy."

"Yes, Jews believe that it is heresy for a man to claim to be God or the Son of God. They, like us, believe in only one God—not two or three, no duality or trinity."

Her eyes flared. "Do you want to hear about Jesus or not?!"

He puffed his cheeks and exploded some air. "Yes."

"OK. So when Jesus was in his thirties, he began wandering and preaching and performing miracles."

He leaned his head back and looked down his nose. "We believe in his miracles."

"Then how can you *not* believe that he was God?"

"The miracles were Allāh acting through Jesus."

She was vexed. "Oh! You twist everything...Well, anyway, Jesus changed water into wine, brought fishermen a multitude of fish, healed a leper, and raised men from the dead. And he cured a paralytic, and made blind men see, and made a mute man talk, and he fed five thousand people with five loaves and two fishes, and did lots of other things."

"Yes, we believe these things."

"He preached many lessons that we live by today. Jesus said, 'The Lord God is one Lord, and thou shalt love the Lord thy God with all thy heart, and with all thy soul, and with all thy mind, and with all thy strength,' and 'thy neighbor as thyself'—both Mark and Luke say that—and you must love your neighbor even if he's poor, starving, naked, or dying. That was Jesus' parable of the Good Samaritan."

Atif countered. "We declare that there is no God except Allāh, and that Muhammad is the Messenger of Allāh. And we worship only one God, Allāh. We've always been monotheistic. And we give Zakāh to the poor every year—two and a half percent of our wealth."

Amy pushed on. "He preached many lessons in the Sermon on the Mount that were against Jewish teachings. Where the Old Testament said, 'Thou shalt not kill,' Jesus said 'Thou shalt not keep anger in your heart.' Where it said, 'Thou shalt not commit adultery,' He said, 'Whosoever looketh on a woman to lust after her hath committed adultery with her already in his heart.' Where it said, 'Thou shalt not put your wife away without a written divorce,' He said, 'Thou shalt not divorce or leave your wife.' Instead of striking back when someone hurts you, Jesus said you should 'Turn the other cheek,' and where it said, 'Love thy neighbors and hate thine enemies,' Jesus said, 'Love thy neighbors and thine enemies.'"

"I can see why they were against him. He was quite radical."

"And the Bible says that if we want salvation—if we want to get into heaven—we must have faith in our Lord Jesus Christ—we must be saved."

Atif slowly waved his head back and forth.

Amy continued: "And the fruit and proof of this faith is good works that we do. In Ephesians, Paul wrote, 'By grace you have been saved through faith. And this is not your own doing; it is the gift of God, not a result of your works, so no one may boast.'"

He gave her his rapt attention.

"So because Jesus is in our hearts," she explained, "we feed the hungry, give water to the thirsty, clothe the naked, help the sick, and people in prison. Jesus said, 'Inasmuch as ye have done it unto one of the least of these, my brethren, ye have done it unto me.' That's why I'm planning to volunteer to help home-less people in Washington or Baltimore this summer or help in a soup kitchen."

He nodded and looked away. "That's good. And we give charity to help needy people, too, in addition to the required Zakāh, and we have our own assistance organizations—ICNA Relief USA and the Red Crescent Society."

"Good. But of course, there's more to the story. In addition to his other teachings, Jesus kept telling people that he was God, and that violated Jewish law. And in John, it says that the Jews wanted to kill him because he'd broken Jewish law by performing a miracle on the Sabbath, and he'd said that God was his Father, and that made him equal with God, and that was blasphemy. Jesus even said, 'I and my Father are one.'"

"I don't believe what John said."

Amy's eyes blazed. "Don't interrupt! So the chief priests asked the Romans to execute Jesus, and he was put on trial, but the Romans found him innocent of breaking any Roman law."

"Did they let him go?"

"No. The religious leaders convinced Pontius Pilate to execute him, and they tortured Jesus and nailed him to a cross, and he died in a few hours."

"The Qur'an says he wasn't crucified. Allāh just made it appear that he was."

"Oh, please. The Romans crucified thousands of Jews, and they crucified Jesus."

"We believe that they did not kill him at all, but Allāh made it look like they did, and that Allāh raised him up unto Himself. That's in, uh, Surah 4."

She grimaced. "All right, let me finish, Atif. This is my story of Jesus. The Bible says they crucified him, but then he came back from the dead and ate with his eleven disciples, and told them to go into the world and preach the gospel to every creature."

"We don't believe he came back from the dead."

"That doesn't surprise me. And this might be the most important thing: he told the disciples, 'He that believeth and is baptized shall be saved; but he that believeth not shall be damned.' That's what Mark says in chapter sixteen."

"You really know your Bible."

"I've studied it all my life, Atif, especially with my grandma Rebecca. But you memorized the Qur'an, didn't you?"

"Yes, when I was young. But that was by rote in Arabic. I didn't know what it meant. But I have studied the English version quite a bit since then."

She closed her eyes, reopened them, and looked at him. "Grandma taught me that scripture, 'For God so loved the world, that he gave his only Son, that whoever believes in him should not perish but have eternal life.' That's all you have to do to be saved from hell, Atif—believe in Jesus Christ."

"Like I said, we don't believe that, Amy. We must love and obey Allāh and follow the five pillars to go to heaven."

She gazed at him sadly, began fidgeting, and then lowered her head and closed her eyes.

"Are you...praying for me?"

Her lips kept silently moving.

CHAPTER 12
TEA

The great room on the back of the house awaited the guests. It was a two-story space with a stone fireplace on the back wall, which was flanked by vertical windows a total of eight feet high. On the opposite side, an open stairway led to the second-floor balcony. The kitchen and dining nook, which were one-story spaces, adjoined it. The living room on the front of the house was much too small and confined for the party.

Salma had arranged the furniture in the great room into three conversation areas. A two-person sofa with end tables and a glass-top coffee table was against the left side high wall below three large canvas prints of Lahore: the Badshahi Mosque, Chauburji Gate, and Lahore Museum, all in heavy dark brown frames. Tapestries and paintings of geometric designs decorated other walls.

By the walkway to the entrance and facing the fireplace was a three-person sofa with companion chairs at each end, plus a coffee table and end tables. A blooming jasmine plant, two feet high—the national flower of Pakistan—sat on the end table, its white star-shaped blooms rising above leafy branches, attracting visitors with its sweet perfume. On the right, backing up to the kitchen, sat another small sofa with end tables and chairs surrounding a coffee table. The furniture was tufted brown leather, clean and masculine.

Muhammad Pasha, the computer engineer, his wife Inaya, and two sons, Ali, fourteen, and Akbar, nine, arrived twenty minutes after the invitation time. The boys carried tablets for playing games. Ahmed and Salma greeted them at the door and escorted them into the great room.

"Men sit here," Ahmed told Muhammad with a smile, ushering him to the sofa on the right. Ahmed sat in the chair with his back to the fireplace and windows.

Salma led Inaya to the sofa facing the fireplace, and she herself sat in the chair at the end near the wall. "The boys may want to go into the living room," she said, and they happily escaped.

Nadira brought each person hot spiced tea with two sweet biscuits on the saucer.

"Nadira, tell Atif that the guests are arriving."

"Yes, Ami."

She went to the basement, and they ascended together. Atif joined the men, shook hands with Muhammad, and sat on the small sofa by the kitchen and facing the high wall and prints.

Half an hour later, the bell rang again, and Ahmed and Salma welcomed Sadiq Malik, his wife Nawaz, and daughters Jasmin, twenty, and Abeera, fourteen.

"And this is Jasmin," Nawaz said proudly.

Salma smiled. "Oh, we're pleased to see you, Jasmin. Come in. I understand you are at Bryn Mawr."

"Yes. I'm a junior."

"That's wonderful."

All the women wore shalwar kameezes—tunics reaching to the knees with sleeves to the wrist, and baggy trousers extending to the ankles. They varied in color, pattern, embroidery and neckline, but Jasmin's was sleeveless and embroidered with decorative flowers, and the trousers were dark gold. She was tall and slender, slightly tan, with full lips, a straight nose, and penetrating brown eyes. She had a long tan scarf draped around her neck.

The men wore dark coats over patterned shirts, open at the collar, and dark trousers, except that Atif wore no coat.

Ahmed led Sadiq to the chair on the right facing the fireplace. "This looks like the men's section," he joked, and shook hands with Muhammad and Atif.

Salma brought Jasmin to the men's group and introduced her to Atif. "This is Atif, my son, who is a premed student at Maryland."

They smiled distantly and shook cool hands; Atif's head and eyes turned slightly downward and to the side. Jasmin backed away and quickly looked at Salma, who led her to the sofa on the wall with the pictures of Lahore. Her mother Nawaz sat on the longer sofa facing the fireplace, and Salma sat between them on the chair. Jasmin's sister Abeera sat on the other end of the sofa, next to Nadira.

The men discussed the progress on the masjid. "The masons will start laying block next week," Ahmed told them. "Then the week after that we can begin the roof."

"It's coming together," Sadiq said.

"If there are no more surprises from Breckenridge and his inspector!" Ahmed growled.

Salma began quizzing Jasmin about her Middle Eastern Studies courses.

"We study history, culture, and politics from Morocco to Afghanistan. It's been quite interesting. It even includes archaeology and art history."

"What are you thinking of doing after you graduate?"

Jasmin smiled pleasantly. "Probably graduate school. I'm not sure in what yet. There are so many interesting areas. But I might move back to Washington—for the politics and job opportunities."

"That's nice. You know, you two college students should talk." Jasmin blushed, and Salma rose, crossed the room, and made the same suggestion to Atif. "You know, you two college students should talk, Atif. Jasmin has been studying some very interesting subjects at Bryn Mawr. Please go talk to her."

All the adults at the party were in on the plot, and Ahmed looked at Atif.

"I will."

Atif rose, and with his head down, crossed to the other sofa. He pointed his hand at the empty space next to Jasmin and looked at her. She remained turned toward the women, but nodded in assent.

He sat and asked, "So…how do like Bryn Mawr?"

She looked down demurely. "Very much. I've learned a lot about the Middle East there, and at Haverford."

"Oh, you can take courses there, too."

"Yes, and at Swarthmore. And you're at Maryland?"

"Yes. Premed. I'm a bio major."

"Heavy on science and math?"

"Yes."

She looked away. "We're more into liberal arts."

"What are you studying?"

"Middle Eastern Studies."

Atif could hardly stand it. He was waiting for it to end. "What's that?" he asked. "History?"

"And politics and culture."

"Uh-huh. Do you like it?"

Her eyes were losing focus. "Yes. Do you like premed?"

"It's interesting. I have to take it to become a physician."

Duh, she thought. "Uh-huh."

They hit a drought from lack of interest. Neither could think of anything to ask that really justified the effort of running air past vocal cords and forming lips and tongues into discernible sounds.

Finally Atif rose and said, "Nice talking to you, Jasmin," and hustled back to the men's section, having fulfilled his obligation.

"How did you like her?" his father asked, almost in a whisper, as he sat down.

"Very nice, very intelligent," Atif whispered, his head bobbing.

Soon they were talking about medical malpractice insurance and the computerization of the medical industry.

Jasmin was outraged (and a little hurt) that this premed student from the local state college would ask her a few questions, quickly lose interest, and abruptly rise and say, "Nice talking to you." Oh! But what was this about anyway—an arranged marriage? What were her parents thinking of? She would be damned if she would let her parents pick her husband. And he's not even from the Ivy League. She would pick her own, thank you. And not some dullard with years and years of school ahead of him.

"So did you like her?" Salma asked Atif after the guests left. He was helping Nadira take dishes to the kitchen.

"She was nice," he said, nodding his head.

"You know, she's not engaged and has no serious suitors."

He peered at her face. "Mother. Is that what this is all about? Are you trying to arrange a marriage between us?"

"Atif. She is a fine, well-educated girl from a good college and a wonderful family, and she's a Muslim, and her family's from Lahore. She shares many of our values, and I think you should consider her."

"Mother! I'm not ready to get married! I have five more years of college and five years of residency before I can start practicing. I can't even think of girls now!"

She paused in thought, and then said, "Well, if you do think of girls, here's one you might think of. But a girl like this won't be available forever. And you know...your father and I married when he was in medical school."

"I'll keep that in mind, Mother."

Nadira had overheard the exchange and whispered to him in the living room, "And Atif's in love with Amy."

His face reddened and his lips crushed each other in a grimace.

The next week Miguel and his crew sprayed tar on the outside of the basement walls and applied thick plastic film to it. They installed exterior drain pipe around the bottom on the outside, covered it with gravel, shot in place by the gravel truck, and filter fabric to keep dirt from clogging the gravel. Then Dan supervised the compact track loader in pushing dirt against the foundation, which was safe to do, now that the twelve-inch thick concrete walls had the added support of the reinforced concrete floors on top and bottom.

Next, the eight-inch concrete blocks for the above-ground walls were delivered. From the top of the basement walls protruded the rods topped with white safety caps—two feet high and four feet apart—and at corners and by doorways. Every movement was under the watchful eye of the security cam.

"What are you going to do next?" Jesse asked his dad in the trophy room.

"I don't know yet. Gerald says he has a few more tricks up his sleeve, but I don't know if he has anything that will actually kill the damned thing."

CHAPTER 13

THE PROM

The doorbell rang, and Eunice called from the living room where she was reading, "He's here!"

"Ask him in," Amy called down the stairs. "I'll be there in a minute."

Eunice greeted Stewart in the reception hall. He was wearing the usual black tux and bow tie, and carried a corsage box in his left hand.

"You look very nice," she said, smiling.

Amy glided down the massive stairway in her lime gown and jarring orange granny shawl. Stewart blinked and said, "You...you look...lovely tonight, Amy. What a...striking dress."

"I'm glad you like it."

He handed her the box, and she opened it to the customary corsage. She smiled. It was an orangey orchid with black spots that clashed perfectly with her gown. He tried to pin it on her, but she said, "Let me do that. We don't want to have to call the rescue squad."

They descended the steps between the six two-story columns and climbed into the black limo with Joe and Connie, friends from Amy's high school, and set out for the hotel in Baltimore. Amy was glad there were four of them so that she wouldn't have to talk one on one with Stewart. He and Joe could talk sports, and she could talk about more interesting things with Connie.

The seats formed an L. The boys sat in the rear facing the front of the car with the girls on the side facing the bar. Football dominated the boys' talk, plus plans for college. Joe was going to Towson, another Maryland state university, which was also where Connie was enrolling.

"Is Stewart going to Maryland?" Connie asked.

"No, Wisconsin." She saw his eye stray toward her.

Connie put her hand beside her mouth and said, "How can you keep an eye on him there?"

"We're setting each other free while we're in college. And if we're still hooked on each other after that, we can tie the knot then."

A concerned look overtook Connie's face. "Oh."

The boys overheard her, and Stewart blushed. He was still in denial.

The driver pulled into the line at the old hotel and dropped them at the front door. They entered the lobby and then made a trip to the restrooms.

"So are you two breaking up?" Joe asked while they waited outside the restroom.

Stewart looked grim. "It's what she wants, not me."

"Well, is she dating someone else?"

Stewart shrugged. "I don't know. Her family is suspicious that she is, but they don't know anything. She always goes to the mall on Saturdays, but usually doesn't buy anything."

"Ooo."

"Her brother has tried to follow her, but can never find out where she goes."

"That does not sound good at all, man."

Stewart frowned. "She can be kind of sneaky sometimes. I don't trust her."

"Hey, one of us ought to go in and get a table."

"I'll go," Stewart said.

The girls returned and Joe led them into the ballroom, which had a high ceiling. The DJ was set up on the bandstand stage at the opposite end and was playing dance music. A buffet on the side held finger sandwiches, snacks, and soft drinks.

People sat at tables around the perimeter, but some were visiting friends or getting food, and others were already on the floor, moving to the music. Most boys were wearing black tuxedos, but the girls' gowns broadcast an array of colors. There was a low roar of laughter and conversation.

"Are we still a couple, Amy?" Stewart asked as they danced a slow one at the end of the evening.

"Stewart, you know how much I like you. But you're going away in the fall, and we already decided to let each other date other people and get back together when we're sure we're right for each other—we already decided that."

He looked down at the side of her head while they danced close. "You decided that, Amy."

She pushed away and looked up at him. "I really think it's best for us, don't you? Marriage is a serious thing: it's sacred—it's for life—and we've got to be sure."

He was quiet. She thought he was about to cry.

A fast song started, and she said, "Come on. Let's do this one."

At home at the door, he held her and tried to kiss her lips, but she turned her head.

"Oh," he gasped, nearly choking up. Then anger surged through him. "OK, Amy. If that's the way you want it." He turned and strode to the limo.

Yes, Stewart. It's the way I want it.

They were sitting in the shade across the picnic table from each other. Atif was morose, and he had said little in the car on the way to the park.

"What's wrong?" she asked him.

He turned his head down and to the side and said, "You know what's wrong."

"No, I don't, Atif. What is it?"

He looked straight into her eyes. "First I think you are my friend, and then I find that you are duplicitous!"

"What?"

"You are pretending to be my friend."

"I am not. I *am* your friend."

"You are going with a boy named Stewart, a rich boy from out of town! Don't deny it! Nadira says that many people saw you dancing with him at that prom."

"Yes, that's true, but—"

"But what? That says it all. You are going with him."

She gave him her earnest look. "No, Atif. I broke it off with him."

"You what?"

"I broke it off. I told him it was because he is going to the University of Wisconsin next year, which is far away, and I'm going to Maryland, and we each need to be free to date other people to decide if he and I are really meant to share the sacred vows and be married for life."

He stared at her. "But that's not the real reason?"

"No."

"I told you that you are duplicitous!" nodding violently. "So what was your real reason? You've already found someone else?"

"I don't know, Atif. Maybe," she said sweetly, smirking within.

"And who is he?" he demanded.

"I can't tell you." She reached her right hand across the table and took his. "But I will tell you when I know it's right."

He felt electricity flowing through her hand into his until it became too intense, and he had to jerk his hand away. "Ugh! Women!"

She smiled.

After regaining his composure, he asked, "I give up. What questions do you have for me today, Amy Breckenridge?"

She looked up into the canopy of leaves and then back at him and said, "Just two. First, why do Muslims hate Jews? I read on the Internet something about a boulder saying, 'O Muslim! There's a Jew hiding behind me, so kill him.'"

"Yes, that's in one of the hadith books written by men who recorded things they heard Muhammad say. It's not in the Qur'an."

"So Muhammad wanted to kill the Jews. And why do Muslims want to destroy Israel? That's my other question. Another place I read said that Muhammad said that he would expel all the Jews and Christians from the Arabian Peninsula."

"I think that's in another hadith book. But Amy, I'm not a religious scholar."

"Well, I'm sure you know some things. The Internet says that there are 2.2 billion Christians in the world, 1.6 billion Muslims, and 1.1 billion Hindus, but only fourteen million Jews. And six million of them live in the United States and six million in Israel. But Muslims want to eliminate all of them and destroy Israel. Why? That's like what the Nazis tried to do."

He turned away and frowned. "I do not appreciate your comparing Muslims to Nazis. There are Jews living in Muslim countries all over the world, and Muslims are not trying to eliminate them. And my father has worked with many Jewish physicians and has held many in high regard."

"Don't Iran and ISIS want to destroy Israel?"

"They're terrorists, not Muslims."

"Iran?"

"It gives money to terrorist groups that attack Israel, like Hezbollah, which is Shia like Iran, and even Hamas, which is Sunni."

She looked at him quizzically. "But don't all of Israel's neighbors want to destroy it, and lots of other Muslims, too? Why?"

"It goes way back, Amy. The Jews claim a right to own and occupy Israel, even though it belongs to the Palestinians."

"It does?"

"In Genesis, it says that Allāh promised the Land of Canaan, which is now called Palestine, to Abraham's offspring, and Abraham had two sons, Ism il and Isaac."

She nodded. "Yes. I know that story. But we say Ishmael."

"Yes, well, the descendants of Isaac were the Jews, and those of Ismāil were Arabs. And Ismāil was born first, so Jewish law says that *he* should have inherited Palestine—the Arabs, not the Jews. However, because Ismāil's mother was a handmaiden to Isaac's mother, the Jews claim that Isaac and the Jews inherited Palestine."

"So? These stories are thousands of years old. How can they make any difference today?"

"Because they're why the Jews say they have a right to Israel."

She gaped at him incredulously. "Is that the only reason Muslims hate Jews?"

"Actually, Muslims don't hate Jews. This is a political problem. The Jews claim that they have a right to live in Israel, and they've dispossessed the Palestinians, imprisoned Palestinians in Gaza, and blocked the movement of goods and people to and from Gaza, and taken land from the Palestinians for settlements on the West Bank. And taken land from Jordan."

"Most people here think the Jews deserve to have a homeland after the Nazis and their allies killed six million of them in World War II. Six million! Including women and children."

"But do you think that gives them the right to take land from the Palestinians?"

"Oh!" she recoiled. "Do you think religions will ever stop fighting, Atif? Over ancient arguments. Old-World arguments. Sunnis and Shia always blowing each other up. And Muslims and Christians and Jews always fighting too. Why can't they remember that they all worship the same God?"

His face grew somber. "I don't know."

She paused, and then looked up at him. "But all Muslims don't hate Christians, do they?" she purred.

"Only Christians who side with the Jews over Israel. Not really. I don't hate Jews…Do you know what, Amy? You sure love to argue. You should join a debate team."

She smiled. "I've had years of practice debating my parents."

On the way back to the car, she began walking backwards and grabbed his right hand.

"What are you doing?" he asked.

"I want to hold your hand, but I can't put my dirty left hand in your clean right hand, so this is all I can do—walk backwards."

"You're crazy!"

"Yes, Atif. Crazy about you!" Then she pulled him to her, threw her arms around his neck, and began kissing his face. He jerked her close and said, "Amy—"

"Shut up."

Her mouth found his, and they closed their eyes and kissed until they were breathless.

"Oh, Amy. What will we do?" Then he said, "No. We cannot get involved. I have eight or ten more years of college left."

"We are involved. And I have lots of college left, too."

"Yes."

They got into the car and she laid her head in his lap, nestled in, and put her hand on his leg. This time he didn't protest, but quickly turned the key, jammed the accelerator, spun out of the gravel, and leaped onto the road—before anything else could happen.

The eight-inch-thick concrete block walls began to rise. Two masons on scaffolding were building stair-step corners, four blocks high at a time, and stretching taut strings between them, and measuring for openings and offsets. They troweled mud (mortar) onto both long sides of the blocks, "buttered" the end of the previous block, and eased a new block into the mortar so that it almost touched the strings that stretched between the corners, lifting it over the bars that rose from the basement walls. On every third course, the masons inserted galvanized wire ladders into the mortar to reduce wall cracking from expansion and contraction due to moisture and temperature changes. Since the finished surface of the mosque was to be stucco, the masons did not "strike" a concave surface in the mortar joints. They simply scraped off any protruding mortar with their trowels.

Laborers on the floor mixed the mortar, shoveled it into buckets, and dumped it on the masons' mud boards. A forklift raised a pallet of blocks up to where laborers could carry them to the masons.

They placed eight-inch offsets on each side of the two large doorways on the front of the building and beside the windows on the east end and topped them with semi-circular arches in an Islamic style. The opening on the left—the main entrance—was recessed ten feet to allow protection from rain and snow. It opened into a spacious collection area where the men would mingle at Jumu'ah, place their shoes in the bins, and use the restroom and ablution room, prior to entering the prayer hall. On the left was a small wing enclosing the U-shaped fireproof steel stairway to the basement. Women would normally enter the basement and pray there.

The top course all around was U-shaped blocks that would form a beam when filled with concrete. The masons inserted long steel rods vertically through the block wall down to the concrete foundation wall—four feet apart—to meet the rods that extended up from the foundation. They wired these vertical rods to horizontal rods they placed in the U-blocks all the way around the building. Finally, the pumper returned, and the crew filled the cavities around the steel rods with concrete, reinforcing the entire structure.

The next day, the stucco crew arrived. Three men began troweling two coats of cement, a total of one-half inch thick, all over the walls—filling all voids, hiding all blemishes, and smoothing the arches over the doors and windows. They sprayed water on the cement twice a day to keep it from cracking, thoroughly wetted it, and applied the finish coat, doing large expanses with two- and four-foot trowels. This coat was mixed with reddish-brown sand, the color of the Badshahi Mosque in Lahore, the fifth largest in the world.

The following week, Kyle Matthews returned, and he and his men stood on scaffolds at each end to bolt the double-pitched top chord steel truss joists to the walls. The slight pitch on the top chord of the trusses would permit rain to drain down the roof to inner drains on both sides of the building and down interior pipes to the ground. The truck delivered the forty-two-foot-long joists, and the crane swung them to the men on the scaffolding. As they were set, the bridging was installed. Then the men began screwing the corrugated steel decking on top.

The roofing contractor installed an air-barrier film on top of the decking, an air-barrier board on top of that, a vapor retarder above that, a four-inch thickness of high-efficiency rigid foam insulation, a cover board, adhesive, and a waterproof "rubber" membrane on top.

Now the mosque, with strong walls and a roof to shelter the congregants, stood proudly and defiantly by the highway.

CHAPTER 14

THE PAMPHLETS

The meeting in the trophy room started at the usual time—seven-thirty. Amy listened attentively to the disembodied voices as they floated up like candle smoke toward the cathedral ceiling and through the wall to where she sat in the corner of her closet. She could hear her father warmly greet each arrival, and she was sure that Jesse was there too.

"I'll call this meeting to order," Randall said. "I'm glad you all could come." She could picture what he wore at dinner—his white, button-down dress shirt, tie, and button-up cardigan. "Let's start with a prayer." Heads bowed and eyes closed. "Dear Father in heaven, we ask that you be with us tonight and give us some new ways to lance this boil that's growing on our land. We have tried so many ways to break it, but still these strong red walls keep rising from the ground. Help us find the way to destroy it forever. And keep our children away from the moozlim Satan. In the name of our Lord and Savior Jesus Christ, Amen."

The men quietly echoed, "Amen."

"Well, it looks like all they have to do is finish the inside and landscape it, and they can move in," Randall began. "Do you have any ideas, Tom?"

"First, I have to say that I think they've done a professional job so far."

"Yeah—it's going to be a real good-looking mosque, as mosques go," the deep voice joked.

They all groaned.

"Until those walls come a-tumblin' down," Randall added. "It's never too late."

"I can just see Osama bin Laden's brother riding up to it on a camel," another said.

"What about a dome or minarets?" Dirkson asked. "Are they going to have those?"

"No. They couldn't afford all the bells and whistles," Randall explained.

"You know, the outside goes up fast," the builder said, "but they still have a long way to go before they get their CO."

"CO?" Dirkson asked.

"Sorry. Certificate of Occupancy from the inspection department. They have to pass inspections on the plumbing and sprinklers, wiring and heating, and air-conditioning and insulation and drywall. And outside, there's grading and parking-lot striping. And then there's all the handicap stuff—ramps and doors and parking and signs and so on. They've hardly started. It'll be six months to a year before they can move in."

"Well at least we have some time," one voice said.

"But it's going fast," another said. "And these guys seem determined. That time will fly by."

Randall agreed. "I'll talk to Gerald. It seems like there's a lot more we can do to stop them before they get that CO."

The mosque moved forward inexorably, like the turning of the earth. Next came the framing contractor and pallets of steel studs and plates. He began in the basement and worked his way upstairs, cutting up the spaces into rooms, and building stud walls against the concrete block walls to house insulation and electrical wiring and switches. It took two men a week to complete them, with Dan and Lonnie assisting, checking plans and helping snap red chalk lines on the concrete floors to mark the location of the bottom plates, corners, and doorway openings. The basement held the prayer room for women, ablution facilities, and classrooms for children and for instruction in the Qur'an, as well as restrooms, offices, and storage rooms.

The following week, Damon inspected the work but could find no defects. He left no red cards indicating denial of approval and no instructions as to what steps had to be taken to pass a reinspection.

Amy went out in the morning to run some errands, and when she returned and walked into the kitchen, Eunice was waiting for her.

"Amy. Explain these." In her outstretched hand were the pamphlets about Islam.

Amy tilted her head and frowned. "What? What are those?"

Eunice shook them at her. "You know perfectly well what they are. They're all about Islam. Jesse found them on your bed."

Her mind swirled back to when she was reading them. She knew she had hidden them and was trying to remember if she had put any marks in them or left any stickies.

"I don't know anything about them, Mother," she said innocently. Then she scowled and looked at her brother. "Maybe Jesse *put* them on my bed. Did you ask him?"

"You're lying. Tell the truth!" Eunice yelled.

"Do you think I would have left them on my bed? If I was trying to hide them from you, do you think I would have been that careless or stupid—that I would want someone to find them?"

Moving past Eunice, she turned the corner toward the kitchen. "What was he doing in my room, anyway? He must have gone in there to plant these on my bed."

"Stop lying! Stop it!"

She splayed her arms in supplication. "I'm not lying. I don't know anything about them. Ask Jesse about them." She stalked into the kitchen.

Eunice took a step toward her. "Come back here, Amy. Right now."

"If he said he found them on my bed, he's lying," Amy spoke over her shoulder.

"This is not the end of this. When your father sees these, you'll be in big trouble."

"Tell that to Jesse!"

"You better go up and pray about this, Amy. Pray!"

Amy stomped up the stairs to her room and messaged Atif, "They found pamphlets. Trouble. LU."

That was the first time she had ever said it, and she meant it. "A B w U," he replied.

Randall arrived home from a stockholders meeting at the bank shortly after noon in his business attire. Eunice told him in the kitchen while she patted hamburger meat for lunch.

"You're not going to want to hear this."

He looked at her. "What?"

"Jesse found six brochures about Islam on Amy's bed."

"What?"

He laid his notebook on the table.

"They tell all about Muhammad and Islam and terrorism and God. They even had the audacity to do one about Jesus."

"Did you question Amy about them?"

"Yes, I asked her about them. She denies knowing anything about them. She says Jesse must have planted them there." She put the six patties in the pan and turned up the flame.

"She's lying," he growled and sat down at the kitchenette table.

"I'm sure she is."

"But where do you think she got them?"

She shrugged. "I don't know. Maybe from her Muslim friend at school." The hamburgers began to sizzle.

"She has a moozlim friend?" he said, frowning.

"Yes."

"Do you know her name?"

"No, but I think she's a senior."

He turned his head sideways. "Maybe we'll see her and her family at graduation."

"That's Tuesday morning."

"You know, I hate to think about it, but it's possible her father is Ahmed Bhati. There aren't that many moozlims around here."

Now the aroma of browning meat filled the air, and the hot grease sputtered. He watched Eunice go to the cabinet, take out plates, and walk into the pantry.

"I still wonder where she goes on Saturdays when she says she's shopping," Eunice said as she came out carrying a package of buns. "She hardly ever buys anything."

"Jesse has been following her, and she always goes to the mall, but he never can keep up with her."

"She just vanishes," she said. "Well, call her for lunch, and see if you can get at the truth."

He rose, went into the hall, and shouted, "Amy. Lunch," and then called up the back stairs for Jesse.

Eunice put the plate full of sandwiches on the narrow table in the kitchen, plus plates, glasses, soft drinks, a bag of chips, a plate of baby carrots and broccoli florets, onion dip, and napkins. Jesse and Amy loaded their plates, put ice in their glasses from the dispenser in the refrigerator door. They single-filed to the table next to the wall of the trophy room. Eunice and Randall took their places at the ends of the table, and the children sat on the side.

Randall led them in a brief prayer, took a big bite, and began. "What's this about pamphlets, Amy?"

She shrugged and raised her eyebrows. "I don't know anything about it. Ask Jesse."

"OK, Jesse. What's the story?"

He looked sideways at his sister. "I found six pamphlets on Islam on Amy's bed."

"What?" Amy put down her burger. "He's lying. He did not find any pamphlets on my bed, unless he put them there."

"OK, OK. They weren't on her bed," he admitted. "They were in her desk drawer."

She sat back and put her hands on the sides of her chair. "What? You were going through my desk drawers?"

"Yes."

"You know you're not allowed to go through my stuff."

"Oh, but Amy," Jesse said. "You've been acting strange lately. We don't know what you're up to."

"Daddy. Did you tell him he could go through my drawers?"

Randall looked straight through her. "Like he said, Amy. We want to find out what you're up to—breaking up with Stewart, disappearing on Saturdays at the mall, making friends with a moozlim girl at school. What is going on? Do you have a moozlim boyfriend?"

She wagged her head. "No, of course not. Where would you get that idea? And Jesse is lying about finding pamphlets in my desk, unless he put them there."

"I am not lying, sister. You are. I even found some yellow stickies in those pamphlets, just like you put in things you read."

She gave him a cruel look. "Oh, that's some powerful evidence. Everyone uses yellow stickies, dumbo. You probably put them in yourself just to try to trap me."

"You know I love you, Amy, and we want what is best for you." Amy grimaced. She hated when he acted like he was an adult and she was a child.

Eunice piled on. "We all love you."

"Humph," Randall snorted. "Well, this is going nowhere. Just remember, Amy, we're watching you, and so is God."

Gazing up at him like she was his little girl again, she said, "B-but you know I believe in Jesus Christ as my Lord and Savior. You know that."

"I'm not sure we do, Amy," Randall said.

She looked at each of them, put her face in her hands, and began sobbing, her whole body shaking.

"We need to pray about this in church tomorrow," Eunice added.

That night, when they were getting ready for bed, Eunice told Randall, "Maybe we need to get her away from here—get her mind on other things."

"What—like to a camp or something?"

"Yes, but I think that would be too short. She needs to be away from this boy for a long time."

"You think it is a boy, then?" he asked.

"It has to be, the way she's acting. And I think it's a Muslim boy."

"God save us!" he said, pulling his pajama top over his head.

"It's probably too late for her to become a camp counselor somewhere—camps are probably staffed up."

"Maybe we could have her volunteer for a work camp," he suggested, "building houses somewhere."

"That's an idea. I think Habitat's still working along the Gulf Coast and in Haiti."

He took off his watch and put it on the end table. "But I don't think we want her around all those black people, do we? That would be asking for trouble. We don't know what might happen to her in either of those places. Why don't we ask around at church tomorrow about what mission trips are available and see what she might be interested in."

They pulled into the God's Word Church, which was on a highway north of Chelmsford. Everyone was quiet.

"Let's see if we can find some divine guidance today everyone," Randall said, "and our way to the light."

It was not a mega-church, but several greeters met them with enthusiastic smiles and said, "Welcome to God's Word." The band—guitars, drums, digital piano, and bass—was playing up-beat Christian praise music. Several hundred people—nearly all white, including many families with children—filled half the pews in the sanctuary. In the center of the room on the wall behind the pulpit and stage was a large empty cross signifying that Christ rose from the dead. An altar beneath it contained candles and flowers.

A young couple began the service by singing "With all I am (Jesus I believe in you…I will worship you …)"

The pastor based the sermon on Mark 16:9–16: after Jesus rose from the dead, he appeared to Mary Magdalene and two others, but when they told the other disciples about it, they wouldn't believe them. So Jesus went to the eleven as they ate and upbraided them for their unbelief, and afterward said to them, "Go ye into all the world, and preach the gospel to every creature. He that believeth and is baptized shall be saved; but he that believeth not shall be damned."

During the closing prayer, Amy thought of Atif and began sobbing. He couldn't be damned!

She was sitting next to Jesse, and when he noticed her crying, he stiffened, drew his chin in, and looked sideways at her, puzzled and embarrassed.

In addition to the regular offering, there was a special collection for the church missions, and anyone who felt a calling to serve God on a mission trip was asked to please go to the Hope Room after the service.

The congregation rose and sang an old hymn to a swing beat: "Jesus, Savior, pilot me, Over life's tempestuous sea…"

After the benediction, the band resumed its joyous music, and they made their way with the others to the narthex.

"Why were you crying in there, Amy?" Eunice asked as they left the sanctuary.

"Nothing," she said, still sniffling.

"She was feeling guilty about lying," Jesse explained.

She turned her head toward him. "I was not, you insect. But I bet you were."

Randall asked her, "How would you like to hear about the mission trips they're putting together? That might be a good adventure for you this summer, and you don't have anything else planned anyway, do you?"

"I don't think I'd be interested. I'm planning to volunteer to help homeless people in Washington or Baltimore or work in a soup kitchen. Or help out on the farm. And I'd like to take some tennis lessons."

"Well, I'd like to hear about these trips," Jesse opined. "And I'd also like to go on one of those canoe trips up in Minnesota or Canada."

"Why don't you go on all of them," Amy suggested.

They walked down the hall to the Hope Room and went in. Only a few families joined them, since most people had already made plans for the summer. The committee chair had a laptop connected to a projector and screen and scrolled through a website while she spoke. She showed them what trips were still available for this summer for teens, adults, and families. The trips were one or two weeks long, and expenses and airfare were paid by the participants. At this late date, there probably wouldn't be time for local fundraising. There were still some openings for Africa, Asia, and South America, and for the United States, where the work included talking to homeless people and helping in soup kitchens, but there was nothing in Washington or Baltimore.

Amy listened with half an ear while glancing out the window and daydreaming about Atif.

"Is there anything you might be interested in?" Randall asked. "There are lots of poor souls out there who need your help."

"Not really. I plan to help poor people in Washington or Baltimore, but I don't see the need to go overseas or to Chicago or Philadelphia. I'm really not interested in traveling out of the country or even to those cities. And anyway, these trips are really short. They might be too short to do much good."

"Uh-huh," Randall said, looking at Eunice, convinced now that their daughter was seeing a Muslim boy.

CHAPTER 15

GRADUATION

Graduation was held on Tuesday at ten o'clock in the University of Maryland basketball arena, where many high schools held their ceremonies. Randall navigated the dark blue Cadillac Escalade SUV through the gaggle of cars into the parking lot, and he, Eunice, Amy, and Jesse walked through the crowd toward the entrance, Amy in her flowing black gown, carrying her flat black hat.

She was not excited in the least about graduating. It was just one small step into her future. Her 4.3 grade point average (higher than 4.0 because of advanced placement classes) was not high enough for valedictorian or salutatorian, so she would receive no special accolade, but Randall and Eunice were proud of her. She was pleased that her GPA was high enough to gain admission to the university in College Park.

Amy kept looking around for Nadira, who also was graduating. She had messaged Atif, and he and his parents would be attending, in spite of his father's busy schedule. With so many people—students, family, and friends—they might not meet at all.

"Don't even look at me," she messaged. "And tell Nadira not to look at me. We can't let them know we know each other! LU."

Amy separated from her family and followed the students into the practice gym to line up in alphabetical order. They would have to be seated in rows facing the stage in the same order. Everyone had to be in exactly the right position so that when the principal called his or her name on stage—reading from the diploma—he would hand it to the correct student. There could no mistakes.

Audience seating was first come first served in the cavernous basketball arena, which seated nearly eighteen thousand people. Amy's high school crowd filled less than a quarter of the seats. People entered at the lower levels along the sides to get the best views. Randall, Eunice, and Jesse sat high in the center to get a bird's-eye view of the students entering in their black gowns and flat black mortarboard caps with gold tassels, sitting in lines of folding chairs on the brown varnished wooden floor. Randall carried his camera with telephoto lens.

The small high school orchestra on the floor in the rear played inspirational music and some songs expressing "farewell," which all students would be saying to friends as they scattered into the world of work and college. From in front of the stage, the choir sang "We've Only Just Begun," and "You Are the Wind Beneath My Wings." The public-address system and arena distorted the sounds with hollow echoes.

The school superintendent introduced three rows of dignitaries on the stage, the salutatorian and valedictorian gave inspirational speeches to cheering students, and then rows began standing and forming lines that circled down the center aisle, up onto the stage, and back around to their seats.

Randall focused his video camera on the stage and waited. "Nadira Bhati," the principal's voice thundered over the speakers, and Randall pushed the button as the principal handed Nadira her diploma. Then he noticed the direction she was sending her excited smile as she crossed the stage to go to her seat, and he followed it to the left side of the arena, about half-way down. He began scanning the crowd with his camera, but was unable to identify his nemesis, Ahmed, and his family. This he would try to do at home.

"Amy Breckenridge," vibrated the loudspeaker, and Randall quickly swung his camera back to the stage.

After the ceremony, he, Eunice, and Jesse went to the discharge point for the students outside the stadium tunnel. A crowd had gathered to meet the graduates.

Randall perused the faces until he found Ahmed. He told Eunice and Jesse, "Wait here," and moved closer to his quarry. *There he is,* he thought, *the boy.* Then he raised his camera, focused it, and began recording the Bhatis, including their son. When his line of sight was blocked by the crowd, he abandoned the effort and returned to Eunice and Jesse to wait for Amy.

While waiting, he reviewed the pictures until he found a clear one of Atif. He showed it to Eunice. "There he is—that Bhati boy. It could be him."

Amy emerged from the stadium tunnel with Nadira. They both were carrying their caps, and searching for their families. Nadira found hers, and Amy glanced at them, but tore her eyes away. Then she waved above the crowd, hoping to find her own family. Jesse saw her and waved back, and she returned the wave and began moving through the people toward them.

They smiled and congratulated her, but then Randall said, "Amy. Look at this picture. Do you know this person?"

Amy stared at Atif's image blindly and looked at her dad. "No. Sorry. I've never seen him."

Jesse said, "Sure you have. It's Nadira's brother."

"Oh. Is that who it is? Interesting. No, I've never seen him before."

He looked at her suspiciously. "Lying's a sin, Amy."

"Then you shouldn't do it, little brother."

"Well, let's go eat and celebrate this occasion," Randall gushed. "We're very proud of your accomplishment, Amy."

"And your 4.3 GPA," Eunice added. Jesse's was 3.4, but this wasn't the time to bring up that.

That night, Randall and Eunice consulted in their bedroom. "He's the one. I'm sure of it," Randall said shaking his head. "Ahmed's son!"

She raised her right index finger to her mouth. "Shh. Not so loud. She might hear. But I think you're right. And Jesse said he heard that Nadira's brother was going to Maryland, and was pre-med, like he's following his father's career."

"But we can't have her hooking up with moozlims. She might become one herself. We've got to stop this—break it up!"

Eunice began removing her makeup at the vanity while Randall gazed out the window past the portico to the street. "That's why she broke up with Stewart," Eunice said. "That's why she wanted to be free to date while they were in college. And that's why she's not interested in going on a missionary trip. It has nothing to do with her not wanting to travel. She wants to stay here to be near that boy!"

Randall turned toward her. "You're right. But what are we going to do? We've got to get her away from here—away from him—until she finds someone else to love or this boy loses interest."

"Where can we send her to keep her away permanently?"

"Well, we could send her to college out of the area, instead of her going to Maryland," Randall said, walking over to his chair. "We've got to get her away from that school!"

"And it's got to be far enough away to keep her from coming back—out of state."

"We can take away her car," he suggested as he sat down.

"She won't need that at college."

"And I think it needs to be a Christian college," he said, "to get her back on the path." He began untying his shoes.

"But what do we do about this summer?" she asked "We have to get her away from here right now."

"Yes," he said as he pulled off a shoe. "Well maybe we can find a school with a summer session. Let's check the Internet. Then tomorrow I can make some calls to get her in."

That night she messaged Atif. "Something's going on. Dad took photo of U. Asked if I knew U. I said no. They don't believe me. Don't know what will happen. LU."

The next afternoon, Eunice called up the stairs for Amy to come down. "We need to have a meeting with you."

Amy descended the stairs, and Eunice added sternly, "In the trophy room."

Amy was anxious. *What is this about?*

"Amy. Sit down," Randall ordered. Amy sat on the brown leather sofa while her parents hovered. "Amy, we've decided that you will begin Steurer University immediately, in their summer session."

"What? I'm going to Maryland."

"No. We've decided you'd do better at a Christian college."

"What? Why?"

"You seem to be going astray, Amy—getting interested in Islam, and in that Bhati boy."

She scowled. "I am not."

"We're not interested in hearing you lie anymore, Amy," Eunice said.

"I'm not lying. What evidence do you have that I'm interested in a…Bhati boy?"

Randall glared at her. "It's decided, Amy. You're going. We're taking you tomorrow. They've already started classes—yesterday—so we have to enroll you immediately—as soon as we get there. You can pack tonight."

"Tonight?! Where is it?"

"Steurer, West Virginia."

"Where's that?"

"It's in the southern part of the state. Beautiful country. You'll love it."

"What about my car?"

"You won't need a car," Eunice said.

She stomped her foot. "I'm not going."

"You are still our daughter, Amy, and you are a minor, and you will do what we tell you to do," Randall said in his military voice. "And we say you are going, and that's the end of it."

"And what if I refuse?"

He crossed his arms and jutted out his chin. "We take your car and ground you. You will not leave this house for any reason until you are eighteen—in July. At that time you will be on your own. You will have to move out, and we will no longer support you, and we will write you out of our will."

She choked and started to cry.

"You have a wonderful life ahead of you, Amy," Eunice added. "But we cannot let you destroy it by getting involved with a…an infidel!"

Amy messaged Atif. "They're making me go to Steurer U., a Christian college! I leave tomorrow for four yrs. It's in south WV, six hrs away, and I won't have car! If I don't go, I'm grounded to the hse with no car until eighteen in July, then move out with no money! ☹ LU."

"Don't lose hope. LU." That was the first time he had said it. She was thrilled, but terrified.

She found the Steurer website and began to read. There were so many rules. *It's a prison*, she thought.

Then she found the packing list, and ran to the top of the stairs, and screamed, "Mother!"

Eunice came to the bottom, and Amy said, "I'm not going. I can't possibly get this together tonight."

"I'll help you. We'll do the best we can. And we'll bring you anything else you need later."

"I don't even know what courses to take."

"Well, you know what you were going to take at Maryland. We'll just find similar courses, plus some Bible courses."

She rode in the middle-row bucket seat behind Randall. The third row and seat beside her were folded down and piled high with baggage, TV, DVD, stereo, laptop, desk lamp, pillow, bedding, laundry basket, backpack, trash can, cleaning supplies, desk supplies, flashlight, and a hundred other essentials.

"This is not happening. You can't do this to me," she said as they turned from the Washington beltway onto Route 66 West.

Randall glanced into the rearview mirror. "Accept it, Amy. Just relax and accept it."

As they turned onto Route 81 for the long haul south, she sobbed, "Why are you doing this?"

"Someday you'll thank us," Eunice said. "We are saving your immortal soul, Amy. You have sinned."

She slept most of the way. She didn't dare message Atif. If they caught her, they'd take away her phone. She felt like Joan of Arc being marched to her pyre, but she decided to go along with their plan until they left the school, and then message Atif and decide what to do.

CHAPTER 16

STEURER UNIVERSITY

R andall pulled into the lot, parked, walked up the steps past the Greek columns into the administration building, and found the registrar's office. A middle-aged woman with medium blond hair asked if she could help them. Randall said that their daughter would like to register as a residential student starting with the summer session, and that he had called earlier to make the arrangements.

"Amy Breckenridge?" the woman asked.

"Yes," Amy said, looking crushed in her wrinkled blouse, jeans, sandals, and hair that screamed for a brush.

"You're very late to register, but you're lucky: we still have a room in Bridge Hall. You'll be sharing it with Amanda Hipkins, Amy. She happens to be the prayer leader for that suite. She'll lead your prayer meetings three times a week. They're compulsory—part of the Steurer program to assist students. Here's a packet of all the information you need to know."

Randall's and Eunice's heads were bobbing down and up like apples in a tub of water.

Mrs. Hopper assured Amy, "Amanda's a really nice girl from Wheeling. Her father's a minister."

Randall smiled. "That sounds good."

"Your other suitemates are from all over the state—Elkins, Morgantown, Charleston, and somewhere east, I think. How does that sound, Amy?"

"Fine." *Just let it be over.*

Amy registered for freshman English and math, Randall wrote a large check, and Mrs. Hopper asked a student assistant to take them to Bridge Hall. They began unloading, and soon the car was swarmed with students giving them a hand.

Her suite had a small living room with two love seats and two lounge chairs and a TV in the corner. Behind them on one wall was a counter with a bar sink, mini-refrigerator and microwave. There were three bedrooms, each with two single beds, two bureaus, two desks, and a closet. They all shared one bathroom with a shower, two toilet stalls, and a double-sink vanity. In Amy's room she noticed that there was no stereo or TV, and on the wall was a large picture of Jesus with a beard and flowing brown hair.

Three of her suitemates were watching a soap opera on TV when she arrived and were interested in meeting her.

"I'm Brittany. I'm from Morgantown," a girl with a curly brown pixie said. "What's your name?" Each sentence ascended at the end.

"Amy Breckenridge. I live near DC."

Brittany looked at her with interest. "Oh, that's a long way."

"Yes. My parents really liked this school. I hope I do."

"And I'm Ashlee, from Charleston," she drawled. "Nice to meet you." She had reddish-brown hair with a top knot.

Amy turned to the next girl. "I'm Amanda," said a short girl with brown pigtails. "I'm your roommate and the group prayer leader. I'm from Wheeling."

"Nice to meet you all."

"Not all. I think Emily's under a tree somewhere, studying. She's from Elkins, and she wants to graduate in three years. And Fran is probably out running."

Randall poked his head in. "Well, it looks like you're in good hands. We're gonna take off now. Be good, and stay close to the Lord."

"Yes, Daddy," she chirped. *You bastard.*

Atif was distraught. He hadn't heard from Amy all day long. Where was she? What was happening? He knew that she was on her way to some small Bible college in West Virginia, far away from Washington. He wondered how they could ever be together.

Salma sensed that something was wrong when he walked into the kitchen from his car on the way to the basement. "Are you all right?" she asked at dinner. "You seem—nervous...and distracted."

"Yes, of course I'm all right."

Nadira saw him too and knew that he wasn't, but said nothing. After dinner, in privacy, Atif told her all about it.

"Oh, poor Amy."

Amy and Amanda went into their room.

"Dinner's at five," Amanda said.

"I'd like to take a nap before that. It was a long trip."

"Sure. I'll wake you up. Then after dinner, we'll have our prayer meeting here. And tomorrow's Friday, so we have convocation in the chapel at ten o'clock. And I guess they gave you your class schedule."

"Yes."

As soon as her parents left, Amy closed the door, curled up on her bed, and pulled out her phone.

There was a gentle rap, the door opened before Amy could say anything, and Amanda stuck her head in. "Excuse me, Amy," she said in an unctuous voice. "It's school policy to leave our doors open six inches."

"What? Oh. OK." She was stunned. *No privacy.*

She had wanted to call Atif and talk to him, but now she thought she better just text him. She would call him later, when she was outside.

She wrote, "A. I'm here. Mom, Dad left. Met suitemates. Going to dinner soon. Then prayer meeting with suitemates. Miss you. LU, XXOO ~A." and pushed "Send."

In less than a minute, she received, "Miss U 2, so much. Think about you! LU2, but can't drive there & back. Too far! Too much time. They'd suspect. ~Dr. B."

"Dr. B! Don't worry. I'll get back somehow. I won't be here long. ~A LU."

Atif blinked back a tear when he read that. "LU." he responded.

That was Amy's challenge: how to get back.

She lay back, closed her eyes, and slept until she heard Amanda's voice—sweet, pious, manipulative: "Dinner, Amy."

"OK. Thanks."

She stood up, walked to the bathroom, splashed some water on her face, ran a brush through her hair, straightened her blouse, went into the living room, and told Amanda, "I'm ready."

Amanda scanned her outfit. "Oh, wait. I'm sorry. We have to wear shoes to the dining hall. We can't wear sandals. Do you have some shoes you can wear? The jeans are OK, I think—if they're not too tight."

Oh, my God, Amy thought. "Are running shoes OK?"

"That'll be fine."

"Just a minute…" She took her shoes and athletic socks out of her duffel bag and sat on her bed. "What, they don't want boys looking at my toes?"

"That's right. Some boys might get the wrong idea."

Amy burst out laughing as she pulled on a sock.

Amanda turned her head and scowled. "You don't know boys."

"Oh, yes I do."

Amanda continued to frown. "Some of them are bad."

They proceeded across the quadrangle to the building containing the dining hall and passed some other students.

"I'm sorry I laughed," Amy said. "I just think most boys look at your figure, not your toes."

"If you have a figure like yours, maybe."

"Thanks for the compliment. But I'm not much interested in boys, anyway."

Amanda stared at her curiously. "Oh? All girls are interested in boys," she said definitively. "You must have one back home then."

This was getting too personal. "Yes, but we broke up. He's going to go to college in Wisconsin, and we decided to set each other free so we could date other people and find out if we were really right for each other."

Amanda squinted suspiciously. "I've always thought that if you get a good one, you should hang onto him, but that's just me. Say, tell me why you came here, if you don't mind me asking."

"My parents wanted a Christian college."

"But why did you matriculate for the summer session?"

Oh. You know big words. "Well, my summer job fell through, and I didn't have anything to do, so they suggested I start now." *That's plausible.*

"But you hadn't applied here last winter or in the spring."

"No, I couldn't make up my mind what school I would like best. We kept looking at catalogs."

"But admissions said your father just called up and told them he wanted you to start here right away and money was no problem and that your grades were straight A."

Amy was about to scream, *Shut up. It's none of your damned business*, but said, "That's what happens when you let things go to the last minute."

They bounced up the outside stairs, with Amanda's pigtails swinging back and forth.

They passed some boys, who gave Amy a quick appraisal. One even turned to get a rear view. She walked to the serving line where they picked up their trays. Amy glanced around. There was a salad bar, a hot-food section with two older women servers—one black and one white—a hot sandwich bar with hamburgers, a dessert bar, soft-serve machine with toppings, a soda machine, and a cooler with milk and bottled drinks. The aroma of meat made Amy suddenly hungry. She picked up a salad, hamburger, and drink and went to the seating area, which had long tables decorated with vases of plastic flowers. She aimed for a table with a group of students, so she might not have to sit with Amanda.

Brittany, the girl from Morgantown with the curly pixie, caught her eye first, and she joined her and Ashlee, the girl from Charleston with the topknot, and two boys. One boy was slender and the other heavy, and both were muscular. They rose to meet her. "I'm James," said the thin one. "Andrew," said the other.

"I'm Amy."

"She's from DC," Ashlee said with her slow drawl.

"What brings you way down here?" James asked.

Amy put on a serious expression. "My parents wanted me to go to a Christian college, and they liked this one."

"Do you do everything your parents like?" Brittany asked.

"Sure. Don't you?" Amy said slyly.

Brittany grinned. "You bet. And everything they don't like, too."

The boys broke up, and students from other tables looked over at them.

"Sh-sh-sh-sh," Ashlee whispered. "You'll get Amanda over here, and we wouldn't want that."

Amy looked over her shoulder toward Amanda, who was sitting with Emily. "No?"

"Uh-uh. She'd have us all praying for each other's virginity!" Ashlee quipped.

The boys guffawed.

"Ashlee!" Brittany whispered with a smile. "You'll get us thrown out, honey."

"That wouldn't be all bad, now would it?"

Amy was wondering if this was the fast crowd and if she really belonged. She didn't think so. But she was interested in exploring the possibility of expulsion. She also wondered why these other girls were here. Were they being punished too? Not Emily. She was trying to graduate in three years.

CHAPTER 17

SIN

In the dorm before the prayer meeting, Amy sat on one of the sofas in the living room, Amanda in one of the lounge chairs, and Emily in the other.

Amanda was asking Amy what her father did when Brittany and Ashlee stumbled in laughing, Ashlee saying, "That James is a hunk."

"I think I'd like to try Andrew first."

Amanda looked up and snapped, "Girls! That's not permitted here. You know that."

Amy noticed Emily frowning.

"Oh, yes. We can only hold hands," Brittany sang, looking at Ashlee mischievously.

They plopped down on the other sofa.

Amanda addressed them: "Amy was just telling us what her father does."

"And what's that?" Ashlee asked with a smirk.

"He's a farmer. He has a dairy farm and a dairy and store."

No one was impressed.

Emily asked, "How many cows?"

"About seven hundred."

"Oh. That's one of those factory farms," Emily said.

"Not really. The biggest dairy farm in the country has thirty thousand cows."

Her eyes grew. "Thirty thousand! Amazing."

"Does he give them drugs to make them give more milk?" Brittany asked.

"No. We don't do that."

A tall girl with long blond hair trotted in wearing running shorts, a T-shirt, and Sauconies.

"You're late, Fran," Amanda said.

"Sorry."

Brittany edged away from her. "Ew. You're sweaty. You stink."

Fran sat next to Amy.

"You know, Amy, one thing you're going to have to watch out for here is the random drug testing," said Brittany.

"Oh, I'm not into drugs."

Ashlee breezed in. "But I heard that they're going to start random pregnancy testing next."

Brittany broke into laughter and asked, "So we'll know when to get a procedure?"

"And we must be careful, girls," Ashlee admonished. "You know half of American babies are born to unwed mothers."

Brittany rolled her eyes. "Now there's the road to instant poverty!"

Amanda frowned. "Girls! You are being very bad."

Pairs broke into separate conversations, and Fran engaged Amy. "I'm Fran, by the way."

"Hi. I'm Amy. I run too. How far did you go?"

"Oh, six or seven miles—I ran for about an hour. There are some nice trails around here through the woods. But it's hillier than where I'm from."

"Where's that?" Amy asked.

"Charles Town."

Amy leaned closer. "That's not far from where I'm from—near DC—north of the beltway—in White County. It's pretty flat there, too."

"So why are you here?" Fran asked. "Did you do something bad, too?"

"No. I just didn't get together my plans for the summer quickly enough," Amy said, "so my parents talked me into starting school. What about you?"

"My mother wanted to get me out of town so she could make time with her boyfriend, and she thought Steurer would be a good babysitter for me."

"Oh. Did your parents split?"

She nodded. "Yeah, like half the couples in the country."

"I'm sorry for them," Amanda interjected. "Divorce is a mortal sin."

Fran rolled her eyes, and Ashlee jumped in from her conversation. "Who's divorced?"

"Fran's parents."

"Mine too," Ashlee said. "So I guess they're all going to hell forever. Wow. Wait till I tell them."

Fran smiled at her. "I'm not worried. My dad's a lawyer. He'll argue his way out of it at the pearly gates."

"Sin is not to be taken lightly," Amanda said, shaking her head and making her pigtails bounce. "We might as well start the meeting. Turn off your cellphones, please." She waited a minute, and then said, "Let us pray." She closed her eyes and knitted her fingers, and the others followed, except for Ashlee and Brittany. "Dear Lord. Forgive us our sins. We know we are sinners. We can't help it. From Adam and Eve's original sin in the garden all the way to us. People have always been bad. We know that even if we try hard, we just can't help ourselves. Help us to know that when we believe in the salvation of Your Son our Lord Jesus Christ that through him we will be forgiven, because He died for our sins. Help us to give ourselves to Jesus and not to any mortal being. In Jesus Christ our Lord's name, we pray. Amen."

The girls mouthed "Amen" as quietly as they could, so they wouldn't be heard.

"Tonight I thought we would talk about the Ten Commandments," Amanda continued. "To break them is to commit a serious sin. I'll read them, and then we can discuss them. They're in Exodus 20." She went to the bookmark in her old black King James Bible.

"The first one is, 'Thou shalt have no other gods before me.' What does that mean?"

Some of the girls looked to the side, others into their laps.

"Come on, girls. It means we can't be like Hindus, you know, with all their gods, or those African tribes, with all theirs..."

There's only one god. That's like Islam...and Judaism, Amy thought.

"OK, the second one is, 'Thou shalt not make unto thee any graven image, or any likeness of anything that is in heaven above, or that is in the earth beneath, or that is in the water under the earth. Thou shalt not bow down thyself to them, nor serve them: for I, the Lord thy God, am a jealous God.'" She looked up and around. "So do we ever make graven images—idols that we worship?"

Emily suggested, "We take lots of photos." Instantly, the others hated her for speaking up.

Amanda brightened. "Do we ever worship them?"

"I guess lots of people worship rock stars and their pictures."

No one else contributed.

"OK. Let's go on. The next one is, 'Thou shalt not take the name of the Lord thy God in vain.'"

"No one ever does that," Fran joked.

"No one but everyone," Ashlee said.

"Going on. 'Remember the Sabbath, to keep it holy. Six days shalt thou labor, and do all thy work: But the seventh day is the Sabbath of the Lord thy God: in it thou shalt not do any work.'"

Fran smiled. "I guess all those sinners at the mall are going to hell then—all those people working and shopping on Sunday."

Brittany looked around at all the girls. "Just the clerks. Shopping's fun, not work."

"Seriously, girls," Amanda chided. "The clerks wouldn't have to work if we weren't shopping."

Fran looked at her. "So we're responsible for their eternal damnation? God."

Emily shook her head disapprovingly.

Amanda looked at her Bible without commenting. "The next one is, 'Honor thy father and thy mother.'"

"Shit," Ashlee cursed. "My father cheated on my mother, and I still have to honor him? The hell with that."

"Please watch your language, Ashlee," Amanda cautioned.

Fran rolled her eyes. "And my mom cheated on my dad. Am I supposed to honor her?"

Amy yearned to talk about her parents, but couldn't. She would have to bring in Atif, and she didn't want to do that.

Amanda ignored them and went on. "OK. This one's easier, 'Thou shalt not kill.'"

"What about in war?" Amy asked. The other girls looked at her, surprised that she had joined in.

"War's OK," Fran explained with a grin. "We can kill as many people and kids and mothers as we want to in war. That's no sin."

"We're talking about personal sins here," Amanda said, "not errors that countries might make."

"What about killing in self-defense? That can't be a sin, can it?" Emily asked.

Amanda shook her head. "I don't suppose so. Here's the next one. 'Thou shalt not commit adultery.'"

Ashlee exclaimed, "God! That'll get my dad the fire and brimstone."

"And my mom," Fran added.

Brittany chimed in, "And millions of other people."

Amanda poked at the Bible with her finger. "Yes, if they haven't accepted Jesus as their personal savior and begged Him for forgiveness. Let's go on. 'Thou shalt not steal.'"

"Like Wall Street bankers?" Emily asked.

Amanda wanted this discussion to end. "And 'Thou shalt not bear false witness against thy neighbor.'"

Fran smiled. "Yeah, you can't lie about them in court, or the judge'll get you."

Amanda sighed in relief. "The last one is, 'Thou shalt not covet thy neighbor's house, nor his wife, nor his manservant, nor his maidservant, nor his ox, nor his ass, nor any thing that is thy neighbor's.'"

"But keeping up with the Joneses is the American way," Brittany argued, running her fingers through her short curls. "That's what makes the economy work."

Fran grinned. "And women are always coveting their neighbor's ass, especially if he has a good one. That's why there's so much running around."

Ashlee gasped in mock horror. "Fran. It's talking about his donkey, not his ass."

"Oh. His donkey! Well I know lots of girls who covet their neighbor's donkey, too."

The girls broke up.

"Fran!" Amanda shouted. "You're being obscene and sacrilegious. That's a sin, too. Oh, get thee behind us, Satan." She paused a moment as the giggling dwindled. "We will now recite the Lord's Prayer." *They won't dare besmirch that.* "Let us pray together. 'Our Father, which art in heaven. Hallowed be thy Name. Thy Kingdom come. Thy will be done in earth, as it is in heaven. Give us this day our daily bread. And forgive us our debts, as we forgive our debtors. And lead us not into temptation, but deliver us from evil. For thine is the kingdom, the power, and the glory, forever and ever. Amen.'"

"Amen," they repeated.

Amanda rose, shook her head at the girls in exasperation, which made her pigtails twitch, and said, "Next time we will be serious, girls, or there will be consequences."

"Oh, no," Ashlee cried in faux fear.

"Someday God will bring another flood," Amanda said, "and cleanse His earth again of all this sin just like when Noah built his ark."

"You mean like when global warming melts all the ice and the oceans flood the cities?" Ashlee asked.

Brittany sneered. "We'll be long gone before that happens."

The girls dissolved into their rooms, except for Amy. She slipped outside and around a corner into a shadow and speed-dialed Atif.

CHAPTER 18
OPTIONS

"Atif?"

"Amy?"

She leaned against the brick wall of her dorm. "Oh, I miss you so much. And I'm so far away. But I want to hold you and kiss you and kiss you."

He was in his bedroom reading at his desk, and he put down the book and rubbed his eyes. "I miss you, too, Amy. I think of you all the time. When can we be together again?"

"I don't know," she said. "I have to think everything through. But I will be back soon. They can't do this to me. They can't! And they can't do it to us."

She told him about the trip and registration and the girls and dinner and the prayer meeting, and about discussing the Ten Commandments.

"The Qur'an includes most of this guidance by Moses, but it doesn't say 'Thou shalt not kill.' It says we should 'not take life—which Allāh has made sacred—except for just cause.'"

"I remember. We talked about that at McDonald's. But remind me."

"Homicide by an individual is a sin because life is sacred. But capital punishment through due process of law, or life taken in a just war that is decided by a lawful government—they are permitted, as is life taken in self-defense."

"Really, most Christians believe that too."

"Oh, yes, and it also doesn't say we have to rest on Sunday. But it does say we have to go to Friday prayers—it's obligatory."

She lifted her right foot and placed it on the wall, bending her knee. "Do you believe that God created the heavens and earth in six days?"

He leaned forward. "Amy, a day is a revolution of the earth. Does it make sense that Allāh related His creation of all the stars in the universe to the turning of our small planet earth? Maybe He did, but I think these words of Moses were written by a poet."

"Do you believe that man is sinful?" she asked.

"Do we believe in original sin passed on to us from Adam and Eve?"

"Yes," she said. "We believe in it, and that all people are sinful. And that Christ was crucified for our sins, and the only way to be saved from hell is to be saved by Jesus Christ and do good works. Jesus died for our sins, Atif, and John said, 'For God so loved the world, that he gave his only begotten Son, that whosoever believeth in him should not perish, but have everlasting life…'"

"You said that before."

"'…For God sent not his Son into the world to condemn the world; but that the world through him might be saved. He that believeth on him is not condemned, but he that believeth not is condemned already, because he hath not believed in the name of the only begotten Son of God.'"

He sat up straighter. "Wow. You know that by heart.…But no. We don't believe in the original sin. We believe that people are originally good. Satan seeks to misguide them, as he misled Adam and Eve. But Allāh forgave them—Allāh will forgive us too if we sincerely regret what we've done, resolve not to do it again, and make amends for it. But anyway, Allāh removed Adam and Eve from Paradise and made them live on earth, but he wasn't blaming them or punishing them."

"That's different from what we believe."

"Uh-huh. And their descendants will do good things and bad things throughout their lives, and Allāh will judge them and decide whether they will go to heaven or hell. They will be judged only on what they themselves do—not for what Adam and Eve or other people have done. That wouldn't be just…"

She leaned the other foot against the wall and switched ears.

"…And people have free will, although Allāh knows what they will do. They can't be saved just by saying they believe in Jesus—we don't believe Allāh had any children—and we don't believe that Jesus died for our sins."

Amy added, "We also believe in the second coming of Christ. You don't believe that, do you?"

"Yes, actually, we do, but I'm sure it's different."

Amy said, "We believe that Christ will come to earth for a second time and defeat Satan and establish the Kingdom of God on earth for a thousand years. Then the wicked and the righteous will be resurrected and judged and sent to heaven or hell forever."

"Yes, our belief is different. Many Muslims believe that Jesus will descend to the earth, kill the Antichrist, convert everyone to Islām, and rule justly for forty years. Then he will die. And then Allāh will raise the dead and judge each person, and if the person did good deeds, he will go to paradise, and if he did bad deeds, he will go to hell. That's kind of a summary of it."

"Oh, my, that's quite different from our belief." She frowned. "You know I'm worried about you, Atif—about your immortal soul if you don't accept Jesus Christ as your Lord and Savior."

"And I worry about yours."

Amy saw someone enter her shadow.

"Gotta go. I love you so much."

"I love you, Amy. Take care."

A voice asked, "Is that you, Amy?"

She recognized Amanda's voice. "Yes."

The dorm leader came around the corner. "Who were you calling?"

Amy stiffened. "That's none of your business."

"I'm just supposed to help you students."

You're a student, aren't you? Amy thought.

Amanda stood there. "Are you coming in? It's nine-thirty."

Amy stood motionless. "I'm allowed to be out here until ten, aren't I."

"It depends on what you're doing."

"Oh!" Amy shouted and stomped her foot. "Yes, I'm coming in. What are you, our jailor?"

"I'm just trying to help."

They went through the living room, where Ashlee and Brittany were watching TV. They looked up, amused at Amy's peevish face, and Amy and Amanda went into their bedroom.

After unpacking her bags and putting away the clothes in the bureau and closet, Amy lifted the TV onto the bureau, made her bed with sheets, blankets, and a pillow, and put the light on her desk, supplies in the drawer, and the waste basket in the corner. All the while, Amanda sat on her desk chair and interrogated her about her family. Amy was not evasive, but kept the answers short, never embellishing.

"You know, Amy, I hope you don't get mixed up with these other girls. I don't think they fear Satan. They could take you down a path to sin and corruption."

"Duly noted."

She sat on the bed and pulled out her packet. It was time to begin analyzing how to get out of there.

"If you have any questions, let me know."

"Thanks."

She looked at the campus map, first—dorms, classroom buildings, library, recreation center, student center, ball fields and track, parking, etc. and class schedule. Then she thumbed through the student handbook and reviewed the rules. Each one was something that could result in expulsion, and that meant a trip home. There were separate dorms for men and women.

She looked at Amanda. "Are boys ever allowed in the girls' dorms?"

"No."

"Are girls allowed in the boys' dorms?"

"No."

That's an angle.

No overnight guests. *That's out. I won't have any overnight guests here.*

Be in dorms at ten every night, midnight on Friday and Saturday. *I could stay out too late, but I doubt they'd throw me out for that, unless I kept at it.*

No alcohol, tobacco, or drugs. *I don't use them.*

Random drug testing, and expulsions for positive tests. *Too iffy. Anyway, I want out of here now.*

Handholding is approved, nothing else. No couples in parks, parked cars, or unlighted areas after dark. *Incredible. But I won't be doing anything with boys.*

No shorts in class. *I have some shorts. That's a possibility.*

Jeans with no holes are approved as are pants, and dresses or skirts extending four inches or more below the knee. *I could hem up some skirts…or just not hem them down!*

Modest one-piece swim suits. No facial jewelry.

"Are earrings facial jewelry?" she asked.

"Yes. The Lord wants us to be the way he made us. Most of us don't even wear makeup."

"Oh, good. That'll save time."

Weekly convocation. Prayer group meetings three times a week with your group leader in dorms to pray together and study the Bible. Students sign out when leaving campus.

No tardiness or skipping class.

No cheating on tests. No plagiarizing from the Internet. *Who would do that? It's so easy to discover now with search engines.*

Honor code for academics and social behavior. *I bet Amanda would love to turn in any of us for a violation. That would prove she was doing her job!*

Promptly at eleven, Amanda told the girls in the living room to turn off the TV—"Time to go to bed"—and they went into their rooms, Brittany with Ashlee, Emily with Fran.

In her own room, Amanda dropped to her knees and prayed silently for several minutes, and then climbed into bed. At eleven-thirty she got out of bed and told Brittany and Ashlee to stop talking and laughing or they would be in trouble, and to be sure to pray. By the time she came back, Amy had already prayed, *Oh, dear God. Get me out of this prison. Tell me what I should do to get back to Atif. Save me....Please....In Jesus name, Amen.* Then she lay in bed, head under the covers, weeping silently, so not to be heard, and waited for an answer.

Ahmed came in from the garage, uncharacteristically ecstatic. "The first phase of our masjid is taking shape!" he announced to Salma, Nadira, and Atif as they sat in the great room before dinner. He slipped off his navy blue suit coat and laid it over a chair. This evening, the air was filled with the aroma of chapati bread, beef kebab, and spiced tea. "The walls and roof are done, the stucco is beautiful, and the plumber, electrician, and the heating men are working. Dan said that next week he will begin the insulation and wallboard. Then the tilers will work on the walls and floors of the bathrooms and ablution room and other floors and decorate the mihrab niche. And the carpenters are building the minbar pulpit. And someday we'll have domes and minarets and adornment with mosaics and tapestries and calligraphy. But now we have a beginning. And it's made of materials that won't burn—they can't burn it down like those other mosques. And Breckenridge has not been able to stop us!"

"Shh-shh-shh-shh," Salma said with a finger over her lips. "Don't tempt Satan!"

Atif demurred. "Breckenridge is not Satan. He's just evil."

"But Satan guides him," Ahmed said.

"Yes, and Breckenridge follows. And earns our vengeance," Atif said, thinking of both the mosque and Amy. He looked ready to rain fire on Sodom and Gomorrah.

Nadira bathed him with sorrowful eyes. When he had shared his secret with her that Amy's father had sent her away, Hamlet's words to Ophelia had raced through her head, "Get thee to a nunnery," but she had kept it to herself.

"Our success is better than revenge," Ahmed said to Atif. "Breckenridge may do his worst, but still we shall prevail, if it be in Allāh's plan."

Atif looked skyward. "If we only knew what was in Allāh's plan. But I don't think we should celebrate yet."

"You seem quiet lately," Salma said to him, "like you're carrying a heavy load."

"Oh, I am. My studies. They're quite heavy, but they're fascinating, too." He blinked back an invisible tear.

"What are you studying now?" Ahmed asked.

"Cell biology is the hardest. It's highly complex—their structure, organelles, life cycle, division, function…what they consume, and what their waste products are. And there are so many different types in nature—maybe billions—single-celled organisms and specialized cells in multi-celled organisms like plants and animals. White cells warring against bacteria in our blood. And there are prokaryotes and eukaryotes, and I could go on and on. It's astonishingly complex. And many of them are part of us, but they act on their own."

"Following Allāh's commands," Ahmed added. "But yes, they're very complex, and you must know how they interact, too. Like how bacteria attack lung cells."

Atif nodded instead of replying, in order to end the lecture.

Amy woke up at three, madder than a wounded bear. She was not putting up with this. She would get home any way she could, and it would be soon.

But how would she do it? Take a bus? Hitchhike? Ride with Fran (does she have a car)? Could Atif pick her up?

But wait, if she just went home, they would either ground her or bring her back.

She could get expelled. She could break the rules, cheat, sleep in class, not do her work. But she did not want to end in disgrace. Anyway, they would say she did it on purpose, and she would be grounded for sure.

No, she had to find something that would prevent her from going to class, but something she wouldn't be responsible for. She needed to get sick. That way she could be excused for missing classes, failing, and could be sent home where she could recuperate near Atif. And it needed to be a sickness without symptoms—one that she could simulate without a doctor or nurse questioning her.

Searching on her phone, she checked on mononucleosis but found that it has definite symptoms—fever, sore throat, swollen lymph glands, headache—that wouldn't do. Lyme disease had a rash and flu-like symptoms, fatigue, and body pains. That would be chancy, and it would take too long to diagnose. What she needed was one that had no clear symptoms—one that would be easy to fake.

She searched on depression and found lots of symptoms she could imitate: downcast mood, loss of interest, narcolepsy, overeating or anorexia, fatigue, difficulty concentrating, lack of energy, and suicidal thoughts.

There were other symptoms she could fake, too, such as chest pain, headaches, stomachache, and nausea.

Then she considered taking antidiarrhea medicine. Too much of that would stop her up and give her cramps and nausea and awful pain. She knew that from experience. Oh, she couldn't do that.

She hated that her parents were going to turn her into a deceitful person, but she didn't care—it was their fault. And could she really fool them? And would they let her out of the house even if she did?

He clicked Amy's number. It buzzed and buzzed. He left voice mail: "Call me." Then he messaged her: "Miss U. I could drive down, rescue the fair maiden, & bring her home—if you had a place to stay here. I don't care if Abu and Ami found out. LU, ~Dr. B."

An hour later, he received her message: "Miss U 2. If I just came home, I'd have nowhere to stay except my house. I'd be grounded: no car, no money. I wouldn't be able to see you. I'd be in prison just like here. And they'd take my laptop."

He clicked on the microphone symbol and spoke into his phone, and then sent his message: "Yes."

She tapped the keyboard of her phone in the dark. "I could break rules and get expelled. But that would hurt my reputation. I don't want that." She clicked send.

"I agree."

"I could pretend I was sick—take antidiarrhea medicine. Mom and Dad would have to take me back."

This scared Atif. "Please don't harm yourself, Amy. Don't take antidiarrhea med. It will make you really sick."

"I could act depressed—sad, not interested in anything, tired, suicidal thoughts."

"No! They will put you away or put you on drugs that will really mess up your mind."

"I thought of that."

He reiterated: "Amy. Do nothing that would make others harm you. Please do not act depressed."

"OK. But anyway, I think if I got sick, Mom and Dad would think I was faking and keep me locked up at home just like if I dropped out. I would be at fault."

"Any other ideas?"

Amanda stirred in her sleep.

"Yes. Resign ourselves to being apart. Send emails, messages, calls. And if I show them I am on the path of Christ, maybe they'll eventually unleash me, and let me run free. To you."

"I hate that we are letting your parents win."

"Me too. But only for a while. And I can keep asking you questions about Islam, and you can keep teaching me."

"But I can't hug you and kiss you."

"You'll have to do it like this: XOXOXO."

"OK. XOXOXO LU, ~Dr. B."

"LU2 XOXOXO ~A." She turned it off and held back a sob.

CHAPTER 19

THE RAMP

Gerald Damon parked on the highway shoulder and strode toward the mosque. Outside, a bulldozer was putting a final grade on the lot and parking area, while Lonnie and another man shot grades with a laser level. A loader was digging the dry storm-water detention basin at the rear of the property. The smell of damp earth was in the air, as well as the groans of the equipment as it moved the recalcitrant dirt. Inside, the heating and air-conditioning subcontractor and plumber were finishing their work, and the drywall crew was hanging fire-resistant wallboard on the walls and ceiling of the prayer hall.

Dan met him at the door under the portico, and greeted him, "Good morning, sir."

"I see you're doing your grading now. You must be about ready to build the ramp."

Dan jumped. "The ramp? What ramp? There's no ramp on the plans."

Damon sneered. "Well, you better have your architect draw you up one then. It's gotta go from the rear of your exit stairs on the upper level down to the rear door downstairs with handrails on both sides."

"What? We don't even have a rear door upstairs."

The older man's jaw stiffened. "Well, I guess you'll have to put one in then. You have to have a way to get those wheelchairs down to the lower level and the parking lot. You can't just push 'em down the stairs. That's not safe."

Dan began looking left and right and asked, "Can't they go out this door and down the driveway?"

The inspector frowned. "Now, that's surely not safe, not with cars out there. And your driveway's too steep anyway. They might lose control and end up in a ditch. The ramp can't be steeper than one inch fall in a twelve-inch run. So if you have a twelve-foot rise, floor to floor, that's a hundred and forty-four inches, so the ramp has to be a hundred and forty-four feet long, plus turning places and five-foot-long horizontal resting places every thirty feet, so it'll have to be maybe…let's say…about a hundred and eighty feet long."

Dan gasped. "A hundred and eighty feet! That's almost three times as long as the mosque."

Damon stroked his chin. "Yes. Looks to me like you'll have to have a rectangle-shaped ramp to accommodate that and bring it back to the basement door."

"A rectangle?"

"Yes. And that'll mean it'll have to change direction three times. You'll have to run it against the wall of the building, and then turn away from it, and then back the other way, and then back to the building, ending at the basement door. And every time it changes direction, it has to have that five-foot by five-foot level turning place. And, of course, it'll all have to have a roof over it to keep out the rain and snow."

Dan gawked at him. "What? You're talking about building an-other building behind the mosque!"

"Something like that. Well, you people should've put in an el-evator. That might have been cheaper. You weren't thinking about people with disabilities now, were you?"

"Why does it have to have a roof? Sidewalks don't have roofs."

"Listen," he said, staring into the young man's eyes. "It has to be functionally equivalent to facilities for nondisabled people. People with disabilities have to have equal access. The law says you can't discriminate against them. And those stairs inside have a roof now, don't they?"

"But...but your planning department approved these plans without a ramp."

"They approved what you gave them, yes. But let me tell you something, if you don't put a ramp on this mosque, not only will I not give you a CO, but you'll have the disability groups out here picketing you and suing you, and you'll get calls from the Department of Justice Civil Rights Division too, and I don't think you'd want any of that."

"N-no, sir."

"Good. Glad you understand. Now before you get all that dry-wall up, I better do a check on the handicap provisions inside to make sure you comply—you know, door sizes and swings and distances beside doors so wheelchair users can reach the door handles and bathroom stalls and toilet heights and grab bars and light switches and all that stuff, cause I don't think you were thinking of those people."

Dan shuddered. "I've been building it all to the plans."

"They better be right."

They walked through the building with Dan holding the plans and Damon directing his practiced eye toward every door, and holding his folding rule up to every toilet, outlet, and switch box, measuring their distances from the floor.

After an hour, he said, "Looks like you're in pretty good shape in here. Too bad about that little old ramp."

You would wait until the job was almost done to tell us about that, Dan thought.

Damon looked at his watch, said "Gotta go," and walked briskly to his car.

Dan hastily called Maskeen. "We're in trouble. Someone forgot the handicap ramp."

Maskeen was sitting in his office at his computer. "The what?"

Dan spoke like a mortician. "We have to have—"

"Speak up!"

He cleared his throat. "We have to have a one-hundred-and-eighty-foot-long ramp on the back of the building to connect the top of the exit stairs to the bottom."

"One hundred and eighty feet long! Why?!"

"It has to be a really low slope so people in wheelchairs can pull their way up, and it has to have level places for them to rest every thirty feet, too. And the inspector said it has to have a roof over it to keep off rain and snow."

Maskseen began tapping a pen on his desk. "A roof!"

"And he won't give us a certificate of occupancy without it."

"Oh! They have us trapped. We have no choice. We can't hold it up with any legal action. We need to get the architect out there right away to design it. Then get it approved by the building department, and build it fast. This is going to hold up everything—maybe a month or more—and it will cost a fortune."

They hung up, and Maskeen called Ahmed and left a message.

Ahmed called back a short while later from his office at the hospital, Maskeen described the situation, and Ahmed agreed that he should call the architect, Alec Smith. Maskeen did so and told him about the job. Smith made an appointment to see Dan the next morning, and arrived at the mosque at about ten.

Dan and Lonnie helped him take some elevations on the upper and lower floors and the ground outside with his laser level. Dan told him what Damon said about disability group pickets and Department of Justice.

Smith shrugged. "He was probably exaggerating, but I don't think we want to risk hooking horns with them."

"That inspector would wait until the end of the job to tell us about the ramp," Dan told Smith. "It's almost like he wanted to spring it on us."

"I'll stop by and pick his brain about what he expects, so at least we're on the same page."

Smith pulled out his phone, called the building department in Chelmsford, and was lucky to catch Damon in his office and available for a quick meeting.

Smith walked in, they shook hands, and Damon invited him to sit.

"I'm sure you're familiar with all the ADA requirements on ramps, so I won't go over them. What do you plan to build it out of?"

Smith stroked his bushy brown mustache with his forefinger and thumb and said, "I plan to use six-by-six treated posts—ground contact grade—set on concrete footings extending to the frost level, and to use preserved wood joists, spindles, and railings above ground, and composite decking on the joists."

Damon jutted out his chin. "What about the roof?"

"Some of the six-by-sixes will continue to roof level. I plan to design a shed roof with wood I-beam rafters extending from the mosque wall out over the ramp and cover it with corrugated glass fiber sheets to let light into the mosque windows and the ramp area. The ramp will form a rectangle, just like you suggested, coming down from the top floor and making three turns to reach the basement door. We'll work out the details before we give you the plans."

Damon gazed out the window. "And I guess you'll have the roof overhang the ramp? If it doesn't, the littlest breeze'll get it wet or icy."

"Yes. I think it will overhang two feet on each side. But the only way to really keep the ramp from getting wet would be to put sidewalls on the ramp. I don't think the government would expect us to do that!"

The inspector smacked his lips. "Yeah, but that's a good idea, Alec. Put walls on it."

The architect's eyes grew. "It might be cheaper to just put the ramp in a separate building."

Damon nodded. "That's a better idea. Put some walls around it with windows in 'em for light. And then put some heat and air conditioning in it so it's equivalent to that stair enclosure."

Smith swallowed. He was digging himself in deeper and deeper. "And insulate the walls?"

The inspector gave a nod in the affirmative. "Yes, sir. Gotta make it energy efficient." He wove the fingers of his hands on top of his desk and looked at the ceiling. "And those walls and roof would make it an interior exit ramp, so you'll have to make the walls one-hour fire rated with fire-rated drywall on them, and the ramp and roof will have to be fire-retardant treated wood or concrete."

"Fire-retardant treated wood or concrete," he repeated. Now he knew the inspector was pulling his leg. So he decided to go along with the gag. "It would be better if I designed it with one of those moving sidewalks so no one would have to push the chairs."

Now Damon knew that Smith had caught on, and he broke into a grin. "Now you're thinking. But it would have to have a reverse on it, or better yet, two separate walkways so the chairs can go both ways. Don't want 'em to run into each other. That would be dangerous."

"You had me going there, Inspector. But seriously, do you think the ramp should have a roof over it with an overhang?"

"Yes sir, I do. That shouldn't cost these people that much. They've got plenty, from what I can see."

"OK. I'll be back with some plans next week."

Ahmed was pacing in the great room. "A handicap ramp a hundred and eighty feet long with a roof over it!" he exclaimed to Maskeen and Atif. "I hate to think what Mr. Stanley will charge for that! We'll definitely have to arrange with the bank for more money for this. I've said it before: Breckenridge is behind this. He's trying to stop the masjid by making us run out of money so we can't get our occupancy certificate!"

"But I do think the inspector is right that a ramp must be required on the masjid for people who use wheelchairs," Maskeen said.

"But a hundred and eighty feet long?"

"I think that length is calculated according to requirements in the building code."

"Oh, that's ridiculous."

Atif tilted his head. "I don't know. I've seen some students in wheelchairs pulling themselves up those ramps at school. It's hard. They can't always find someone to push them. They have to do it themselves if they want to go to class. They usually end up pulling themselves up using the handrail. I don't know what they do when it's icy or snowy or when it's raining. They don't have roofs."

Smith submitted the plans to the building department and gave sets to Damon and Maskeen, and to Dan for pricing. The department expedited the review, and Dan quickly got his ramp contractor to price it out and told Maskeen, and he passed it on to Ahmed.

"Thousands and thousands of dollars! And do you think that's a fair price?"

"Dan says it's high because of all the changes in level, and the railings on both sides all the way around it. And some of the six-by-six posts extend all the way from the footings up to the roof beams, and they all had to be a higher grade of treatment because they're in contact with the ground. He says he has to get twenty-four-foot-long six-by-sixes for some of the posts to support the roof, and they're special order. He said the labor on it is extensive, and he has to hire a specialty contractor. All those posts have to be in exactly the right place. He was apologetic, but firm, but I do think he's being fair, to us, and to himself, of course."

"And the roof will block the masjid windows on that whole side. All you'll see is those glass fiber sheets. That's terrible."

"We have no choice," said Maskeen.

"Couldn't we run the ramp away from the building so it wouldn't block the windows?"

"Hmm. I'll ask the architect."

"You could," Smith told Maskeen, "but only about twenty feet of the roof would be attached to the mosque wall. It would still be a rectangle, but it would project about seventy feet away from the mosque wall. That would make it less resistant to wind uplift. But it could be done."

"We would prefer that, if you can make it work."

"It will take another week to draw the plans."

"Please do it. We can't have those windows blocked."

Again Smith submitted the plans to the building department and gave sets to Damon, Maskeen, and Dan, for pricing. An addition was the rain gutter on the lower side of the roof. Again the department reviewed the plans quickly, and Dan had his ramp contractor price it out.

This time the price was even higher. "Higher! Why more?" Ahmed asked Maskeen.

"They have to rent a crane and a bucket-boom truck to set the big lam beams supporting the roof, and they have to anchor the roof and beams on both sides to the ground with guy-wires attached to concrete dead men—large blocks of concrete in the ground—on both sides. Otherwise the wind will carry it away. Oh, and you also have the gutter and downspout on the low side—but that wasn't much extra."

"Who's ever seen a ramp with a roof. Bah!"

"But this time they can use a conventional plywood and asphalt roof on it instead of glass fiber panels, so it should last longer."

John Quiggley, the ramp contractor, couldn't schedule the job for several weeks, but fortunately, the ramp wasn't delaying any work inside of the mosque.

Dan rented a small track loader, and he and Lonnie leveled the area where the ramp would go and where the materials would be stored. The manufacturer required two weeks to build and deliver the big twenty-foot-long laminated beams that would support each side of the roof and the I-joists that would span from beam to beam. The large steel brackets to attach the beam to the six-by-six posts and other materials were delivered as well.

When all the materials were on site, John came out with a helper and spent a day staking it out and marking where the many post holes and the eight deadmen would go, setting stakes in the ground and pulling strings to align them. Dan and Lonnie helped and supervised.

The next day Quiggley brought a power augur behind his pickup, and drilled the sixteen-inch-wide holes for the posts. They called for inspection, and Damon arrived an hour later, checked the plans, the hole sizes and depths with a tape and measuring pole, making notes as to the depth of each hole, and left. The next morning they cleaned out the holes, and the truck brought concrete, which they wheeled up a slope over eight-inch boards and dumped into each hole. On three holes, they had to carry the concrete in five-gallon buckets. There were too few holes to use the pumper, and it couldn't place the concrete accurately enough anyway—there would be concrete spilled all over the ground.

Damon came back the next morning and checked each hole again to make sure the concrete was at least eight inches thick. "You're a little shy on this one," he told Dan, "but I'll let it go."

They sighed in relief.

He thinks he's God Almighty, Dan thought.

When they were loading up their trucks to leave, Dan told Quiggley and Lonnie, "I've never seen a ramp with a roof over it."

"Neither had we. But this is just a shed roof supported by two beams and twelve posts and attached to the wall on one end."

Dan was leaning against the basement wall with his arms crossed. "And held by guy-wires and eight deadmen to keep it from blowing away."

"Yes—it won't be hard," Quiggley said. "But there are a whale of a lot of post holes for the ramp underneath the roof."

"Maybe that's why he let that one hole go 'shy.'"

"Maybe he was already feeling guilty for making you do this thing."

"He's never felt guilty about anything else," Lonnie groused.

Quiggley looked up into the air, visualizing the structure. "The thing is, the slightest breeze will blow the rain and snow right under the roof onto the ramp."

Dan gazed across the field. "He knows that."

"Why don't you ask the owner if we can build some walls on it to keep out the rain."

Dan made a gruesome laugh. "You want to get me fired?"

"Well, why didn't they ask for a hearing?"

"If they did or tried to sue the city, it'd delay the project. No, we're stuck. We just have to do what the idiot says and be done with it."

Lonnie looked at them gravely. "I'll bet that Breckenridge is laughing his head off."

Dan turned to go up the hill to his truck. "I'll be back." He had an errand in town.

When he returned, he told Lonnie, down where Quiggley was working, "The crew laying the water and sewer lines is getting close to the corner of the property. There's a big-track backhoe digging its way toward us from town laying sewer line beside the shoulder, eight feet deep. And another hoe is following it—digging the water line—you know, in a separate trench. It's only three feet deep. It has to be five feet away from the sewer trench."

"And I see the loader's grading the turning lane by the highway."

"Yep. Things are coming along."

"What about Internet?"

"High-speed Internet comes later in a separate trench, and of course, the power and telephone come off the poles along the highway."

Lonnie raised his eyebrows optimistically. "It won't be long before we have water and sewer."

"The sooner the better. Until we get hooked up, we won't know if the plumbing leaks, or all the faucets and drains work in the bathrooms or that room where they wash their feet."

"And we won't know if the sewage pump works."

"Yeah, and we can't get our plumbing approvals and CO until then either," Lonnie said. "So we can't finish the job."

CHAPTER 20

PHONES

"Please, Mommy. Let me come home!" Amy sobbed into her cellphone. "I want to come home!" Amy was outside in the shade of the dorm in the late afternoon, away from doors and windows.

Eunice was sitting at her desk in the trophy room. "No, Amy. You have to stay there and learn what you've done wrong."

Amy stomped her foot in the grass. "I haven't done anything wrong!"

Eunice squinted. "You know you were seeing that boy."

"What boy?"

"Don't lie to me!" she shouted. "That Muslim boy."

"You can't prove that," she said, suddenly the lawyer. "You can't prove anything. Jesse lied about not putting those brochures in my desk and admitted to putting them on my bed."

"Amy! Respect your father and mother. Tell the truth!"

"I am, Mommy. Please let me come home." She stared at the ground, then at the dorm across the courtyard. "I hate it here. I hate the other girls. They're bad girls. They're not Christian. They'll teach me bad things, I know it."

"It's a fine Christian school, Amy. Don't you pray together every night in your dorm?"

"Yes. Three times a week."

"And at convocation and worship?"

"Yes, Mommy."

"But you still say the girls are bad."

"All they think about is boys and sex. That's why their parents sent them there."

And that's why we sent you there, Eunice thought. "Then you need to help them too, Amy. Help them become better Christians."

"I can't take it here."

"I'm sure you can. Lots of girls get homesick away from home. You'll adjust. Just dig into your studies. And stop thinking about that Muslim boy! He's going to end up in the fiery place, and you don't want to go there with him!" She stood up to go into the kitchen.

Unless I save him, Amy thought. "I can't study! I'm too upset."

"You better study, girl. You are not going to waste our money down there. Now get busy." She hung up.

Immediately, Amy called Atif and clicked on the video.

"Hi, Amy," came the soft reply and gentle face. He was in his basement cave, reading, and she was still outside.

"Oh, Atif. I can see you!"

"And you look beautiful, but so sad."

Amy tilted her head to the right and pulled back her long dark brown hair behind her ears with the fingers of her left hand. "She won't let me come home. I begged. I pleaded. I argued. I told her how bad the girls here are, and how I'm too upset to study."

"I'm sorry."

"She said that I was to stop thinking about that Muslim boy, or I would go to the fiery place with you!"

...unless you become a Muslim, he thought.

She looked at him. "I told her there was no Muslim boy!"

"You lied."

She jutted out her chin. "She makes me lie. It's her fault."

"Yes."

"What am I going to do?"

"Like you said before, we just have to be patient, and things will change. Pretend to adjust…So anyway, in the meantime…do you have more questions about Islam?"

Amy sighed. "Oh…OK." She looked up in thought, and then asked, "Do Muslims believe in…evolution?"

"Do you?"

"No, we don't. We believe that God made Adam and Eve and human beings descended from them."

"Well, Muslims believe that, too. But I think many of us believe that Allāh started and guided the process in which man evolved from minerals into plants and then into animals, and it didn't happen instantaneously. The Qur'an says that a day in the sight of the Lord is like a thousand years in our reckoning."

"So you believe in evolution."

He shrugged. "Yes, I believe in natural selection and evolution. In biology, we constantly see bacteria mutating to become resistant to antibiotics, and many animal species have become naturally immune to poisons given off by other plants or animals. And there are innumerable other examples in nature. But I also believe that Allāh guides it all. He did not just put the earth in orbit like a spinning top and let His natural laws and accidents and survival of the fittest determine everything. The Qur'an says, let me think, 'Nothing will happen to us except what Allāh has decreed for us.' He is the creator and sustainer, and he determines everything."

She wrinkled her forehead. "Hmmm. So you believe in predestination."

"I believe that we are part of Allāh's plan. He has given us free will to do good or bad, and he knows what we will do and decides at the end whether to be merciful and reward us with paradise or to punish us with hell."

He looked to the side, distracted by the thought of his studies, and then glanced at his watch. "I have to go."

"O—kay," she sang. "I'll let you."

"Bye."

"I love you," she blurted before he could click off, and she puckered up and gave him a gentle kiss.

He returned it. "I love you, too."

She decided to go for a run before dinner, and put on her shorts, T-shirt, and shoes.

Outside, she found Fran in a sleeveless T-shirt and orange running shorts with a headband over her blond hair stretching her long, tan legs on the stairs.

"Are you going out or coming back?" Amy asked.

She looked up. "Going out. Want to come?"

"As long as you don't go too fast. I'm pretty slow."

Fran led her behind the men's dorm and library and onto a path into the woods.

"I try to avoid peeping Toms while I run," Fran said. "I don't want to excite any of those boys so I'd have to outrun them."

Amy laughed. "I know what you mean."

"Do you have a boy at home?"

"Yes. That's why I'm here. My mom and dad don't like him, so they drove me down here and left me."

She looked dumbfounded. "Wow! Aren't parents amazing. My mom didn't like my friends either. She kept claiming she smelled weed on me."

"Did she?"

"I'll never tell."

They bounded around a curve and through a narrow place in the undergrowth. Then the trail opened up under some large trees. The scent of rhododendron blossoms filled the air, and their ears caught the echo of a wood thrush.

"How did you get here?" Amy asked.

"I drove."

Amy lit up. "So you can go back anytime you want?"

"Not exactly. She took my credit card, so I can't buy gas and can't get a motel."

"Far-out!" Amy exclaimed. "I have a credit card, but I don't have a car!"

"Sounds like a perfect match!"

They tromped around a bend, and then Amy said, "So you live in Charles Town?"

"Yes."

"That's near DC!"

"A little over an hour away."

They started up a hill and had to quit talking. At the top, they stopped to rest on a log that had fallen across the path.

"Maybe we could go home together sometime," Fran suggested.

"I'd have to work out some things first, though. I don't have anywhere to stay if I go home."

Fran looked astonished. "You mean they'd kick you out?"

"I don't know. But I know if they did let me stay, they'd ground me and not let me drive my car. I know that."

Fran raised her eyebrows. "Well, couldn't you sneak out of the house and have your friend pick you up?"

"Then I *would* get into trouble."

"You've gotta be brave, girl." Then Fran leaped up and said, "Race you back!"

They took off, and Amy found herself falling behind. Around a bend, she found Fran waiting with her hands on her knees, smiling. "Hey, do you know where I can get a joint? I need one bad."

"Runners don't smoke pot!"

"Some do. That's how we get that runners' high, the easy way."

Jesse came down the back stairs from his bedroom into the kitchen where Eunice was grilling steaks and vegetables on the gas range. "Smells good, Mom."

"Wash your hands. It'll be ready in a minute, and you can help carry it to the table."

Randall came in the side door through the kitchen into the lavatory, greeting Eunice on the way. He washed his hands, and then went to the trophy room, sat down, and turned on the news. When Eunice and Jesse walked in carrying the plates of steaks and bowls of vegetables and potatoes, he turned it off, rose, and came to his seat. "Looks good, Mama."

They folded their hands and bowed their heads, and Randall prayed, "Bless this food to our body and us to Thy service, and be with our Amy in West Virginia, Lord, too. Help her to find you, Lord, in the name of Jesus Christ, our Lord, Amen. Let's eat!"

They passed the food around family style and loaded their plates.

"So what did you do today, Jess-bo?" Randall asked.

Jesse said proudly, "Pete showed me how to 'pregnate a cow."

"Yeah? Did you actually do it?"

He smiled. "Naa. Not yet. He showed me how on one, and then he made me watch that video on his tablet."

"Yeah, you have to have x-ray vision to do that job—to know where that cervix and uterus are so you know where to put the sperm."

Eunice looked at her husband. "Randall, this is not dinner talk."

"Sorry. I'll catch you later, Jess-bo, but I'm glad you're learning the business."

They ate in silence. Then Randall said, "I wish I knew how she was doing down there."

She raised her eyebrows. "I spoke with her this afternoon."

He raised his head. "Oh?"

She summarized their conversation and said, "I told her to stop thinking about that Muslim boy, and she said that we don't have any evidence that she was seeing a Muslim boy, and I said, 'Stop lying,' and so on. I finally told her to get busy, and that she was not going to waste our money down there. Oh, if we only knew how much time she spends calling that boy."

"All you have to do is look at the numbers she's calling on the telephone bill," Jesse said.

"What?" Eunice asked.

Jesse added, "And we can get the name of the people she's calling from the number."

"We can?" Randall asked.

"Sure. I can do it for you."

"Do it." He stabbed a piece of steak with his fork, stuffed it into his mouth, and began grinding it with his teeth. "Then we'll have some evidence to show her."

After dinner, Jesse came back into the trophy room and asked if they had an unlimited calling plan, that the phone company didn't list numbers for unlimited calling. "You'll have to switch to pay-per-minute."

Eunice looked concerned. "But if she's calling very much, that'll cost a lot more."

"That'll be money well spent," Randall said, "to get at the truth, once and for all."

"To catch her in a lie. I'll change it tomorrow."

A few days later, Jesse came in with a printout of their online phone bill including the list of phone numbers. They were few—only two or three calls a day—all to the same number in their area code, but not to their own number. The printout told exactly when the calls were placed and their duration. Some were for over thirty minutes.

"Did you trace the number?" Randall asked.

"Yes. Here's the report."

"Last name: Bhati," Randall read. "I knew it! The surgeon who's building the mosque."

"Or his son."

Eunice said, "Well, I'm sure Amy's not calling the doctor."

"Call him up, Jesse. Call that number and see if you can get that boy's first name. Say, let's see, say, 'Is this Dr. Bhati?' and if he says 'No, who's this?' be friendly and say...say, 'This is Dr. Paul from the hospital. Who's this?' and if he says 'How did you get this number?' you say, 'He gave it to me. He must have given it to me by mistake. Who are you?' and if he says, 'His son,' you say, 'Oh, and what's your name?' and after he gives it to you, say, 'Well, please tell him I called. Thank you. Goodbye.' Be nice."

Jesse looked at him and his mother with a grin. "I'll try."

He pulled his cell from his jeans pocket and dialed. "Dr. Bhati?" he asked in a deeper than normal voice. "This is Dr. Paul from the hospital. Who's this?...Atif?...His son? Oh, I guess he gave me your number by mistake. Please tell him I called. Thank you."

Randall looked at him. "Atif, is it?"

"Yes."

"Great job, Jesse. You almost sounded like a phee-zicion."

"I knew she was lying," Jesse said of his sister.

Eunice nodded. "We all did, honey. What do you think we should do next, Randall?"

He thrust up his chin and growled, "Cancel her cellphone."

Eunice disagreed. "But what if she needs us?"

"Everyone's got a cell now," Jesse said. "She can get through."

"He's right."

"She won't call us. And we won't be able to call her. And she'll just use someone else's phone to call him."

"I've got another idea," Randall said. "We can put one of those parental control apps on her phone. That'll tell us where she is and let us monitor who she's calling and sending messages to and what she's saying."

Jesse blinked. "I heard that sometimes they don't work too well. She might be out of network down there. And she could just leave her cell in her room and go anywhere and you'd never know where she went. And she could erase her emails and texts after she sent them. And, anyway, you'd have to have her phone to put one of them on." He was mostly blowing smoke, but he was afraid they might put one on his phone some day and steal his privacy.

"Oh...well...OK. Maybe we should just wait. We can tell her what we found out from the phone company and see what she says. And now that we switched to pay-per-minute, we can at least keep track of who she's calling."

In his study carrel in the University of Maryland chemistry building, Atif pulled up the hospital website on his laptop, clicked on "staff," and visually scanned the names and pictures. *So many nationalities... Arab, Pakistani, Indian, Asian, African, Black/African American, and Jews and other Whites and Hispanics...the United Nations*, he thought. He reached the bottom. *No Dr. Paul. Ha! I'll tell Abu when I get home.*

Ahmed came in the front door, put his briefcase in his office, and entered the great room. Nadira was with him. She was helping in his medical office and riding with him when she wasn't taking the bus. Today she wore a brightly embroidered short-sleeve kameez tunic over baggy tan shalwar pants, a long red sash over her shoulder, and sandals with gold straps. After laying her electronic notepad on the island, she began setting the table for dinner. Salma was preparing baingan bharta—roasted eggplant, tomatoes, and garlic—and roti flatbread, and the aromas permeated the area.

Ahmed put his briefcase in his study, went into the great room, and sat down facing the fireplace wall. "That smells wonderful, Salma."

"Hello, Father," Atif said, after coming up from the basement. "You must hear this. I had a strange phone call today."

"Oh? What?"

"It was from a man claiming to be Dr. Paul from the hospital. He wanted to speak to you."

Salma looked up in interest.

Ahmed squinted. "I don't know a Dr. Paul—at least I can't think of one."

"I searched the hospital staff website and couldn't find a Dr. Paul."

"Interesting."

"He said, 'Please tell him I called.'"

Ahmed shrugged.

"Oh, and he asked, 'Who's this?' and I said, 'His son, Atif. How did you get my number?' and he said, 'I guess he gave it to me by mistake.' Then he said, 'Please tell him I called.'"

Ahmed raised his eyebrows. "That is strange."

"He was very friendly, and his voice sounded young, almost boyish."

"What?" Salma exclaimed. "What do you think he was after?"

Nadira put down a handful of silverware, and said, "Maybe he was after your name."

Ahmed looked over his knitted fingers at Atif. "Hmm. He had your number and my name, but he wanted your name. Why? What could he do with that?"

"Get other information about you, Atif?" Nadira suggested.

"This is suspicious," Ahmed said. "And that makes me think about our enemy, Breckenridge! Could he be up to something?"

Atif thought it might have something to do with him and Amy, but he couldn't say that, and he knew that Amy had a brother a year younger than her who could have made the call, but he couldn't bring that up either.

Nadira suggested, "If I were you, Atif, I would change my passwords, just to be careful."

"Ugh. I don't have time for this. I need to study."

"I think you should do it," Ahmed said.

Salma agreed. "You never know what people will try to do."

Nadira shook her head. "And now they know your name and cell number."

"I wonder if they know how to hack into my files. Maybe I should change my cell number, too."

Ahmed's brow furrowed. "Yes. Do it."

"I bet now that they know my name, they're going to search it and try to learn as much as they can about me. Maybe I need to do that to them."

"Let me do it, brother. You have to study!"

Atif was seething. "We have to start fighting back against this Breckenridge! We should have started that from the beginning and not waited until now. We need to get something on him to get him to stop attacking us! Maybe get the town behind us."

"He has too much power around here," Ahmed lamented. "Too much land and too much money. And his family goes back hundreds of years. We're just immigrants."

"Not me," Atif snapped. "I was born in this country. And you're citizens. And I say we still need to get something on him and fight him. Everybody's got some skeleton in his closet."

"But Atif. You have to study!" Salma cried. "You can't let your grades go down."

Ahmed stared at him. "And you have to learn all the material, too, and retain it, to be a good physician. No cramming."

"It won't take me long."

CHAPTER 21

MOVING BONES

"What's holding us up now?" Ahmed asked Maskeen over his cellphone as he was getting ready to leave the house to go to his office. Maskeen was sitting in his SUV after having checked the job.

"Four major things," Maskeen said. "The grading, curbing, and paving of the parking lots, and the extension of the water and sewer service from the town. Oh, and the county road permit, and that depends on construction of the turning lane on the highway, which they're working on now, and the sidewalks by the highway."

"The sidewalks to nowhere," Ahmed growled, "that don't connect to anything because there aren't any on the adjacent properties! Oh, these American codes and regulations!"

He went out the door and walked into the garage, and then asked, "When will they be done?"

"We requested the utility work months ago, but it was approved only last month, and the contractors have started it but aren't finished. Until the water and sewer are connected to the building, the inspector won't give us our occupancy permit. And Dan said the grading of the parking lots will begin as soon as we have a few dry days, and the curbing and sidewalks by the highway and the paving will be after that."

"Yeah, Clyde, it's me," Randall spoke into his phone. He had just grabbed a bagel and some coffee for breakfast, and was standing at the side door in the trophy room. "What are you doin'?"

"Changing the oil in the 7R."

"I got another job for you."

Clyde leaned against the side of the seven-foot-tall tractor tire, crossed his ankles, and asked, "What?"

"We better meet. Peter's gone today, isn't he?"

"Yeah. He's down at the sale."

"What about the other guys?"

"Two are cutting hay down at the southern end, two in the dairy barn, a couple of 'em are in the birthing barn..."

Randall interrupted. "OK. What say I meet you up at Cool Spring and Jaybird Road in an hour?"

"Sure."

"Thanks. And bring a pick and shovel."

Randall pulled his black four-door pickup down the farm road to the rendezvous point. He got out, carrying a yellowed roll of maps. Clyde was already there.

"How ya doin'?" he asked Clyde.

"Pretty good." The endless fields were fenced along the road with weathered posts, some rotted at the base and held up by rusty barbed wire. The rich, pungent smell of alfalfa hay filled their nostrils. Randall laid the maps on the hood of Clyde's old truck, looked up, and asked, "Say Clyde, do you know where that old graveyard is in the woods somewhere up here in the back ninety in the northeast quadrant?"

"Whoa! Lemme think. I don't believe I've even heard of it." He looked out across the meadow now.

"It's in the middle of the woods, and there are just a few little headstones and sunken places with trees and bushes all around them and scrub trees between them, and you can't read the writing on the stones anymore, as I remember."

Clyde looked at Randall. "When was the last time you saw them?"

"We used to play in there around Halloween when I was a kid. Rumor was that it was an Indian graveyard."

Clyde raised his brows and snickered. "So you think you can find a graveyard you played in forty years ago?"

Randall shrugged. "Maybe not quite that long ago."

Clyde knew he was serious now. "Do you think the headstones are still there?"

"We've never cut timber in there. I'll bet they're still there. Here, I'll show you where they are on the farm plat." He unrolled the maps, spread them out, and went to the page showing the northeast quadrant. "It's somewhere up here," he said, pointing his finger straight down and then drawing a circle with it. "Feel like taking a walk? The weather's good." The sun was darting between fluffy white clouds and then hiding.

"Sure, sir, but what's this all about?"

"You'll find out. Come on. You drive, so you remember where we went."

They climbed into Clyde's pickup and went bouncing down the farm road to a dirt crossroad, turned right, drove a mile or more through hay fields and untilled land, turned down another road with only one pair of wheel tracks and grass between them. Up a grade where the tracks became rutted, Clyde said, "I know why you wanted me to drive my vehicle." They laughed.

The road turned a bend and entered a stand of trees that soon became a dense hardwood forest of white oak, maple, birch, tulip, and sycamore trees with serviceberry and holly bushes in the shade on the floor.

Clyde looked over at him. "You mean to tell me you can find those stones now?"

"I bet I can, Clyde."

They drove another quarter of a mile until they started up another grade. "Seems to me it's up on this hill. They always put them on hills when they could, to get them closer to the Lord…or the happy hunting grounds." Clyde looked at him like he might be supernatural himself.

Randall looked up through the windshield and then hung his head out the window and gazed at the woods and up at the trees. "OK, here. Stop here." Clyde braked. "Let's take a walk. Bring the pick and shovel."

He took out his compass to get his bearings, and up they went, winding around bushes and trees, through small clearings, past shale outcrops.

Randall said, "I have the feeling it's around here. Take a good look."

They began searching the ground, and Clyde pointed to a lump covered with decomposed vegetation and some slightly sunken ground nearby, and said, "What's that?"

"Could be a headstone," Randall said. "And it looks like the plants around there are kind of stunted and the ground's sunk-in a little. Could be where a coffin's rotted away in there and collapsed. Yeah, let's look."

They walked over and began kicking off soil and leaves, and then dropped to their knees and brushed away the thick shroud of moss and tree litter with their hands until they could make out the rectangular prism of stone with faint depressions where words were once carved.

"Bingo," Randall said, picking one up. "Here we are."

"OK. Now are you gonna tell me why we're here?"

"Sure. Clyde, I want you to dig up this grave and get me a skull and a skeleton."

His eyes leaped. "What?"

"Yes! I already started digging it up when I was a boy, but I gave up."

"And you want me to finish it. Isn't it illegal—digging up graves?"

"I don't know. Maybe. But what they don't know can't hurt them." He grinned.

Clyde looked askance at the grave. "Who's in there?"

"I can't say. Could be my great-great-grandfather! Anyway, dig him up, and get the skull and skeleton, but leave the casket, if there is one, and leave any cloth or anything else you find, and fill the hole back up and put leaves over it when you're done."

Clyde snickered. "And what are you going to do with a skull and a skeleton—put 'em on the wall in your trophy room?"

"No, no, no. It's what *you're* going to do with them, Clyde, not me."

At two in the morning, Clyde parked on the back road a short ways from the mosque property. Under an overcast night sky, he approached Father White Highway through the brush and scrub trees carrying a pointed shovel and heavy-duty black-plastic leaf bag full of bones over his shoulder, and a flashlight. At the trench, which was just higher than his head, he laid his baggage down, slid in, pulled in the bag and shovel, carried them through the heavy steel trench box that the workers used to prevent the dirt walls from collapsing onto them, went to the farthest end where no pipe had been laid, and began digging a hole into the wall of dirt at the bottom of the trough. After carving out a cave three feet deep, he unfastened the bag, dumped out the bones, and stuffed them in, head first. Then he filled the hole with dirt, just as Randall had prescribed, walked to the other end of the trench, climbed out, and skulked away into the brush.

At six in the morning, the four-man utility crew arrived, drank coffee from their thermoses in the dim light, and walked to the big track backhoe, which sat ready to dig at the end of the trench, and the small rubber tire backhoe-loader parked by the road, which was for moving dirt. Traffic guards put up one-way signs on the highway and began holding their signs up: "STOP" and on the reverse side "SLOW." Two workers jumped into the ditch and found a safe place inside the trench box. The track hoe operator climbed up, cranked-up the rumbling behemoth, reached out the steel arm with the toothy bucket on it, and proceeded to take his first big bite of dirt. Up came the soil and rock, and up came the bones, which he unceremoniously dumped on the pile by the road.

"Stop!" yelled Phil, the crew chief, one of the men in the box. "What're those white rocks in the dirt?"

"Look like bones!" said the other, Phil's helper.

Phil took a closer look. "They better not be. If they are, we have to stop diggin'!"

Various profanities fractured the air.

The helper asked, "So what do we do now?"

"I think we have to call the police," Phil said. "We might be in the middle of a crime scene. Some murderer might have buried a corpse here."

"Might be Jimmy Hoffa."

"Who?"

"That union guy—they never found his body."

Phil nodded but didn't laugh. "I'll call it in." He climbed out of the trench, and the other man followed. Then he took out the phone from his hip holster and dialed 911. "Give me the police.".... "Local, I guess. Chelmsford.".…"No, it's not a real emergency, I guess.".…"OK. Let me write it down. Hold on." He took out a small spiral notebook from his pocket and a pen. "OK. Shoot."

"What's the problem?"

Phil wrote down the number and then hung up. "They want me to call the police directly because it's not an emergency. Damn guy. He could've switched me over."

He dialed the police number and told the operator about the bones, and was told the department would send out an inspector. Two of them arrived an hour later. Everyone was standing around drinking coffee and smoking. It was Sam, the taller one, with a roll of yellow tape, and his shorter colleague, Bud.

"Now, where are these bones?" Sam asked.

Phil showed them the bones in the pile of dirt. Some were exposed, some half-buried, but the skull was not in sight.

Sam bent down and pulled out a thin one more than a foot long, brought it to eye-level, and studied it. "This doesn't look like a fresh bone to me. Looks like it's been in the ground a long time. The worms and bugs have eaten it clean. And there's no sign of a casket, and I don't see any cloth or anything, so it doesn't look like a regular burial, unless it's been in the ground a long time."

"Are you sure it's not a deer or a pig?" Bud asked.

"No, it doesn't look like an animal—it looks human. But I doubt if we have a homicide here, Bud, unless it's a really, really cold case." They both laughed. "I don't know what it is. We better tape it off and call for the forensic anthropologist. Let him figure it out."

"You mean we have to stop working?" Phil asked.

"I'm afraid so. And leave everything just as it is. Don't touch anything."

"What? For how long?"

Sam looked him in the eye. "Until the crime lab examines the site and sends the bones to the medical examiner. He does a forensic analysis to determine how old these bones are, whether they're male or female, and their ancestry. It shouldn't take more than a couple of weeks, unless it's part of a graveyard."

"A couple of weeks!" Phil wailed.

"That's right. It could be a lot longer. And listen—until they decide what to do, this is a crime scene."

Phil looked worried. "B-but that'll hold up construction of the mosque."

"That's too bad. Let's tape it off, Bud—around the pile and around the ditch. We'll come back later and cover the pile with a tarp."

"And we can't move this dirt off the shoulder?"

Sam looked at the mound of dirt. "I guess you can move that little bit," he replied, pointing to a small pile on the edge of the highway. "But you can't disturb the bones. Leave the big pile the way it is. The crime lab investigators will want to come out here and dig out the bones themselves. And if the bones are less than a hundred years old, this is a crime scene, and we have to investigate it as such. Even if the case is cold."

Phil muttered an obscenity under his breath, and then asked, "What happens then?"

"Well," Sam said with a shrug, "if the bones are over a hundred years old, then the archaeologists have to determine if this is a grave site, and if these are Indian bones."

"Indian bones!" Phil said in surprise. "What if they are?"

"If they are, then the Commission on Indian Affairs has to supervise the dig and make sure that the remains are treated with respect."

"Respect!" Phil yelled. "What about respect for us?! We have a job to do."

"So do they. They have to supervise the reburial of the bones if that becomes necessary."

"This could take months!"

Sam scowled. "Don't yell at me. I didn't write the laws. But, yeah, sometimes it does take that long, I've heard it said, although I've never dealt with a case like this before."

Phil looked at Sam. "Sorry I shouted, officer. It's not your fault." Then he turned and said, "Excuse me. I gotta make a call."

"A skeleton in the sewer ditch?!" Ahmed asked Maskeen, putting his pen down on his office desk. The accountant was sitting in his SUV at the jobsite. "And they're stopping the water and sewer installation for months? I know who's behind this. This is not a coincidence!"

"Yes. You're right."

"Call a board meeting for tonight…at eight…at my house. Tell them it's mandatory. I will ask another doctor to do my surgery. We have to fight back!"

The eight members of the board plus Atif sat around the great room solemnly listening to Maskeen describe the problem and the potential for months of delay. The group included a hotel manager, lawyer, another accountant, and an engineer.

"We'll have to start repaying our loan before we even get use of the building," the lawyer griped.

"And if we don't have use of the building, we'll have lower attendance and less Zakāh," the accountant added.

Another said, "And that means that *we* pay more out of our pockets."

Ahmed growled, "This is no coincidence. That devil Breckenridge is behind this. I mean, tell me what is the probability of finding skeletal remains right at the end of the trench we are digging for our sewer line—and outside the scope of our security camera. This was no accident!" He slammed his fist down on the arm of his chair. "Someone put those bones in the trench. And it must have been Breckenridge or one of his henchmen."

"What can we do?" asked the accountant.

They argued heatedly for most of an hour. Then Ahmed barked, "We must hire a private investigator to find out where those bones came from and who put them in the ditch!"

"That's expensive," the lawyer said. "You don't think the police can investigate?"

"No, I don't. They are either corrupt or incompetent or anti-Muslim. Remember, they never found out who vandalized the foundation."

Atif decided to speak. "We should get our friends at the church to picket the site with signs. We can call it what it is: a fraud committed to stop the construction."

Before they left, the group decided to wait a day or two before hiring an investigator, to see what the police would do.

CHAPTER 22
THE SKULL

The crane and bucket boom truck were on-site when Quiggley arrived. He used the crane to raise one end of the six-by-six vertical posts in place while he rode up in the bucket boom, trimmed them to the correct height with a chain saw, and helpers attached temporary diagonal braces to them, down to stakes on the ground. Then the crane raised the big laminated beams, and Quiggley bolted them to the tops of the posts. When these were set, the crane lifted wood I-beam rafters, which Quiggley and his helpers attached to the top of the "lam" beams, allowing them to overhang the roof two feet on each side of the beams. Next, they nailed inch–and-a-half thick two-by-six tongue-and-groove sheathing to the top of the rafters. They attached steel cables from the top of the eight posts to the concrete deadmen buried in the ground to keep the wind from carrying the roof away. Lastly, the crane hoisted tar paper and asphalt shingles to the roof, and two of the men nailed them down with power nailers.

"There," Quiggley said as he climbed down the ladder. "The stupid thing is finished."

Dan gazed up at it and his eyes followed it as it went along the building, then turned away from it at right angles, resting on the posts and beams, then made a U and returned to the building, with hips at each turn. "It's a beautiful roof," Dan said, "even if it is useless. You did a great job." He had observed the process, intending to make suggestions, but they weren't needed. Quiggley and his men knew exactly what they were doing. In fact, Dan learned from them.

"It'll keep the rain off our heads while we're building the ramp," said one of the workers.

"If the wind don't blow," said another.

"I've never seen a U-shaped roof before," said a third man.

But now, looking off in the direction of the utility crew on the highway, Dan could no longer hear the grinding sounds of the hoes and wondered why they had stopped working. He sent Lonnie over to find out what was happening—they needed those pipes!—and he returned with the bad news: bones.

"That's all we need is another holdup," Lonnie said.

"Something's fishy," Dan said. "Something's rotten in Denmark."

Quiggley and his men began building the ramp under the roof, bolting treated joists to the posts and screwing plastic decking to the joists, at right angles to the direction of movement, to make a smooth surface. Great care was given to the slope of the joists and to the regulation regarding a level resting place for wheelchair users every thirty feet or less, and five-foot-square landings at each turn, and making the ramp wide enough to keep thirty-six inches between the handrails on the sides.

Out at the highway, Clary Fennel, the crime scene investigator, passed the one-way section of road with traffic guards holding signs that read "SLOW" on one side and "STOP" on the other, and the tent-shrouded pile of dirt at the end of the sewer trench with the yellow "CRIME SCENE DO NOT CROSS" tape around it.

She parked the silver White County Police CSI van in front of the police cruiser, swung open the door, and emerged wearing a yellow hard hat, loose-fitting button-up shirt with the sleeves rolled above her elbows, tan cargo pants, and work boots. She was over forty and short with tan muscular arms. Putting her camera case strap over her shoulder, she glanced at the sky. There was a high veil of clouds, but no rain was approaching. Occasional cars passed, and the drivers slowed down and gawked to try to understand what was happening.

As she walked to the tent, Clary pulled on latex gloves, so that her DNA would not contaminate the site. Sam and Bud met her. "Afternoon, ma'am," Sam said. "I'm not sure what we have here— just some bones in the dirt. They found them right at the end of the trench they were digging."

"That's peculiar."

They led her to the tent. She gave the area a cursory look, and then took out her camera and began photographing: the drainage ditch beside the road, the brush and scrub trees beside the ditch, the end and sides of the trench, the steel box, the excavating equipment, and the shoulder containing the pile of dirt with the ends of bones projecting. In the trench, she noted that the top strata of unexcavated soil was mostly dark humus—topsoil—and below that was orangey clay. She replaced the camera, set the case down, squatted, pulled a narrow trowel from a holster on her belt, and began digging around a large bone.

"Find anything?" Sam asked.

She looked up at him. "This will take a couple of hours, officer. You might as well take a load off."

They walked to their car, and she went back to the van, swung open the rear door, and took out an augur—for bringing up soil samples from different depths—and her probe, a four-foot long stainless steel rod with a small ball on one end and a handle soldered at right angles to the other end for gripping with both hands. The probe was used to check for differences in soil density (and for finding rocks and bones).

She began probing the pile, holding the waist-high handles with both hands and pushing the rod down into the soft dirt until she felt something solid. Then she extracted the probe, moved to the side a few inches, and kept probing until she had a mental picture of where the bones might be. She put wood stakes in the corners of the area.

Returning to her vehicle, she retrieved a shovel, a tarp, and a shaker screen. This device was sixteen inches square with four-inch-high boards on the sides and a quarter-inch mesh screen on the bottom. A metal leg went from one side of the box down to the ground, across the ground sixteen inches, and up to the other side of the box.

She spread the tarp on the ground, laid the shaker board down flat, and began shoveling dirt from the area of the bones into the box. When it was full, she put her foot on the bottom part of the metal leg, grabbed the handles on the box, swung it up to waist height, and began shaking it back and forth so the dirt went through the mesh and anything larger than a quarter of an inch was left on top of the screen.

Brushing the last of the dirt through the screen, she found gravel and pebbles and several small bones from hands. These she carefully laid on the tarp.

Like a small but efficient sandboni, she cleaned the pile of all the larger rocks and bones, which she began reassembling into the shape of the skeleton to determine whether any puzzle pieces were missing. After a few hours, she went to the van, climbed in, pulled off her gloves, and ate lunch—a sandwich, coffee, and an apple. Sam and Bud stopped by and she gave them a report.

"I haven't found much yet. A few bones, but I can't say anything definitive about them. And the dirt is mostly orangey clay, so I can't say anything about that either."

"When do you think you'll be done?" Sam asked.

"Oh, when I'm finished, I guess." She grinned at him. He laughed, and Sam and Bud went back to their car.

She continued to work late into the afternoon until she had a pile of dirt larger than the size of the backhoe scoop and many bones, large and small, arranged into the skeletal shape on the tarp.

Then her shovel hit something large and solid. *Eureka*, she thought, *the brains of the outfit.* She dug it out and held it up for Sam and Bud to see, if they were looking, along with people in an SUV that almost skidded to a stop before it rolled by. The jawbone was still attached, and the teeth were in place, and it was full of dirt, which she studied closely. The dirt was orange in color but flecked with humus and was different from the dirt at the bottom of the trench. *Aha!* she thought. *Me thinks I smell a rat! The soil's different in the skull. And there were slivers of wood on the shaker screen—remains of a coffin, I bet—but I didn't see any wood particles in the dirt in the sides of the trench near where the backhoe dug.*

She climbed into the trench and put a couple of cups of the orangey clay from the sides of the trench near the bottom into a plastic bag, marked it, and photographed the location. She did the same halfway up the trench. *No humus in this clay*, she thought.

She laid down the skull at the top of the skeleton and took a photo, and then carried the sample bags to the van, climbed in, started the engine, turned on the AC, ate another sandwich, and drank some lukewarm coffee.

Sam knocked on the window and yelled, "What do you know now?"

She rolled it down and said, "It appears that we are victims of a hoax, Sergeant Sam. I am nearly positive that these bones were moved here from somewhere else and placed in this trench."

Sam scowled, and said, "Oh? How do you know that?"

"The orangey dirt inside the skull is flecked with dark humus like the seams of humus you find in the mixed-up dirt where a grave has been filled-in after a burial. The humus is the dark top-soil from the top of the ground and the orangey dirt is the clay or loam below it. There are also slivers of wood in the skull left from the coffin after it rotted. When the coffin rots, the ground caves in and dirt fills the space in the coffin. The body's already decomposed, so the ground water just washes the dirt mixture and slivers of wood into the bones, like we have in this skull. But the other dirt in the pile is orange clay, so it looks like whoever did this dug out a hole in the clay, placed the bones into it, and backfilled it with the same clay. But they did not replace the dirt in the skull. That came from the original grave where he dug up the bones. That's my theory. I'll want confirmation of the soil samples from the soil scientists in the crime lab before I make a final determination. You detectives can begin looking around for an empty grave, though. I'm sure it's out there."

"How much longer do you think you'll be here now?"

"Another hour, maybe. Then I want to see if there are any good footprints I can get from the trench."

She found a group of prints around where the shovel last scooped the earth, and one where someone had climbed out of the trench, and made three plaster casts, but she didn't know that Clyde had already tossed his boots off the Bay Bridge into the middle of the Chesapeake Bay.

Before she left, she photographed the dig site and bones, put the bones and skull in a plastic bag, and carried them to the van.

The next morning, she met the soil scientist in the crime lab, showed him the photos of the site, and held out the skull for them to take a soil sample. They said they would call after they had done their analysis. She also phoned the county historian at the historical society library and, just to be sure, asked if she could look at the historical maps of the area to see if there was a gravesite where the bones were discovered. The historian returned her call later with a negative report, which was further support for the hoax theory.

Furthermore, the crime-lab soil scientist confirmed that the two soil samples were from different places.

After a four-day delay, construction of the sewer and water lines resumed. Randall drove by, saw the backhoes at work, and was livid. *God Almighty! How can I stop these terrorists from building this mosque!...*An ominous look gripped his face....*Maybe there's only one way.*

A story about the hoax made the Washington Post front page, bottom left. People with any information about it were asked to contact the White County Police Department.

"I knew this was no coincidence!" Ahmed told the reporter when he called. "After all, what was the probability of finding skeletal remains right at the end of a trench we were digging for our sewer line? But you must know that this was not a harmless hoax or prank. This was a deliberate attempt by anti-Muslims to stop the construction of our mosque. And I know who is behind it—the same one who moved our property stakes and vandalized our footers. Of course, I can't prove it, so I won't say who it is."

Friends from three of the churches in town responded to the article by calling Ahmed and expressing their sympathy and support, and Ahmed and Imam Mufti sent a carefully crafted letter of thanks to Clary Fennel, with copies to her superiors at the White County police crime lab, the county executive, the Chelmsford chief of police, and the mayor.

Flyovers by the state police chopper were unable to locate the empty grave deep in the Breckenridge woods, covered once again with leaves and shielded by overhanging limbs of a large oak.

The skeleton was sent to the Medical Examiner's office in Baltimore, and the report from the forensic archaeologist came back two weeks later saying that the deceased was a Caucasoid male from the late eighteenth century. They would need to advertise the bones, and if not claimed, after a year they would be reburied in a pauper's cemetery.

CHAPTER 23
HOMEWARD BOUND

The utility lines were connected and the parking area graded, and this week Miguel and his crew were installing curbing and gutter forms along the highway turning lane, the access road, and around the parking areas, and sidewalk forms along the highway and in front of the mosque. Dan and Lonnie were checking the slope of the forms with Dan's level to make sure the gutter would drain rainwater, ensuring that the rebar was properly installed, and seeing that the curb cuts were correctly placed for people using wheelchairs, walkers, and other mobility aids. Gerald Damon came out, inspected, and to their amazement, approved it.

"Make sure you have enough handicap parking spaces," he told Dan. "I'll be watching."

Dan agreed, with dread in his eyes. He knew that Damon would find every mistake he could to hold up the CO.

The next morning the concrete trucks came, one after another, relentlessly pursuing Miguel and his men down the driveway and around the lot, like bulldozers chasing toreadors, as they placed the rocky mixture in the forms and quickly troweled it smooth. Miguel brought two extra men that day to strip off the forms and finish the surfaces of the curbs after the concrete set. They poured the concrete sidewalks along the highway and in front of the mosque, screeded them, and then swept them with brooms to give them a nonslip surface.

The following day, a backhoe loader spread gravel between the curbs and a roller compacted it in preparation for its asphalt surface. The next morning a small paver spread asphalt all over the turning lane, driveway, and parking lot, followed by the roller, which pressed it and smoothed it. Mist rose from the black concrete, and the rich odor of sulfur and hydrocarbons spread through the jobsite.

Breckenridge! How did he ever think of it? Atif wondered. *Bones!* He was in his room at home, sitting at his desk. *The man's a demon!...He must gather miscellaneous information all the time and let it swirl around his brain until he can assemble it into a weapon to use against us—a torpedo....And we must fight him! But first, I must call Amy...to tell her of this latest outrage.*

He called before the crime scene investigator arrived on site, so he didn't know the outcome with certainty. There was no answer, so he left a message for her to call him back.

She did, clicked on the video, and explained, "I was in class," and then said, "Oh, I miss you so much."

He told her about the bones. "It has to be your dad. It's too much of a coincidence to find a skeleton right in the scoop of the backhoe! It's so improbable that it could not have been an accident. They planted it there."

"Will it delay the construction?"

"Yes! They have to stop digging until a forensic archaeologist examines the bones and determines how old they are and whether they're Indian or African American so they know what to do with them, and then they have to check with the local historians and look at the maps to see if there is a graveyard or burial site there to rebury the bones in. It may take months!"

"Can't they just keep working on the mosque?"

"Yes, but they won't be able to tell if the plumbing works until they hook up the water and sewer lines, and they can't get the certificate of occupancy until the plumbing works. But we're not going to put up with it. We're going to fight it—demonstrate, write letters, whatever. This is fraud."

She looked down and said, "I'm so sorry, Atif. And I'm so ashamed that my dad is behind it."

"We can't pick our parents, Amy."

"No."

"But there's something else I have to tell you about." Amy looked up, and he told her about the call from the fake doctor who got him to reveal his first name. "Now he can search on my full name and find information about me. I don't know what else he has in mind. Anyway, I'm changing my phone number."

"To what?"

"I don't know yet. I'll call you when I have it."

I have to learn more about Breckenridge, he mused. *A soldier, hunter, with guns. That's scary.*

He turned on his laptop, searched on "Mogadishu" and quickly found that the battle of Mogadishu took place in 1993. Then he searched on "Silver Stars 1993," and found an alphabetical listing of medal winners with descriptions of each citation. He scrolled down and read:

BRECKENRIDGE, RANDALL

Synopsis:

The President of the United States takes pleasure in presenting the Silver Star Medal to Randall Breckenridge, Explosive Ordinance Disposal (EOD) Specialist (89D), 93rd OD CO (EOD), US Army, for conspicuous gallantry and intrepidity in action against hostile enemy forces while attached to Company D, 85th Infantry Regiment (Ranger), during combat operations in Mogadishu, Somalia, on 3 and 4 October 1993. EOD Specialist Breckenridge was part of the rescue operations following the crash of two Black Hawk helicopters in the streets of Mogadishu and under heavy fire dismantled an enemy mine aimed at US Army Ranger forces who were trapped by the enemy. His actions were in keeping with the finest traditions of the military forces of the United States and reflect the highest credit upon himself and the United States Army.

EOD specialist! He knows all about bombs…and guns. And he's a hunter. And so is his son. What are we dealing with? A heavily armed Muslim-hater who knows about bombs. I must tell Abu. But he will do nothing. He will say we need to be careful and use the police to protect us. But that's not enough! This man's dangerous! Bombs! Guns! We must be able to defend ourselves if he goes crazy! I must get out Abu's gun, and make sure it's ready—just in case.

It was not the first time he had taken out the gun. He had borrowed it once when Ahmed and Salma were at a conference of Pakistani American physicians in Palm Springs, which happened to coincide with a visit from his cousin, Ali Ibrahim, a US Army sergeant who had seen duty in Afghanistan. Atif took the pistol case for the Beretta PX4 9MM from the shelf of Ahmed's closet, they picked up some ammunition at Walmart early on a Tuesday morning, drove to a range in Prince George's County, and Ali taught Atif to shoot. They paid cash to reduce their electronic trail.

In some ways Atif wished Ahmed would discover that he had borrowed the gun so he could have an open discussion with him. Why did Ahmed have a pistol? He was such a devout man of peace. Was there a time when he felt he needed it to protect his family? Was it when they lived in the neighborhood in Northeast

Washington where there were frequent murders when Atif and Nadira were small?

He decided not to tell Amy about the pistol. It was something to keep in reserve, should he ever need it.

"Hey Dad," Jesse yelled as he galloped down the back stairs through the kitchen into the great room carrying some papers.

Randall looked up from his tablet and barked, "What?" He wore the same pinched expression that he'd had since seeing the backhoes resume work on the trench. Eunice muted the TV and echoed, "What is it?"

"I got another printout of her phone bill."

Randall put down the tablet. "What does it say?"

"The calls are still to the same area code, but the number changed. Amy must've told him that we were tracing her calls, so he changed his number—but it didn't do any good. We still know what she's up to. She's still calling him two or three times a day and still making long calls. I wonder what they talk about."

"Damnation!" he roared, leaping to his feet. "Our daughter consorting with a black-faced moozlim! I won't have it! Eunice. Cut off her phone!"

"You know she'll just use a friend's phone or email him."

"They can use video phone calls on a friend's phone to be together," Jesse added.

"We can't stop them," she said, "no matter how far away we send her."

"They can use Facebook or Twitter," Jesse added.

"I don't care," he roared. "Cut her off anyway. I can't stand it."

Amy sat in English class, dreaming of Atif. *Why is he so interested in Daddy's and Jesse's hunting and Daddy's war service? And when she told him that Jesse shot the coyote, Atif said, "They're killers!...But they don't*

225

scare me." What was that? Anger? Bravado? Belligerence? What is he going to do? And what is Daddy going to do now that so many of his efforts to stop the mosque construction have failed? Her mind's eye saw two battle-ships steaming toward each other through fog.

If only she could be there, she could try to protect them both, but especially Atif. He was the one in greater danger if he con-fronted her dad. Atif's right. Daddy could be a killer. He killed lots of animals, and she didn't know if he killed any people in the war. But she knew he lost his temper sometimes. She needed to calm both of them if she could, and try to bring peace between them.

After class, she went to Fran's room and found her reading on her laptop.

"Fran. I need your help."

"What?"

"I need to get home. Are you going to Charles Town soon?"

"I told you, I don't have any money. She took my credit card, so I can't buy gas."

"I remember," Amy replied. "And I have a credit card, but I don't have my car! How would you feel about going home? We can share the driving, and I'll buy the meals and gas. If we left Saturday morning, we'd be in Charles Town by twelve or one o'clock. Then Atif could pick me up there. But where?"

"Atif? Is he a foreigner?"

"No. He's from Chelmsford. He's a pre-med student at Maryland, and his dad's a doctor."

"Oh, well, tell him to meet us at the diner across from Hollywood Drive, the road that takes you to the casino and race track. That's easy to find, and he can wait there."

"Oh, Fran. You're an angel!"

"Anything for young love—yours and mine. But you'll have to give me some money to get back to school."

"Of course!"

She picked up her phone and clicked the on button. Silence. *Battery must be dead,* she thought. She plugged it in to the recharge cord and pushed the button. Again, it would not come on. *The whole phone is dead. Damn.* She went back to Fran.

"I don't know what's wrong with my phone. It won't work. Can I use yours?"

"Sure."

She punched in Atif's number. "Maybe they cancelled my service," she told Fran.

Atif answered and she told him about her phone and told him to put Fran's number in his contacts. Then she told him the plan. He said he would pick her up in Charles Town.

"Where will you stay when you get here?" he asked.

"At home. I'll just walk in the front door and shout, 'I'm home.' I don't care what they do. They can ground me, take away my phone and laptop and credit card and make me stay in my room. Put an armed guard on me for all I care. They won't be able to keep me from slipping out for an occasional run, and sneaking a few calls on their landline while they're out."

"You are a delinquent, Amy, but you're certainly not juvenile. Oh, I can't wait to see you and hold you."

"Me too, Atif. I want to hold you so badly and kiss you."

They left at seven on Saturday morning and proceeded down to Route 81 in Virginia, and then north up the Shenandoah Valley to Winchester, east on Route 7, and north on Route 340 to Charles Town. They made stops near Lexington and Winchester, for restrooms and food, but didn't tarry, and took turns driving, going a steady ten miles an hour over the speed limits, and pulled into the diner at ten after twelve.

Amy ran to the door and stood outside hugging Atif and wouldn't let go. Fran was shocked to see her embracing a man who was obviously South Asian.

"Fran, this is Atif. Atif, this is Fran. Two dear friends. Thank you, thank you for bringing me here, Fran. I am so grateful."

Fran smiled lasciviously. "As I said, anything for love—as long as you give me my money to get back to school."

Amy looked at Atif. "Do you have some?"

"Yes, yes. Is two twenties enough? Otherwise we'll have to find a bank machine."

"That's plenty."

"Anybody hungry?" he asked.

They ate, he signed the credit slip, and they went their separate ways.

In the car, Atif looked at her and said, "Oh, Amy, it's so good to see you again!"

He drove a short way, pulled into a mall parking lot, and stopped.

"What are we stopping for?"

He turned to her, took her head in his hands, and said, "This," and began kissing her passionately. She unhooked her seatbelt to get closer, and gave him her mouth again. She closed her eyes deliriously, and they caressed each other's shoulders and backs.

Then she tipped her head down so her forehead rested on his cheek and moaned, "Oh, Atif. I love you so much. I want you. I want to give myself to you and be one with you."

Suddenly, he pushed himself away, "No, Amy, we mustn't. We can't. But I want you so much, too."

She kept kneading his body. "We can just stop and get a motel room. No one knows we're here."

"No, we can't," he panted. "We are not married. It is…haram—forbidden. Even our kissing and touching is."

"I want to go to a motel," she demanded.

"No. It is sin!"

"Then we will sin."

"No, please, we can't," he said breathlessly. "We must wait. We're not married."

A thought struck her, and she looked into his eyes and whispered, "When are we getting married, Atif?"

"Oh! I am still in school."

"But you said your father was still in college when he and your mother were married."

He looked at her. "But you are a Christian. Would you convert to Islam?"

"No, I can't do that, Atif, but we can still be together. That can't stop us. We love each other."

"Yes."

She looked up at him with dreams in her eyes. "Atif, will you marry me?"

"Oh, yes, yes, Amy, I will."

"And you'll promise to have no one other than me until death do we part."

He nodded. "Yes. I'll promise."

"Do you promise it right now?"

"Yes, I promise."

"I promise it, too. I will have no one other than you until death do we part. So now we're married. Now we can go to a motel."

"No, no, no! You tricked me. It's not official. We must say it in front of the imam and our parents and friends."

"Oh, poo. But it's OK with Muslims if we marry, isn't it?"

"Yes. Muslim women can't marry Christians, but Muslim men can marry Christian women. It's because the husband and father is the imam of the household and leads the family in Salah—that's prayer, and the Christian man couldn't do that."

A car began pulling in next to them. Amy jerked to her side and pulled on her seat belt, Atif turned the key, and they pulled out.

She looked at him. "Now I'm Mrs. Bhati," she whispered proudly.

After they were on a straight stretch of road, Amy said, "And now Jesus and I have the whole rest of our lives to save you from the fiery furnace."

Atif laughed. "And I have our whole life to convert you and save you!"

They drove through the rolling countryside down the Charles Town Pike and for a while were lost in thought. Then Atif said, "Amy. I promised you I would show you a mosque. Do you still want to see one?"

"Yes. Which one?"

"I thought I could take you to the Islamic Center in Washington. It's quite beautiful."

"OK."

They continued onto VA Rt. 7 toward Leesburg, and onto I-66 into the District of Columbia, and then Massachusetts Avenue until they came to the center. It loomed high on the left, its minaret rising well over a hundred feet high.

They parked on a side street and walked through the gate of the wrought iron arrow fence, up a few stairs, between one of five keyhole arches supported by marble columns, and into a courtyard.

"I think we can get in and look around before it's time for Asr—afternoon prayers. There might be a lot of people praying at that time. I think it's at about four-thirty."

She saw a sign that said, "Women's Entrance," and asked if she needed to use it, but Atif said that was only used on Fridays during congregational prayer when women prayed on the lower level because of large crowds.

Amy pulled a scarf from her backpack—the same one she wore to their meetings—covered her head, and tied it under her chin. Atif smiled in recognition when he saw it.

They climbed a few more marble stairs, removed their shoes, placed them in the rack by the door, and went through high wooden doors with carved panels into the great prayer hall. A large chandelier hung in the center of the square room surrounded by marble columns and tiled walls with intricate geometric designs.

"Straight ahead is the mihrab," Atif told her, "that curved niche. It faces Mecca, and that is where the imam stands when he leads the prayers. It is said to be the doorway to Mecca. The imam faces that direction, too. And over on the right, where those stairs go up, is the minbar where he gives the Khutbah—the sermon."

"Oh," she gasped as she arched her head backward and gazed at the top of the dome from which the chandelier was suspended. "It's gorgeous! A star...inside a...an octagon...with stained glass windows in little arches on eight sides...coming down to the square over the prayer room."

"I'm home!" she yelled, bursting through the front door, her backpack over her shoulder.

Eunice raced in from the kitchen. "What are you doing here? Your father won't like this."

"I bet he won't. But here I am."

She passed her mother fast—a moving target, and bolted up the steps toward her bedroom, hitting each one in a drum roll.

"You won't get any food here," Eunice shouted.

"Then I'll starve!" She dropped the words over the railing and they sailed down to the kitchen.

Soon she heard angry voices—her mother asking, "What'll we do with her?" and her father shouting, "We'll kick her out—make her go her own way."

"No, we can't do that. She's still a minor. And anyway, she'll just move in with him, or they'll elope. No we have to keep her in our control, and make her go back to school."

"Then we'll lock her in her room!"

She hung over the railing to listen.

Jesse advised, "Don't forget, she has her laptop."

Randall's eyes flared. He snarled, "Well, we'll take that away right now!"

"She says she'll starve if we don't feed her," Eunice said.

"Let her starve!" he boomed. "No food or water for a few days and she'll be dying to go back south."

Eunice looked up at him. "I'll get her laptop."

"Jesse, you go put one of those little gate hooks on her door," Randall ordered. "That'll hold her for now."

"Do you have one?" He did not want to take off the one on the door between the second floor landing and his private abode.

Randall pointed with his head toward the side door. "Check the tool box in the garage."

Eunice looked puzzled. "But where will she go to the bathroom?"

"Get her one of those bedside toilets for old people and a couple rolls of paper," Randall said.

"And we can't cut off her water. She might die."

Randall looked down out of the corner of his eye. "Hmm. OK. Get her a case of water."

Amy sighed. *Water. And at least they're giving me a pot to pee in.*

She went into her room and quickly hid her laptop under her bed, and then went into the sleeping room and looked out the window. Instantly, she determined that she could go out the window onto the roof of the addition, jump off, and get away. But maybe she didn't want them to know yet that she could do that.

She scampered out of the room across the hall into the bathroom, to use it while she still could, then returned to her room, closed the door, and locked it. She went into her walk-in closet, sat on the floor, and was relieved to hear the drone of the TV and the side door slamming.

She heard the doorknob turn back and forth. "Amy. Open this door."

"Just a minute."

She went to the door and turned the knob, releasing the lock. Leaning against the door, she opened it a few inches.

"Let me in," Eunice demanded.

Amy swung it open wide. "Of course. Come in."

Eunice began scanning the room, and said, "Give me your lap top."

Amy looked away. "I didn't bring it home. I was afraid it would get stolen."

"Stolen? How did you get home?"

She waved her thumb. "I hitchhiked."

Eunice scowled. "Amy! You could have been raped or murdered."

"No, Mother. Not all people are rapists and killers. Some are good Christians."

Her mother's eyes drilled into her. "But you were afraid it would be stolen?"

Amy shrugged. "Yes. And it wouldn't work anyway in the mountains. I would have been out of range."

She's explaining too much, Eunice thought, cocking her head to the side and squinting. "Are you lying again?"

Amy stomped her foot. "No! I didn't bring it home!"

"I'll have to search your room."

"You don't have any right," she said, shaking her head. "This is my room."

"No it isn't. Your room is at Steuer University."

Eunice scanned the room, and then went straight for the bed, dropped to her knees, bent down, and felt underneath. "What's this?" she barked.

"You can't take that!"

"Oh yes I can…liar," she said, pulling it out and standing. "You've forgotten how to tell the truth, haven't you? You have forgotten how to be a Christian."

"No, I haven't. It's you and Daddy who have forgotten."

Eunice brought her arm up and slapped Amy hard across the face. "That's enough!"

"Oh!" Amy squealed, bringing her hand to her cheek.

"And you are to stay in your room."

"Oh, don't worry, Mother, dear. I wouldn't want to be with you and Daddy."

Eunice turned and walked out, and Amy locked the door.

Shortly thereafter, Jesse arrived with a pair of wireman pliers and twisted the gate hook and eye into the door and frame. "There you go, Amy-girl. You're locked in now."

Amy went to the door and tried to open it, shaking it back and forth, rattling it. "Brat!" she yelled.

An hour later, Eunice unhooked the door, turned the knob, which was locked again, and ordered, "Let me in."

Amy opened the door, and Eunice handed her the bedside toilet and two rolls of paper. "Here. Don't make a mess." She turned and walked out.

Jesse brought in the case of water and set it on the floor. "Don't get hungry now, girly-girl," he said with a grin.

"Why can't you help me?" she asked.

"You want me to help a sinner sin?"

"Out!" she commanded, and he pulled the door shut and put the hook in the eye.

CHAPTER 24
PREPARING FOR WAR

At the mosque in Chelmsford, the parking-lot striper and his helper were measuring spaces, marking the ends of the space lines on the asphalt with chalk—nine feet apart—snapping chalk lines between the marks, and following the lines with the painting machine—the airless line striper—which resembled a lawn mower and sprayed paint over the chalk lines. Lonnie was supervising—counting the spaces and ensuring that there were sufficient handicap spaces and accessible van spaces.

Inside, the plumber and heating contractor were doing tests in preparation for the final inspections; tilers were grouting a mosaic design around the curved mihrab, carpenters were installing moldings on the stairs to the minbar in preparation for painting, and the carpet installers were rolling carpet over the prayer room floor. Outside, the landscaper was planting shrubs and broadcasting grass seed and straw over the graded areas and begin the watering. Dan was supervising the cleaning crew, which was washing the tile floors, walls, counters, and windows, and wiping the doors and mirrors, and he was directing his own clean-up crew to do odds and ends throughout the building. Outside, Quiggley and his men were completing the railings on the ramp, throwing scraps of wood into his pickup, and raking the dirt around and under the ramp until it was free of nails and wood.

Ahmed and the building committee would inspect the building the following week and develop a punch list of items that needed to be completed prior to making the final payment to Dan Stanley. When those were finished, Gerald Damon would make his final inspection for the city and hopefully would grant the certificate of occupancy.

Ahmed, who was normally stern and imperturbable, drove by the construction repeatedly, staring at it and effervescing with giddy dreams and prayers of thanksgiving—"Praise be to Allāh, who hath guided us to this!"

The Chelmsford Ministerial Association invited him and Imam Mufti to attend their meeting, at which the clergy lavished warm congratulations on them for their accomplishment.

Meanwhile, as Randall drove by, his vision grew progressively dark and narrow. *Time for the final solution...we have no choice...They've driven us to it.*

There would be no more meetings in the trophy room. This he would do himself, to insulate his friends from prosecution. He would use only Clyde and Jesse.

He spoke to his son alone in the trophy room, witnessed only by the beasts on the walls.

"Jesse. I need your help."

"Yes?"

Amy was dozing on her closet floor. It was the only place where she could ascertain what was happening. In a state of hunger-induced fatigue after three days without food, she picked up on the conversation and began to concentrate.

"You know I've tried and tried to stop that mosque from being built in our town..." Jesse nodded. "We made them resurvey the lot and tear out those footings and double those floor joists and put on a covered ramp, and we put those bones in that ditch and all, and nothing we did stopped them from going ahead. Nothing!"

"I know," Jesse's voice chimed.

"And in a matter of weeks they're going to open that thing up and start preaching jihad to all those camel jockeys and their children, and it won't be long till they're setting off IEDs by our highways and blowing themselves up with suicide vests in our restaurants and buildings. It's only a matter of time before they start trying to take over America."

"What do we do, Dad?"

"We have to end it, Jesse. Once and for all."

His voice trailed off to a whisper, and Amy lost it, though she strained mightily.

Then, it returned and grew louder. "Can I count on you?"

She heard a voice mustering men for battle.

"Yessir, you can count on me."

"Do you think you can do it?"

"Yes, sir. I can do it."

"OK," he shouted. "First we zero our rifles. We'll take those thermal night vision scopes too."

Oh, God, Amy thought.

Then she heard, "Yeah, Clyde, it's me. Whatcha doin'?"…"Yeah, I need some more help."…"No, I don't need any more bones moved." She heard Jesse laugh.…"It's a different job. Listen. Can you meet me this evening in the old barn at the northern end, you know, where we keep the fertilizer and diesel?"

"Uh!" Amy puffed, gaping. She knew what they were used for.

"…About seven. And bring that old two-horse trailer, will you? You know, the one with the tandem axles?"

I've got to warn them as soon as I can, she thought. But…I have to wait for darkness.

She used the time to prepare, putting on her dark gray sweats with a hoodie and her running shoes, finding a flashlight, and then waiting nervously.

She heard her dad's pickup pull out and return late in the afternoon, and then heard her dad and Jesse come in and eat in the trophy room.

Eunice said, "You two are quiet." Amy could almost see them silently nodding and see fear in her mother's eyes.

Then she heard her dad say, "Let's go."

Eunice asked, "Where are you going?"

She heard him say, "Down to the farm," and heard the pickup drive out again.

At about seven-thirty, Amy heard the door close on the lavatory, located off the main hallway and almost below where she sat in the closet. Hearing the sound of flushing, she crept out of the closet, into the sleeping room off the bedroom, carefully raised the left double hung window, lifted the storm window, and climbed gently out onto the addition roof. She lowered the sash, but couldn't turn the lock, and slid the storm window down as far as she could. After easing down the roof, she kneeled, lay on her stomach, hung her legs over the edge, and dropped ten feet to the ground, her flashlight in her hand.

She flew across the yard beside the house and down the road, staying in the shadows, across the road from the streetlights. The air was cool and damp with dew. Afraid to go to his house but wanting to talk to Atif directly, she ran to the only outdoor payphone she knew of in town—one with a blue metal box around it—on the wall of the café next to the theater, and clicked his number.

After a few rings, he answered.

"Atif?"

"Amy! Where are you?"

"I'm at the payphone in town at the cafe."

He jumped out of his chair in his bedroom, began pacing, and said, "I thought I'd hear from you sooner."

"They locked me in my room. And they're refusing to feed me. They're only giving me water. I haven't eaten in three days."

He was aghast. "That's criminal! That's child abuse. But I know you're not a child."

"I had to break out. I climbed out a window just now onto the roof of our addition on the back and jumped to the ground, and I can't get back in without a ladder, but I had to tell you something I heard through the wall. I heard my dad tell Jesse, when they were talking about the mosque, that 'We have to end it. Once and for all.' And then they went out on the farm to adjust their rifle sights."

"Oh! They're getting ready for war!"

"And then I heard him telling someone on the phone to meet him tonight at six in the old barn where they keep fertilizer and diesel."

"Fertilizer and diesel! That's what they make those big bombs out of—like what Timothy McVeigh used to blow up that federal building in Oklahoma City!"

"And he's supposed to bring the two-horse trailer."

"A trailer! To carry drums full of explosive! And your dad learned about bombs in the army!"

"What? What are they going to do?"

He stopped pacing. "They're going to try to blow up the masjid!"

"Oh!" she gasped. "What should we do?"

"Call the police?"

"I don't trust them. They know Dad too well."

"Well, I'll tell Abu!"

"I won't let him do it!" she said angrily. "Maybe…maybe we should wrap a human chain around it. You know, get a bunch of people and all link hands. They wouldn't dare blow it up then. That would be mass murder."

"That's a good idea. We can get people from the masjid."

"And from the other churches in town."

"I'll tell Abu. I'll call you back. What's the number?"

She gave it to him and then waited at the brightly-lit payphone until she saw a police cruiser approaching and hung up and raced by the theater, turned onto the alley behind it, and sprinted between houses and stores until it dead-ended at a side street, and then turned back toward the highway. Seeing no police car, she dashed away toward Atif's subdivision, and after ten minutes, ran up to his front door and rang the bell.

It was the first time she'd been to his home, and she was anxious about meeting his parents. Salma, wrapped in a long robe, opened the door, looked at Amy standing there panting in her running clothes with her hands on her knees. As if sizing her for a shalwar kameeze and scarf, she waved her head back and forth and said, "You must be Miss Breckenridge. Come in."

Nadira stood behind her and whooped, "Amy!"

They went into the small living room on the right and sat— Amy and Nadira on the sofa and Salma on a chair—and waited for Dr. Bhati who came in with Atif behind him, the doctor wearing his white shirt, tie, and dress pants from work, and Atif in a T-shirt and jeans. "Miss Breckenridge?" Ahmed asked.

Amy stood awkwardly, blushing, and said, "Yes, Dr. Bhati. I'm Amy."

He did not offer to shake hands, but sat on the front edge of a large stuffed chair "Please tell me what you heard."

She repeated what she had told Atif and her suggestion of forming a human chain.

"First I will call the police."

He rose from his chair, pulled out his cellphone, and clicked the number.

"Yes. This is Ahmed Bhati. I want to speak to someone about an attempt to blow up the new mosque on Father White Highway."

"Hold on."

There was a minute of silence as he waited, during which he began pacing through the living room, turning, and retracing his steps like a guard at Buckingham Palace. Then he heard, "Yes?"

"Yes. This is Dr. Ahmed Bhati. I live in Oakton Acres off Father White Highway and am president of the board of the Chelmsford Islamic Center."

"Yes, sir. How can I help you?"

"To whom am I speaking?"

"Sergeant Collins."

"Thank you. We have received a report that an attempt will be made, possibly tonight, to blow up our mosque on Father White Highway."

"Really. Who gave you this information?"

"Miss Amy Breckenridge, the daughter of Randall Breckenridge."

"Oh. Is she back? I thought she was going to college in West Virginia."

"She came back."

"And what did she say?"

Ahmed told him.

"Dr. Bhati. This is a very serious accusation she's making about her father, and you know, he's a decorated war veteran from one of the oldest families in the county. I doubt very much that there is any credence to the story. I've heard that this girl has been at odds with her parents for some time and may just be trying to get them in trouble."

"What? So—what? You won't do anything about this?"

"Dr. Bhati. You must realize that our force is spread thin and is investigating many crimes that have already occurred. We can't just drop everything and start investigating some unsubstantiated rumor."

He stopped pacing. "Rumor! This is a report from a well-respected young woman—a graduate of Chelsmford High School."

"Yes, I understand. Well, we'll send a cruiser by the mosque a few times tonight, but I really can't promise more than that, sir. Sorry."

"Can't you park a police car there?"

"I really can't. I'm sorry."

Ahmed hung up. He was furious. "They won't do anything except drive by a few times. We're really on our own."

"Father, we must build the human chain as Amy suggested. He wouldn't dare murder the ministers."

"Yes. I'll make some calls."

"And ask them to come out at night?" Salma asked.

"I think they will understand. And we need all the time we can get."

First he called Imam Mufti, and asked him to contact other members of the congregation. Then he called Reverend Carson, the Methodist minister, who said he'd call the other ministers and the pastor of the Catholic church, and the Jewish rabbi, and ask them to contact others. Next Ahmed called Maskeen, who said he'd call Dan Stanley. Dan said he'd call Lonnie and Miguel, and Miguel said he'd bring his helpers. All would assemble at nine at night. They'd pack food and bring folding chairs and blankets. Amy said they should bring poster board, too, and big markers.

"Do you have any poster board and markers or paint and brushes?" Amy asked. "We must make signs."

Nadira said, "Yes! I'll get some." She ran off to the basement and came back carrying a stack of boards and markers.

Ahmed urged, "Quick, now. Let's change our clothes."

Nadira began sprinting to the stairs, and Salma said, "You're not going, Nadira."

"Oh, yes, I am!" Nadira replied and kept on running.

"What happens if they do blow up the masjid? Are you going to leave me all alone?"

"It's in Allāh's hands, Mother," Atif said.

"I'll make sandwiches," she said, tears streaming down her face.

Just before they left, Atif slipped into his father's bedroom, lifted the case down from the closet, and removed the pistol. He loaded it with a full magazine, put two more in his pocket, and placed the pistol behind his belt under his sweatshirt in the back.

CHAPTER 25

THE MARRIAGE

The mosque was dark when they arrived, except for a spot-light shining on it from the yard in front and a light by the entrance door. Ahmed and Atif parked their cars in front with their headlights aimed at the entrance for additional light, and left them running.

People began arriving well before nine, parking behind the mosque and dragging chairs, coolers, blankets, and sleeping bags to the front.

Ahmed greeted them, thanking them for coming, and address-ing those he knew by name—Reverend Carson, Maskeen, Mr. Stanley, Rabbi Goldman, Father Francis—and many others. Most faces were resolute.

"Thanks for coming, Reverend Carson, and bringing your wife and daughter. You have no idea how grateful we are to you for helping us."

"We have to do it, Ahmed. We must stand up to bullies." His daughter, who was middle-school age, nodded strongly.

Dan Stanley said, "With all the work we've done on this place, I sure don't want some terrorist destroying it."

"Some Islamophobe," added Lonnie.

They took positions near the entrance. The lights shining through the darkness cast an eerie spell over the assemblage.

Soon the church leaders gathered and decided that a prayer service was needed. They collected everyone into a circle at the entrance. Imam Mufti, the lawyer, addressed the group first. "I want to express our deepest gratitude that all of you have come here tonight to help us protect our mosque. We will be indebted to you forever. And we want to thank Allāh for leading you here and answering our prayers. And Allāh, I pray that you will protect these servants and this masjid from the ravages of Satan, our enemy. In the name of Allāh, the Most Gracious, the Most Merciful. Blessed and exalted are You."

Reverend Carson—young, tall, and strong—spoke next. "We are gathered here to help our Muslim friends guard their new mosque from a satanic terrorist set on destroying their house of worship. I think it would be appropriate if I read King Solomon's Prayer of Dedication of the first Jewish temple, on Mount Zion in Jerusalem, built perhaps in 832 BCE and destroyed by Nebuchadnezzar several centuries later. I read from First Kings 8, verses 27 through 30 in the Good News Translation.

> But can you, O God, really live on earth? Not even all of heaven is large enough to hold you, so how can this Temple that I have built be large enough? Lord my God, I am your servant. Listen to my prayer, and grant the requests I make to you today. Watch over this Temple day and night, this place where you have chosen to be worshiped. Hear me when I face this Temple and pray. Hear my prayers and the prayers of your people when they face this place and pray. In your home in heaven hear us and forgive us.

"We all worship one God," Reverend Carson said, "whether we call Him God, Allāh, Yahweh, Adonai, or Jehovah."

Rabbi Goldman, with a black velvet kippah on the back of his balding head and gray hair at his temples, spoke next. "I'd like to begin with a reading from Deuteronomy 6:4–5: Moses said,

Hear, O Israel: The Lord our God is one Lord: And thou shalt love the Lord thy God with all thine heart, and with all thy soul, and with all thy might.

"I'd also like everyone to remember the hundreds of thousands of Jews killed in the pogroms in Russia, the Ukraine, Poland, and Moldova during the eighteenth and nineteenth centuries, and the six million Jews murdered in Europe in the Nazi Holocaust— seventy-eight percent of the Jews in Europe. I ask God, please, do not let religious terrorism take hold here."

Father Francis spoke next, bowing his head and saying, "Let us pray. Father Almighty, maker of heaven and earth, protect us tonight. Save us from intolerance and bigotry. Let us live together peacefully with those who have beliefs different from our own, and let us support each other in doing your divine will. In the name of the Father, the Son, and the Holy Spirit. Amen."

The group dispersed. Dan showed people where the restrooms were in the mosque and turned on lights for them. Then people placed their chairs along the sidewalk and arranged their blankets and sleeping bags for the night. The sky was clear and full of stars, and no rain was predicted. The air was still, damp, and getting chilly.

Conversation was subdued, stunted by fear, but girded by resolution.

Imam Mufti thanked Father Francis for coming and leading them in prayer, and the priest replied, "God will protect us, either here or in heaven."

Atif put two chairs—for him and Amy—near the entrance. Ahmed put his on the other side of Atif.

"Atif," Amy said. "Give me a sandwich, please. I'm starving! I haven't eaten in three days! And a bottle of water, please."

He reached in the cloth bag that Salma had given him and pulled out two sandwiches—roti with feta cheese and pineapple—one for each of them, in plastic bags, and two bottles of water.

"Thanks," she said, and she took a bite, smiled, and then stood up and quickly walked down the line, eating as she went, asking people to come make signs. Reverend Carson, his wife and daughter, and some of the other younger people joined her. In the light at the entrance, Amy gave them poster board and markers and suggested some things to write —"Save the Mosque," "Preserve Freedom of Religion." Others offered their own words—"First Amendment Rights," and "Defend All Religions," "Catholics Support Muslims," and "Methodists Support Muslims." Dan Stanley found some furring strips from a waste pile and cans of paint and brushes, and they traced the lettering with paint and stapled the signs to long furring strips so they could raise them high enough to be seen from the highway. Then they took them to their chairs on the sidewalk.

At about ten-thirty, Imam Mufti began collecting members of the Muslim congregation—the dozen or so people who could come on short notice—to go inside for Ishā prayers.

"I have to stay here," Atif told him, "in case he comes. I will pray here." Ahmed nodded at his son and told the imam that he himself would go with the group. Nadira followed them in. She would pray behind the men.

Inside, they used the bathroom, removed their shoes and placed them on the rack, and entered the ablution room to carry out the symbolic Wudu cleansing. Then they entered the dim, silent prayer hall, and Imam Mufti went to the mihrab and stood with his back to the others who stood behind him placing their toes on lines on the newly-carpeted floor, facing the mihrab. He spoke softly and the congregants mimicked him, so not to disturb the others. Still their voices echoed through the empty room from the hard walls and ceiling—into the anteroom and through the entrance door—praying in Arabic, praising Allāh, asking for refuge from Satan and for guidance along the straight path, praying that the mosque not be destroyed, and testifying that there is no God but Allāh and that Muhammad is His servant and messenger.

Amy heard the reverberations and pictured a Muslim prayer service she had seen in a video on the Internet. Atif felt shy about praying in public in front of nonbelievers, so he prayed silently in his mind, listening to the Arabic sounds originating from inside.

There, inside, the group stood upright in a line, raised their hands to their ears with fingers spread, then placed their hands together just below the navel. They bowed down with hands on knees, resumed an erect posture, went to their knees and placed their forehead, nose, and palms of both hands on the carpeted floor, and then sat upright with their legs beneath them and their hands on their knees, looked to the right and left and at their hands. Finally they rose, moved from the prayer hall into the narthex, put on their shoes, and exited into the glare of the spotlight and headlights.

The night air was cooling and slowly giving up its moisture into droplets of fog.

Ahmed walked down the line to speak to Reverend Carson, to thank him once again for all he had done for them. Meanwhile, Atif and Amy had a whispered tête-à-tête.

"Amy, when this is over, we must get married."

She leaned over to his chair, grabbed him, and almost knocking him over, began kissing him.

"Oh, Amy," Nadira sang. "Tsk, tsk, tsk, tsk."

Atif pushed her away. "Not here, Amy!"

"But you just asked me to marry you! I have to kiss you. What am I supposed to do?"

"What?" Nadira repeated.

He said, "Later, Amy, later."

"Wonderful!" Nadira shouted so that everyone could hear. "They're going to get married!"

Amy was all business now. "OK. Will we be married in the mosque?"

"Only if you decide to convert."

She shook her head. "I can't give up Jesus, Atif."

"Then we will have to find somewhere else. I know. Maybe in the Methodist church—in the basement where we hold our services."

"Yes. That would be OK. And then my friends can come and your friends will feel at home, too."

"But normally my mother would visit your home and bring sweets and a coin wrapped in silk—"

She looked into his eyes. "But Atif. You know she wouldn't be welcome. And I don't even know where I'm going to live. Can I live with you in your family?"

"Oh, Amy, I'm sure Abu and Ami will learn to love you as much as I do, and very soon, especially after what you have done to save the mosque, but you can't expect them to take you in to live with us yet, since we are not married. That would not be acceptable."

"Where then?"

"I don't know. But think of the lilies of the field, Amy. Allāh takes care of them, and he will take care of you and feed you and clothe you."

"Matthew 6:26, Jesus's words. How do you know that?"

"Everyone does, Amy. It's a famous saying."

"I know it's true, Atif. God will show us a way."

"Yes."

Nadira was quiet, so she would not miss a word.

Amy looked worried. "But who will marry us, Atif?"

"Maybe we can have Imam Mufti and Reverend Carson do it together."

"Yes! And we can help them write the service."

Nadira could not control herself. "Yes, yes!" she blurted.

"And then after the wedding, you can come to our house, and we'll have a big party for everyone, right Nadira?"

"A big, big party, brother."

"Let's go talk to Abu, and the imam, and Reverend Carson, Amy."

They sprang up and walked briskly down the walk, all smiles, holding hands.

Ahmed was talking with the imam when they approached.

"Father, and Imam Mufti. Amy and I have decided to get married."

"What?" Ahmed asked. "She's not a Muslim."

"Father, the Qur'an does not prohibit a Muslim man from marrying a non-Muslim woman."

"No...but you're too young, and you're still in school, and you must get straight As, or you won't get into medical school!"

"I'm not too young, and we're in love, and you married Mother when you were in school, and you continued, and you were successful."

"But then you will have children, and that will distract you."

"You didn't, and we can wait to have children, like you did. So please tell Mother that we are getting married."

Ahmed flinched at having his son give him an order.

"Imam Mufti. Can you and Reverend Carson do the service for us? We want to be married in the basement of his church where we now meet."

He looked skeptical. "Have you discussed this with Reverend Carson?"

"Not yet. Let me get him."

While Ahmed quickly clicked his cell phone, Atif and Amy walked down to where Reverend Carson was standing, smiling. "What's going on, Atif?"

"Amy and I are getting married, and we want you and Imam Mufti to do the service in the basement of your church. Will you do it for us?"

Mrs. Carson and their daughter Susan burst into smiles, and Mrs. Carson said, "Say yes, Bill. We must get these fine people married!"

He looked at her. "Well, young lady. Are you eighteen yet? You must be eighteen to be married without parental consent in Maryland."

"I'll be eighteen next month."

"Then I think I should talk to Imam Mufti and Ahmed about this, don't you?"

Atif held up his right hand. "But wait. I have another request. Amy has nowhere to live. Her parents are locking her in her room and giving her no food—only water."

"What?" Reverend and Mrs. Carson said, scowling. "They can't do that," he said.

"That's child abuse," she added.

Atif went on. "She needs a place to live until we are married. Can you help her?"

Susan looked up at her mother shaking her head yes.

Reverend Carson looked at his wife and received her assent. "Yes, I am sure we can do that, Amy."

"Amy, you are welcome to live with us," Mrs. Carson agreed.

"There, you see, Amy. Allāh has provided. Now let's talk to my father and the imam."

Reverend Carson followed Atif and Amy as they marched back.

Ahmed spoke gravely, "I discussed this with your mother, Atif, and you know the marriage tradition is that she and I would make the proposal to Amy's parents and they would have to accept it. But it seems in this case that is out of the question, so Salma has decided that she will go along with your plan, Atif. Thus far, she likes Amy."

"I hope so!" Nadira interjected.

"But she can't live with us until after the wedding."

Reverend Carson informed Ahmed and the imam, "We have told Amy she can live with us until the wedding, and I am willing to assist with the wedding, Mr. Mufti, if you agree, but it will have to be after she is eighteen, in July."

"Yes, I agree."

"And we are willing for it to be held in our church basement, if that is their wish. I have to check it with the board, but I'm sure they'll agree."

Atif smiled. "Then we have a plan."

Amy looked at him, proud, starstruck, and dreamy-eyed. *How did he do it?* "Can I kiss him now?"

"Only once," the imam said.

And she planted one on his mouth and wouldn't let go until he ripped himself away and said, "That's enough! I need air!"

"OK, we must have a little more decorum here, Amy, if you are to be in our family," Ahmed said.

"They're getting married," Nadira shouted to the group.

"That goes for you, too, Nadira." She grinned.

Amy, Atif, and Nadira returned to their chairs near the entrance, and sat for a moment as the chatter around them dwindled and people wrapped themselves in blankets in the cool night air and began again to feel sleep creep into them. Then Amy whispered to him. It was like pillow talk. "What about our children?" she asked. "How will we raise them? We haven't talked about that."

"Hmm. Well, they must go to school to learn the Qur'an in Arabic, and I will teach them about the five pillars and some of the short surahs in the Qur'an."

"Surahs?"

"Chapters. And when we pay Zakāh or visit the sick or elderly, I will tell them that we do it to please Allāh."

"OK, but I must be allowed to teach them the Bible, too, and the stories about Jesus. And songs."

"Like what?"

"'Jesus loves me' and Christmas carols like 'O Little Town of Bethlehem,' and Easter songs like 'Were You There When They Crucified My Lord,' and 'Up from the Grave He Arose!' and spirituals like 'Go Tell It on the Mountain,' and 'Steal Away to Jesus.' They have to learn them."

His head moved side to side as he squinted in the pale light. "OK, but I want to teach them how to pray."

"And to pray before meals."

"That would be all right, but they must also fast during Ramadan so that they learn what hunger is like, and celebrate Eid Al-Fitr at the end of Ramadan, and Eid Al-Adha at the end of Hajj."

"What's Eid Al-Adha?"

"It celebrates Ibrahim's willingness to sacrifice his son Ismāil to God."

"Ibrahim?"

"In the Hebrew Bible, he's called Abraham."

"Oh yes, but we don't believe in human sacrifice."

"But you believe in the Bible, and you believe that Jesus was a human sacrifice to God to save you from your sins—and the sins of Adam and Eve—the original sin."

"Oh, but that doesn't mean we believe everything in the Bible."

"But Ibrahim was only trying to show his obedience to Allāh."

She considered that a moment. "You're right…I guess."

He abruptly turned his focus to the highway as headlights approached and a car sped past.

"OK," she said. "The children can celebrate that Eid Al-Fitr and Eid Al-Adha. But we must also celebrate Christmas and Easter… and have a Christmas tree."

"I think we can celebrate the birth of the prophet Jesus to Mary. But a Christmas tree? That's pagan! So I suppose you want Santa

Claus to fly in with his reindeer and bring presents, too, and for everyone to give presents to each other."

"Yes!" she said emphatically. "They teach children about giving, Atif, and that's important in both Islam and Christianity."

"I think they teach children more about getting things and spending money."

She started pleading with her hands. "But Christmas is a part of our culture. And…it's a time to make children happy. We can't deny them that."

"I think we could teach them more about giving by helping at a soup kitchen or making gift bags for street people."

"Yes, but we can't take the fun out of their childhoods, Atif."

Nadira's eyes were jumping behind closed eyelids.

"Well, I'm not putting up Christmas lights. And don't ask me to go to Easter services with you. We don't believe in the crucifixion of Jesus and him dying for our sins and all that."

"But you said you believe that Allāh raised Jesus into heaven. So we could all celebrate that."

Atif was getting agitated. "No. It's different. We don't believe that Jesus is God or the son of God. We believe that there is no God but Allāh, and Muhammad is his Messenger."

Amy stared into the foggy darkness across the new grass toward the highway, and said, "Well, I still say we're not that far apart."

"And I won't go to communion with you and pretend to eat his flesh and drink his blood."

"We're just going to have to teach our children both religions and let them choose what to believe. I will take them to church on Easter and Christmas, but I think you should go with us."

He gave his head a quick shake. "No. I will take them to the masjid on Fridays."

"When they're not in school. And I will take them to church on Sundays." *That'll be more often than his occasional Fridays. But then he wants them to take Qur'an lessons, too.*

"And what about that Easter bunny and all his eggs? Do we have to have them? They're pagan, too. What is their meaning, anyway? I could never figure that out."

"They're just about the coming of spring, I guess, and about making children happy. We have to make our children happy. The Easter bunny is just like a fairy tale."

"I think it's confusing. Why don't you have an Easter chicken bringing the eggs, instead of a bunny?"

They were silent, and after a while Amy asked, "Atif. What do you think is the purpose of life, I mean like why are we here?"

"Amy, our purpose here on earth is to worship Allāh and him alone."

"And we believe that our purpose is to glorify God. It's the same, I think. We're not so far apart. But when you help cure people, you will be worshipping Allāh, won't you?"

"Yes, helping others is an act of worship."

"Yes, and Jesus said that what we do for the least of our brethren, we do for him."

At quarter to four in the morning, Ahmed's watch alarm sounded. He quickly turned it off, rose from his chair, and shook his son, who was half asleep. Atif again said he would pray later, so Ahmed and the others entered the mosque to say their Fajr predawn prayers without him. When finished, they emerged into the headlight glare and half-lit sky.

Now Atif was wide awake. "Where is he?" he mumbled to himself, feeling under his sweatshirt to be sure the pistol was still there.

Amy awoke out of a fitful sleep. "What?"

"Where is your father? Is he coming?"

"I—I don't know."

"Did something happen?"

"What? Maybe. Lots of things could have happened. Maybe they…couldn't get the explosive mixed right or were missing an ingredient. Maybe they had a flat tire, or someone got sick. Lots of things could've happened."

"Maybe they got cold feet."

"Yes. Or maybe Mom discovered I wasn't in my room, and she called Dad on the phone and told him, and maybe he decided not to do it today."

"Well, we can't stay here forever."

"No."

"Are you sure you heard them correctly, that they were going to mix up explosives and put them in the trailer and use it to blow up the mosque today?"

"That's not what I heard. I told you what I heard. I heard my dad tell Jesse, 'We've got to end it,' and then, 'Can I count on you?' and then Daddy said they had to zero their rifles. And then I heard him tell Clyde to meet him in the old barn, 'where we keep the fertilizer and diesel,' and to bring the two-horse trailer. That's all I heard."

"And we filled in the blanks from that."

"Yes. So do you think they might not be coming?"

"I don't know. Are you sure you heard him correctly?"

"Well, yes."

"How exactly did you hear him."

"I told you. There's a place in the back of my closet near the floor where sounds come up from the trophy room. There must be a hole in the insulation in the wall between the house and the addition or something. I don't know. All I know is that I can hear voices quite clearly from there."

"Huh. Yes, because if you didn't hear correctly, we may have inconvenienced a lot of people for nothing."

She turned red and was starting to burn. "Atif. I know what I heard."

"You didn't misunderstand what he said?"

"No, I did not," she said, emphasizing each word.

"Please don't raise your voice. You'll disturb everyone."

"Well, don't incite me with idiotic questions."

She turned away from him, and he bent over in his chair, turned his head toward her, and said, "I'm sorry, Amy. I don't doubt you. I know you're right. I just hope you're wrong. I guess I'm jittery. It's hard to wait. It's like waiting for a volcano to erupt."

She was silent.

"Does Jesse always do what your dad says?"

She turned toward him. "Yes. He worships my dad."

At about quarter till six, the sun broke over the rim of the earth, flooding the eastern sky with light. Randall pulled onto the highway turning lane fifty yards from the front of the mosque and stopped the big black pickup and the twelve-foot horse trailer. He saw the double-door entrance with the glass sidelights and the semicircular window and concrete arch above it. He saw the line of people sleeping in lounge chairs under blankets and in sleeping bags, with their signs propped up, all across the front of the reddish-brown stucco building. The people were on the white sidewalks in front of the new shrubs and behind the white curb and gutter and the asphalt parking lot with clean white lines, nine feet apart.

"Humph!" he snorted. "To hell with those mush-heads."

Jesse nodded nervously. He was sitting on the passenger side.

"A lot of sinners are gonna meet God today. Yessir! OK, boy, go!"

Jesse leaped out, sprang to the rear of the truck, and started unhooking the trailer.

Atif jumped to his feet and pointed at him. "Who's that?" he asked Amy, who had jumped up from her chair and was standing at his side.

"That's...Jesse!" she replied, shaking her head, still groggy from sleep.

"What's he doing?"

"I don't know."

From down the line, Muskeen shouted, "He pulled that wire from out of the truck....Now he's fiddling with something on top."

"He's turning a big handle," Dan said to Lonnie.

"He's trying to unhitch it!" Lonnie yelled, pointing at Jesse.

Atif growled, "We can't let him. It's probably full of explosives! They'll pull away and leave it. . . ."

"And then blow it up. . . ." Dan added.

Ahmed stepped forward. "And blow up the masjid!"

"Daddy, no!" Amy shrieked. "Stop!"

Randall, elbow resting out the open window, looked back and saw Amy standing beside Atif in the line. *Damnation! What is she doing here?...How did she find out about us?...and who's that beside her?...It must be that moozlim boy.* "Get out of there, girl!" he shouted. "Run!"

"No, Daddy, I won't! I'm staying here."

"Get out. Run!"

She just waved her head.

I can't help it, Randall thought. *She'll just have to be...a sacrifice... to God and our country....These walls must go down!*

The ghosts of Mogadishu were chasing him and getting close. "Goodbye, Amy!" he roared.

"Daddy!"

"I have to stop him!" Atif shouted. He reached behind his back, pulled out the pistol from under his sweatshirt, whipped it around in front of him, went down on one knee, straightened his arms, took off the safety, and began squeezing off shots.

The first bullets missed wildly, but Jesse heard them cracking over his head. He jumped behind the pickup bed, reached inside, grabbed his rifle, and began firing back, pulling back the bolt after every shot and then looking through the scope. First, he aimed at Atif, but hit Amy in the chest. She fell to the ground. Then he grazed Atif in the arm.

Randall watched Amy fall, and gasped.

"Amy!" Atif cried, looking at her, but then turning angrily back to his target. He pulled the trigger, but nothing happened, and he quickly replaced magazines.

"Get down!" Ahmed ordered everyone, and the line of people began diving to the ground.

One of Atif's shots struck Jesse in the forehead at the same time as Jesse hit Atif in his chest. Atif fell writhing to the ground.

Randall looked in his passenger side mirror and watched Jesse falling backward. He slid across the seat, burst out the passenger door, dropped to his knees, and crawled to his son. He picked up Jesse's head in both his hands, looked at the entry hole in his son's forehead and saw blood streaming out from the other side. "No, God, no!" he yelled, and tears filled his eyes. Then anger seized him. He considered unhooking the trailer himself. But shots began flying over his head. Ahmed had taken the gun from Atif's hand and was firing wildly. Randall scrambled back to the cab and dove behind the wheel, staying low. He gunned the accelerator and the truck leaped forward under the cracking of bullets with the trailer still attached.

After driving a short distance, he stopped, looked back in his mirrors, saw Jesse lying inert on the ground and Amy and her friend motionless beside each other, as if laid out in graves, with someone kneeling over them.

Then he pulled away and turned onto the highway. Soon, in anger, he said, "Oh, what the hell," grasped the remote control on the seat beside him, and pushed the button. The explosion blew pieces of the truck and trailer and Randall himself high into the air and knocked down a stand of trees well off the road. The windows beside the mihrab shattered, and the building shook, but stood. Ahmed was knocked from his kneeling position, but the others, still lying on the ground, were only briefly deafened. Detritus from the truck and trailer landed on the road and field all the way to the mosque.

Amy rose to her hands and knees, lunged sideways onto Atif, and with her last breath, said, "I love you, Atif." He held her in limp arms, and they fled the world together.

AUTHOR'S NOTE

*M*asjid Morning is fiction. It is not based on any real events or people, past or present. The setting, White County, Maryland, does not exist. I named it after Andrew White (1579-1656) [https://en.wikipedia.org/wiki/Andrew_White_(Jesuit)], an English Jesuit missionary who helped found the Maryland colony. He left England to escape religious persecution and to convert the native population in America.

For general information, in 2011, there were 2106 mosques in the United States [http://www.hartfordinstitute.org/The-American-Mosque-Report-2.pdf] and more than fifty in Maryland [http://hirr.hartsem.edu/mosque/database.html]. Three in the United States have been destroyed—all by fire: the Islamic Center of Yuba City in California in 1994 [http://www.appeal-democrat.com/news/yuba-city-mosque-fire-anniversary-faith-from-the-ashes/article_2b1b9d8c-a8e3-11e3-9a31-001a4bcf6878.html], the Islamic Center in Columbia, Tennessee in February, 2008 [http://www.realcourage.org/2010/03/tennessee-man-sentenced-to-183-months-in-prison-for-burning-islamic-center/], and the Islamic Society (mosque) of Joplin, Missouri in 2012 [http://www.cnn.com/2012/08/06/us/missouri-mosque-burned/]. In Culpepper, Virginia, in 2016, the county denied a permit to haul waste from a property where a Muslim congregation planned to build a mosque [https://www.washingtonpost.com/local/public-safety/virginia-county-puts-brakes-on-plans-for-new-mosque-was-it-discriminati on/2016/09/18/15101ace-79d1-11e6-bd86-b7bbd53d2b5d_story. html].

More than fifty of 69,738 African American churches have been burned down [http://answers.google.com/answers/threadview?id= 96516], thirty-nine of them in the years 1995 and 1996 [https:// en.wikipedia.org/wiki/List_of_attacks_against_African-American_ churches].

No mosques have been destroyed in Maryland. However, the congregations of mosques, synagogues, and African American churches have felt the need to be on guard with the rise of hate language in the United States. In Maryland, there has been opposition to construction of a few Muslim facilities, such as a pre-K–12 Muslim school and center and future mosque in Howard County. Also, in September 2016, security cameras recorded a tractor-trailer backing into the side of the Islamic Community Center in Laurel—twice—damaging the roof (under investigation).

One mosque built recently is in Lanham, Maryland, the Diyanet Center of America [https://www.youtube.com/watch?v= ckuMmGvbsyY], one of the largest in the hemisphere. Turkish President Recep Tayyip Erdogan, US Vice President Joe Biden, other dignitaries, and thousands of people participated in the opening ceremony on March 31, 2016. Some neighbors opposed the mosque, but the center has opened facilities for use by the community and invited a nearby high school to use its swimming pool.

The Southern Poverty Law Center lists fifteen hate groups meeting in Maryland [https://www.splcenter.org/hate-map], out of 892 in the United States. But there is also a Maryland population that supports dignity and rights for all human beings, and many communities have interfaith organizations and services with people of different faiths working together.

—Richard Morris

ACKNOWLEDGEMENTS

I could not have written this book without the support, wisdom, and expertise of many people: my wife Barbara Morris, who has contributed her reviews and edits numerous times; Rev. Cynthia Snavely, Jay Endelman, home builder, Virginia Grove, Dawud Abdur-Rahman, Mary Jeffers, Rasheed Jelani, Rafay Ihsan, Raaheela Ahmed, Audrey Engdahl, Lobna "Luby" Ismail, Jill Dickey, and Michael Gollin who have provided their knowledgeable scrutiny and feedback. I thank Stanford K. Pritchard, author of *The Elements of Style: Updated and Annotated for Present-Day Use*, plus novels, poetry and plays, for his advice and encouragement. I am grateful to my excellent CreateSpace copyeditor Meera, who was scrupulous in finding my deviations from the *Chicago Manual of Style*. Without all their help, I would not have confidence that my characters are realistic and my descriptions of Islam and Christianity are accurate.

I am grateful to Larry Suid for his Prince George's Community College course on Islam and to Ken Shilling for his religious education course on Islam at Goodloe Memorial Unitarian Universalist Congregation in Bowie, Maryland; to Jake Rollow, Julia Gaspar Bates, and Lobna "Luby" Ismail and the City of Hyattsville, Maryland for their Ramadan Iftar and meetings on Islam at City Hall; and to Imam Ahmad Azzaari, Isa Wada, Dawud Abdur-Rahman, Roulf

Abdullah, Khalil Shadeed, Sharif Salim, and Rasheed Jelani for providing me with tours of five Washington, DC, area mosques. I also thank Susan Pearl, historian, Prince George's County (MD) Historical Society, for information on county historical regulations; Dan Creueling, Prince George's County Parks and Planning Archaeologist; Dr. Dana Kollmann, Clinical Assistant Professor, Towson University, and author of *Never Suck A Dead Man's Hand: Curious Adventures of a CSI,* for her expertise on identification and disposal of human remains; and Brandon Weston Morris for information about high school customs and culture.

In addition to reading portions of the Qur'an, translated by Abdullah Yusuf Ali and published by Tahrike Tarsile Qur'an, Inc., and the online version (wright-house.com/religions), and accounts of the prophet Muhammad's words and actions in various hadith provided on Sunnah.com, I found that that my most useful secondary sources on Islam, were *Islam: Beliefs and Teachings* by Ghulam Sarwar and the *Great World Religions: Islam* by Professor John L. Esposito. I found Sean Sheehan's book *Pakistan (Cultures of the World)* useful for providing background information on the cultures of Pakistan, and especially, the Punjab, where one of my protagonists originated.

I myself was reared in the Christian tradition and have studied it for many years.